HARD FEELINGS
and other stories

Francis King

HARD FEELINGS
and other stories

Hutchinson of London

Hutchinson & Co (Publishers) Ltd
3 Fitzroy Square, London W1

London Melbourne Sydney Auckland
Wellington Johannesburg and agencies
throughout the world

The following stories first appeared as indicated,
and the author and publishers acknowledge with
thanks the permission of the publishers concerned
to reproduce them in this volume:

'Home' and 'A Scent of Mimosa' in *The Times*;
'To the Camp and Back' in *Penguin Modern Short
Stories*; 'A Nice Way to Go' in *New Review*;
'The Fence' and 'Hard Feelings' in *London Magazine*; 'The Love Game' in *Winter's Tales*; and 'The
Collectors' in the *Sunday Telegraph*.

Set in Monotype Fournier

Printed in Great Britain by
The Anchor Press Ltd, and bound by
Wm Brendon & Son Ltd, both of
Tiptree, Essex

ISBN 0 09 127620 9

Contents

To Miriam with love

Home

'ELIZABETH and I have shared our lives for more than a quarter of a century,' Eleanor was in the habit of saying. What she meant was that Elizabeth had shared the expenses of the house for that period, even though she seldom lived in it. 'Why on earth don't you bring the arrangement to an end?' Elizabeth's friends, who were seldom also Eleanor's friends, would ask her; and she would then explain that she was really very fond of Eleanor, that she preferred to leave her bits and pieces in the house than in store and that one day her years of wandering would be over and she would wish to settle down. But the true reason was a mixture of kindness and weakness: she shrank from hurting others partly because she did not like to inflict hurt and partly for fear of retaliation. So in Taos or in Taormina, in Dubrovnik or in Delhi, she would regularly, every month, inspect Eleanor's account and then write her a cheque for rates, repairs, utilities and the wages of whatever 'treasure' was at that moment in process of turning into 'a dead loss'.

The two women were so unlike in every respect that people were puzzled that they should ever have come together, much less continued together for that quarter of a century in which Eleanor took such pride. The most common explanation was that Elizabeth, who had been an orphan brought up by a succession of unloving relatives, found in Eleanor, her senior by sixteen years, a mother-figure; and certainly Eleanor was like many mothers who become fixed points in their children's lives but ones to which the children become less and less inclined to return.

'Elizabeth has to be abroad for her painting,' Eleanor would explain. But there seemed no reason why the watery watercolours of potted plants or bowls of fruit or the façades of houses or churches should not be as easily executed in St John's Wood as in some remote corner of the globe.

Two or three years would pass and then Elizabeth would return, to find that Eleanor had had her sofa re-covered with a particularly hideous chintz, or her room redecorated with a particularly hideous wallpaper. 'I know it's not *quite* what you'd have wanted. But as you probably saw from the account, that little man gave us an absolutely bargain price.' There were innumerable little men in Eleanor's life, who by a process similar to that which turned treasures to dead losses, progressed from being 'wonderful finds' to being 'rotters' or 'utter crooks'. 'You must be delighted to be back,' Eleanor's friends would say to Elizabeth – her own friends usually knew better – and she would agree that, yes, it was wonderful to be back. But after five or six weeks Eleanor would announce to all and sundry, 'Well, Elizabeth is off on her travels once again,' and, after a wine-and-cheese party, Elizabeth would vanish for a further two or three years.

But this time Elizabeth had been away for less than five months; she had come back because the family doctor had told her to come back.

'It's typical of that woman to take herself off just when I need her most. When I think of all that we've done for her. All that trouble with her son, getting him out on bail. That holiday we gave her in Cornwall.' It was Eleanor alone who had decided on the gift of the holiday; but it had none the less subsequently appeared as an item of expenditure in the monthly account between the two friends. 'These people are all alike. No sense of gratitude or responsibility.'

Pink-cheeked and white-haired, her large capable hands resting outside the bedclothes, Eleanor did not look like someone for whom it had been, as the doctor put it, 'touch and go' less than a week previously. Perhaps because she had nursed a deaf father for many years until his death her voice had always seemed pitched to an invisible public meeting; and now, miraculously, it had lost none of its resonant timbre.

'I'll go to the agency tomorrow,' Elizabeth said. 'Anyway, what's the urgency? I can manage on my own for a while.'

But Eleanor refused ever to believe that Elizabeth was capable of housework, let alone cooking.

'I've made you an oxtail stew. I got up after breakfast and did it. As soon as that hopeless home-help had gone.'

'You *what*! But Adams said you weren't to get out of bed except for absolutely essential things.'

'It's not only *you*, dear. It's Miss Saarinen and Bob Graham. I had to think of them.'

'I could have dealt with them.'

'You know you loathe cooking.'

In fact, Elizabeth enjoyed cooking and cooked better than Eleanor; but the older woman had for so many years told all and sundry 'Elizabeth loathes cooking' that in the house in St John's Wood Elizabeth went into the kitchen only to do the washing-up. This Eleanor was always prepared to leave to her.

'They could eat out,' Elizabeth said.

'Then we'd have to give them money for it, wouldn't we? After all, they're supposed to get full board.'

'Eleanor dear, is it really necessary to have these lodgers?' One was a Finnish philologist at the Institute of Education; the other a distant male cousin of Eleanor's, who was working in a King's Road boutique while labouring at a novel.

'It's not *necessary*,' Eleanor said. 'But I do feel that it's, in a way, a duty. After all, they couldn't afford to live anywhere else in central London and we *do* have this big house, which is usually half-empty.' Eleanor liked to maintain the fiction that, though she charged the lodgers twenty-five pounds a week for bed and board, it was only out of kindness that she kept them.

'But if you're ill,' Elizabeth said. 'They must understand.'

'Oh, I shall be up and about in a day or two. These little turns never leave me any the worse for wear. You know that.'

The little turn had, on this occasion, been a massive heart-attack.

'But, Eleanor, Adams says you *must* take things easy. For a long, long time.'

'He's an old fusser.... You don't mind, do you, dear, that Bob is using your sitting room for his study? After all, you can always use mine.'

Elizabeth did mind, especially since her permission had not been sought; but she decided that, with Eleanor so ill, it was better to make no opposition. 'Oh, that's all right,' she said. 'He's welcome to it.'

'That bedroom's so poky. He must have somewhere to spread himself – for his writing, I mean. And he's been paying extra for the use of the sitting room, you know. I insisted on that.'

Elizabeth wondered for a moment why, if he were paying extra for a sitting room that belonged to her and not to Eleanor, she had received none of the money; but that resentment too she put away from her, as though it were something soiled and soiling.

'You look much better than I'd hoped.'

'Oh, I feel perfectly all right. I can't think why that idiot Adams sent you such an alarmist bulletin.'

'Well, I was coming back anyway,' Elizabeth lied. 'I was getting bored with Greece.'

When she had left Eleanor – who had insisted that she must deal with some correspondence – Elizabeth set about exploring the house before the lodgers returned. A few weeks previously Eleanor had written to tell her that 'this perfectly marvellous little man', an ex-marine, had painted the staircase from top to bottom; and now gloomily Elizabeth examined the paint encrusted like inexpertly applied icing to the banisters, the white splashes on a corner of a Bokhara rug inherited from an uncle, and the dents, obviously made by a ladder, on the William Morris wallpaper. It was the only wallpaper in the house that Elizabeth could bear to look at; she had been present at its choosing and for once had held out obstinately against Eleanor's demands for 'something a little less sombre – something gay and cosy'. Presumably, following the usual pattern, another little man would eventually have to be called in to repair the damage caused by the first little man; and so little man would follow little man, on and on *ad infinitum*. Elizabeth sighed, drawing her small pointed chin down on to the neck around which she always wore the same rope of pearls, a long-ago present from Eleanor.

At the top of the large Edwardian house was the attic room in which Miss Saarinen lived. It was typical of Eleanor to favour a man, however young and silly – and her cousin was both – at the expense of a woman, however elderly and worthy. Elizabeth had never met Miss Saarinen, but as she gazed round the neat, chill room, with its low ceiling and its white-wood furniture and its single-bar electric fire, she imagined someone equally neat and chill to match it. No doubt Miss Saarinen had herself knitted the pale blue cardigan that rested over the back of a chair; and no doubt Eleanor had persuaded her, as she persuaded all her female paying guests, that in lodgings in England it was customary to make one's own bed. On the dressing-table there was a photo-graph of a young naval officer with a wide, rectangular face and irregular teeth. Not a son, obviously. And, equally obviously, not a boy-friend. A favourite nephew, Elizabeth decided. She pulled open a drawer and glanced down at a pile of sanitary towels. Somehow she had imagined Miss Saarinen as long past the menopause. Then, feeling ashamed of herself, she pushed the drawer shut with a slam.

The boy's bedroom, which faced south and had two beds in it and received the benefit of central heating, smelled of cigarette smoke, of stale sweat and of something, acrid and vaguely cloy-ing, that was less easily definable. The bed was unmade, because in his case the now vanished treasure had no doubt been instruct-ed to make it for him and he was now waiting for someone to replace her; his pyjama trousers lay on the floor and his pyjama jacket had been festooned over the French nineteenth-century ormolu clock that had mysteriously travelled from the mantel-piece in Elizabeth's sitting room to the bedside table. There were fag-ends everywhere: in a tea-cup on the floor beside the bed, in the fireplace, in an empty soap-dish and even on the windowsill. For a moment Elizabeth decided that she had better do out the room; if she did not do it, then in a moment of madness Eleanor might attempt the task. But she was tired from her flight and tired from the innumerable, complicated mental adjustments she seemed to have to make as soon as she stepped over the threshold of the St John's Wood house.

The sitting room – her sitting room – was as untidy as the bedroom. A caster had come off one of the legs of her pretty little Victorian serpentine-backed sofa and someone, presumably the boy, had used her *Oxford Dictionary of Quotations* to prop it up. There were cigarette-ends here too; three lay in a Sèvres bonbonnière that she had always particularly treasured. It was too bad of Eleanor not to see that her things were properly looked after, Elizabeth thought with sudden anger; but then she relented, reminding herself that Eleanor had no interest whatsoever in 'things': Sèvres or Doulton, Meissen or Denby, it was all one to her.

The boy had cleared Elizabeth's desk of everything on it: the little silver clock, shaped like a church, that she had inherited from a nanny; the large silver inkstand, encrusted with ink, that her mother had once used; the ugly twisiting brass candlesticks that she had brought back from Benares; even the blotter and the lamp and the try ofjpens. All had been ranged about the floor to make way for the typewriter and thespapers scattered about it. She peered at the sheet actually in the machine and read, with bewilderment, 'I was a child and she was a child in this kingdom by the sea, She is older than the rocksss.'

Elizabeth felt slightly sick when she left the little room, crammed with possessions either inherited or collected during her wanderings. It's too bad of Eleanor, she thought again. It's not the first time either. This is *my* room. She's no business to let anyone else use it without asking me. But she always shrank from a clash of opposing wills and now the excuse that Eleanor was in no fit state to take on an argument made her decide that she would have to 'put up with it'. Putting up with it was something for which Elizabeth had a talent.

When abroad Elizabeth had always thought sentimentally of

the house – it was, after all, the only permanent home she had ever known – but now, as she continued her exploration, a curious feeling of suffocation allied with one of despair began mysteriously to come over her. Nothing in the house seemed to belong to her any more, even though everything of any value was in fact hers. All the invisible nerves that had joined her to the Sèvres bonbonnière in which the boy had stubbed out his cigarettes, to the serpentine-backed Victorian sofa or to her desk and everything on it now seemed to shrivel up like the tendrils of a creeper when thrown on a bonfire. She had become all at once a stranger among things strange to her.

In an access of growing panic she pushed open the French windows of Eleanor's sitting room and went out of the airless house into the airy London garden. A hand to her greying hair, a dumpy middle-aged woman with a beautiful, pale, oval face and weak eyes behind gold-rimmed spectacles, she breathed in deeply again and yet again the scent of the phlox from the herbaceous border that ran along one wall. When they had first come to inspect the dirty and dilapidated house just after the war, with its boarded-up windows and its damp-stains and its obscene scribblings on the tattered wallpaper, it was only this garden, dark green, mysterious and whispering, that had attracted her. Everywhere there had been overgrown shrubs; and between them huge docks and towering clumps of cow-parsley and the trailing, murderous arms of wild rose-bushes, festooned with bindweed. It had seemed then to be not a small back garden in London, but the heart of some secret place in the secret heart of the country. 'We'll have our work cut out getting this in order,' Eleanor had said; and the words had even then given Elizabeth a pang. Month by month Eleanor and her helpers – for a time Elizabeth was one of them – hacked and burned and trenched and planted; and long since the former wilderness had shrunk into this neat little jigsaw of herbaceous borders and triangular rose-beds and zigzag crazy paving.

Worst of all to Elizabeth had been the destruction of the drunken circular wooden summer-house at the remotest and darkest end of the garden. Apparently a novelist, long since forgotten but once successful, had lived in the house and had built himself this little revolving hut in which to work. Part of the roof had rotted away; birds had built their nests inside; and it was only by pushing hard that one could persuade the tottering little box to rotate on its rusty track. But Elizabeth – she could not have said why – adored it. 'We *must* have it repaired,' she used to say, and Eleanor would answer, 'Oh it'll cost a fortune, dear. Let's leave it for the moment.' Then Elizabeth went away and when after several months she came back again Eleanor said to her, 'Come and see my surprise for you.' She took Elizabeth into the garden and there in the place of the round wooden summer-house was a sensible square one, of red-brick with leaded window-panes.

Elizabeth was appalled. But she rallied and said, 'Oh, Eleanor, how lovely!'

'It's useful too, because I had a shed made at the back for the mower and the garden tools. I knew you'd like it.'

Elizabeth never used the new summer-house except on the rare occasions when Eleanor carried tea out there. She used to wonder if Eleanor noticed her hatred of the place. Probably not, since she was observant only of things, never of feelings.

Now Elizabeth walked over to it and leant against its door, so that she could look back and up at the house. She could see a shadow move across Eleanor's curtains. That meant that she had got up for something or other. She ought really to go and see what she wanted, but with a brutality that surprised her she told herself: Well, let her get on with it. If she's so foolish, at her age, as to disobey the doctor, then she'll have to take the consequences!

Again she touched her close-cut greying hair, brushing a tendril of it away from her cheek. Was Eleanor going to die? The thought suddenly hit her. The tone of the doctor's letter – 'not at all happy about the long-term prognosis . . . defective valve . . . essential you should . . .' – suggested that she might. Reading the remote, measured phrases in a hotel bedroom overlooking the Lycabettus, Elizabeth had felt a rising nausea that had eventually made her stretch out on the bed, the letter still in her hand and her cheek pressed deep into a pillow. Then she had jumped up and rushed out into the afternoon glare to book a seat on the earliest plane back to England. From then until her arrival she had been unable to force more than a mouthful or two of food down her throat.

But now, her back against the door of the hideous, squat summer-house, she found that, as she asked herself that question 'Is Eleanor going to die?', she could consider it calmly, even coldly, with none of that former flurry of panic and desolation. Eleanor had always seemed so firmly rooted in life, with her positive gestures and her positive decisions and that firm, loud voice of hers. It was hard to think of her as mortal.

Again the shadow moved behind the curtains. Elizabeth straightened and then forced herself to go in to see what her friend was doing.

Supper with the silent Miss Saarinen and the loquacious Bob was over.

'Oughtn't you to be trying to go to sleep, Eleanor dear?'

Eleanor was still propped up in bed, letters scattered everywhere around her. Her glasses were low on her long, bony nose; the grey hairnet she was wearing looked like a cobweb across her forehead.

'Must get through this lot first,' she said.

'Can't you leave them till tomorrow? I could help you. You could dictate to me on the typewriter.'

'I'm hopeless at dictating.' She might have added that Elizabeth was hopeless on the typewriter. 'No, dear, I feel perfectly all right. What you *could* do is make me a cup of Ovaltine.'

'Eleanor – do please stop.'

But Eleanor picked up another letter, her lips moving soundlessly as she read it to herself. Then she looked up over her glasses: 'How was the oxtail?'

'Delicious,' Elizabeth lied. The meat had been glutinous, as it had shredded from the bones; the gravy had been edged on the plate with a hardening frill of yellow fat.

'I sometimes think that I'm the only person who knows how

to cook oxtail properly. The secret is in the time, of course. It must have at least six hours. . . . What about Miss Saarinen?'

'What about her?'

'Well, is she all right?'

'Oh, yes. She wanted to look in and see you but I put her off.'

'Why did you do that, dear? You go on as though I were seriously ill. I'd like to have had a little chat with her.'

'She doesn't seem exactly a chatty sort of person.'

'And Bob?'

'Oh, he chats away all right.'

'Such a nice boy. Oh – that reminds me. He hasn't yet given me his cheque. The rent. Perhaps you could remind him?' She threw down one letter and picked up another. But instead of reading it she again looked over her glasses at her friend: 'It's so nice to have you back, my dear,' she said.

'It's nice to *be* back.'

'I hope you're not going to go gadding off again too soon now. We want really to see something of you.'

'Oh, you're going to have me here for a long time,' Elizabeth said. 'You're going to get sick of me.'

At half past ten Elizabeth again entered Eleanor's room.

'Now, Eleanor, you really *must* stop! Please!'

'But it's only just gone ten.'

With unwonted decisiveness, Elizabeth began to gather together the letters, papers, magazines and books scattered about the bed.

'Dear – you're muddling them all up! Elizabeth!'

'We can sort them out again tomorrow.'

Eleanor sighed. 'So impractical. What's the good of my putting them all in order if you then muddle them up?'

'Now I'm going to bring you a wash-basin here. No, Eleanor, Adams said you were on no account to get up to wash. It's quite unnecessary now that I'm here. I can bring you everything you need.'

Elizabeth began to bustle around, while Eleanor shouted instructions at her. 'No, dear! Not that soap! . . . Don't squeeze so much toothpaste on the brush, just half an inch. . . . If you'd put down the basin, you'd find it easier to manage the jug . . .' Eleanor had the faculty of always being able to make Elizabeth feel incompetent.

It was when Elizabeth was soaping her friend's hands and then sponging them – usually so strong-looking, they now seemed oddly helpless as they lay limply, one after the other, in hers – that the tenderness that had eluded her out in the garden suddenly returned. Elizabeth was relieved: she had feared that all her devotion to Eleanor had suddenly and mysteriously dried at its source. The wedding ring – Eleanor's husband had been killed in the war, after they had been married for only a few weeks – was reassuringly tight on the finger. Even though she had been so dangerously ill, she had obviously lost no weight.

'Such a fuss,' Eleanor was muttering. 'Quite unnecessary.'

When Elizabeth had finished, she asked, 'Now have you all you need for the night?' She plucked away a pillow and began to plump it up. It was strange to be looking after Eleanor, in this total reversal of usual roles, and the unwontedness of it made her feel clumsy and somehow embarrassed.

'Everything, thank you, dear.'

'I've put the bell here. Now ring for me, if you need anything. I'm a light sleeper, as you know, and I'm certain to hear you.'

'Oh, I won't need anything.'

'Would you like one of my pills?'

'Heavens no!' Eleanor disapproved of 'drugging', as she called it.

'Well then – good night, dear.'

'Good night.'

Elizabeth put her lips to Eleanor's forehead. She had always hated physical contact and in the early days of their friendship she would involuntarily stiffen when Eleanor touched her or kissed her, or she had to touch her or kiss her back. But now she had grown used to it.

'Sleep well.'

'It's you who need the sleep. After that long plane journey of yours.'

Elizabeth had told Eleanor that she would bring her breakfast in bed at nine o'clock, after she had got Miss Saarinen off to the Institute and the boy off to the boutique in the King's Road. Miss Saarinen had left promptly at twenty to nine, but the boy, obviously in no mood to hurry, had chattered to her in his pale blue silk dressing-gown, a cigarette dangling from his loose mouth, while she washed up the breakfast things. He had eaten three fried eggs and a number of rashers of bacon.

'How ill *is* Eleanor?' he asked in a loud voice.

Elizabeth lowered her own voice as she answered, 'Very ill, I gather. Far iller than she knows.'

'Don't you think that doctor's got himself into a needless tizz? She doesn't strike me as all that bad.'

'He's a good doctor,' Elizabeth said, wishing the boy would go. She began to set out Eleanor's tray.

The boy put out his cigarette in one of the unwashed plates stacked by the sink and then, whistling under his breath, left the kitchen, taking with him the copy of *The Times* that Elizabeth was about to take to Eleanor. Elizabeth went in pursuit, but he had already gone into the lavatory.

There was no answer to her first knock on Eleanor's door and so she knocked a second time, balancing the tray awkwardly on a raised knee in order to free a hand to do so. After that she struggled with the door-handle and gave the door a gentle push with the toe of her shoe.

'Eleanor!'

Slamming the tray down on to the dressing-table, so violently that a brush shot to the floor, she rushed over to the bed where Eleanor lay sprawled across the bed-rest. The curtains were closed; the bedside lamp was burning.

The counterpane was covered with papers and there were also papers on the floor, making a dry crunching noise, like insects, when Elizabeth trod on them in her panic.

Elizabeth grabbed Eleanor's shoulders and tried to pull her up and back on to the pillows. But even before she saw the swollen purple face, something about the still warm but stiffening flesh under the flimsy nightdress told her that her friend was dead.

'Oh, Eleanor!' she cried out once more, in what was half a moan and half a sob, letting the head fall forward again on to the bed-rest.

She put both hands to her temples, swaying from side to side in a terrible access of grief. Until, suddenly, that undying worm that is present at almost every death-bed, however deeply mourned and however little expected, raised its head in the deepest and darkest recesses of her being and whispered, 'Free! You're free! Your bondage is over!'

Carefully she again attempted to raise Eleanor and this time, shrinking from that obstinate flesh and yet forcing herself to handle it, she at last succeeded. Eleanor's face lay back on the pillows; but it was a subtly different face, not merely because of its dreadful puffiness and its dreadful colour, but because the glasses had fallen off the long, crooked nose.

What on earth had Eleanor been doing? What were all these papers?

Elizabeth peered, picking up first one and then another.

All of them were bills for the last month; and on the bed-rest – a fountain pen had left a smear of ink on the counterpane beneath it – there was the beginning of an account in Eleanor's large, clear handwriting, as of a clever child. Elizabeth read:

June 2nd	Wages to Mrs Turton	£8·00
	Window cleaner	1·50
June 3rd	Bulb for Miss S's room	0·35
June 4th	Early-morning-tea service	12·00

Early-morning-tea service! Eleanor read no further.

In a fury that obliterated all her previous emotions of horror, shock and grief, she thought: Why the hell should I have to pay half for her early-morning-tea service? I've never had early-morning tea once in this house.

A Nice Way to Go

SUDDENLY and simply it had come to him: he had had enough.

Later, he was able to fix the precise moment of that realization, the overhead kitchen light isolating him in a blank world while his hands, twisted by arthritis, fastidiously removed a milky, spear-shaped bone from the fish pie that Mrs Crawford had left for him to warm up for his supper. There was no surprise or shock. Yes, I've had enough, he repeated to himself as, slouched towards the table in his darned cardigan, the transistor radio beside him crackling with yet another news bulletin to which he did not listen, he dug his fork once again into the mush. I've had enough; I'd better do something about it.

There had been a whole sequence of happenings, some important and some trivial, that, a sinuously powerful river, had first carried him towards this decision and had then cast him up on it. He had retired and he and his wife and his already middle-aged spinster daughter had left a large house in Putney for this small basement flat not far from it. His wife had died with the clumsy abruptness with which she had been in the habit of breaking into a conversation or a television or wireless programme to put some question or to make some demand. A year or two later the spinster daughter, a medical librarian, had announced that she was going off to live with a fierce female friend, a gynaecologist, in a damp cottage in the New Forest. He and the Siamese cat had lived on in the basement flat, with occasional visits from the daughter and even more occasional ones from his son and his son's wife and children, and daily ones from brisk, brusque Mrs Crawford, who looked after far too many widowers and bachelors to have time for a chat or even for a gulped cup of tea or coffee.

The cat was old, her mask now tinged with silver and her movements careful and leisurely. She could no longer jump up on to the high brass bedstead but would stand beside it, tail erect, emitting a series of squeaks as of chalk on slate until, throwing down *The Times* crossword in exasperation – every night he went to sleep over it – he would stoop down and lift her up beside him. She smelled musty now, like clothes hung up too long in an untenanted room, and the threads of saliva from her half-open, nearly toothless mouth would smear the eiderdown and sometimes even the sheet. 'Oh, you filthy cat!' he would often exclaim aloud to her, rubbing with a handkerchief; but he felt a curious kinship between his own ageing body, with its aches and stiffnesses and insistence on relieving itself two and three times in the course of a single brief night, and the ageing body of the animal curled beside him.

Then, one night, she did not come to his bed; and when, at last missing her, he clambered, skinny and friable, down out of the warmth of the vast bed and made his way, cursing, into the kitchen and the sitting room, he could not find her. The food lay out for her, untouched, on the kitchen floor, the snippets of melts – he would cut them up carefully with a pair of scissors – now dry and curling up on the saucer like the shrivelled petals of some purple flower. The kitchen window was open on to the exiguous yard that was part of his domain; he must have forgotten to close it, as so often – 'You'll have a burglar in here one day,' Mrs Crawford would tell him, often adding: 'And then where will you be?' But the cat seldom now ventured, even in summer weather like this, out of the flat.

'Oh, damn you!' he muttered, as he unlocked and pulled open the door into the yard and then ventured out, narrow bare feet crinkling at the touch of stone, on to the first of the three steps. He called her name and whistled; ventured up to the next step; called again. Slowly his eyes grew accustomed to the thunder-laden darkness until at last he became aware of the two infinitely small, intensely glittering points of light in the dark shadow under the straggling elder. Again he called her name; but she did not stir. He walked over to her, one bare heel treading on

something disgustingly soft and sticky, and stopped. A branch
of the elder grazed his cheek. 'Oh, silly cat!' She gave a curious
breathy squeak as he lifted her up. She seemed very light,
almost insubstantial. He carried her back into his room, holding
her to his chest with one hand while the other struggled to fasten
kitchen window and door, and then placed her in her usual
place on top of the part of the eiderdown that, in the past, had
covered his wife's humped, snoring form. He leant over and
switched off the bedside light and then put a hand over to the
cat, running one of her ears through forefinger and middle finger.
Something was amiss; and for a while he lay in the dark, the cat's
ear resting between his fingers like a dead leaf, until he realized
what it was. She was not purring.

When he awoke the next morning, with the habitual dizziness
as he raised his head from the pillow and the habitual ache in his
bones as he struggled off the bed, the cat had once more vanished.
In dressing-gown and slippers this time, he searched for her as
he had searched for her the night before; and once again it was
in the yard that he found her, under the lanky elder tree. Her
pale blue eyes, fixedly staring into some space behind him, were
now two misty opals. A thread of saliva trailed from her chin.
He carried her into the kitchen and poured out some cream for
her from a carton almost empty. But she sat before it, where he
had set her down, indifferently hunched. Soon, without his
noticing her departure as he prepared for another day, she had
slithered back into the garden, to take up her place under the
elder.

Somewhere there was a cat basket and eventually he found it,
its wicker thick with dust, under the bed in the room that had
once been occupied by his daughter but was now so often empty.
In the past the cat had always struggled against being placed
inside it; but now, inert and again curiously insubstantial, she
suffered him to pick her up and immure her.

The vet, an elderly woman who was herself like some rangy,
famished cat, briskly palped the sides of the animal with long,
bony fingers, and as she did so a viscous orange liquid, reeking
of decay and death, spread over the slab. 'Tumour,' she grunted

laconically. And then, 'Kidney failure.' The teenage girl, with the red scrubbed cheeks and raw hands, who acted as her assistant, swabbed at the mess, as though it were nothing worse than spilled tea.

The cat lay on his knees as the fatal injection was administered to her. His trousers felt warm and sodden but he did not care. He had similarly held his wife folded in his arms at the moment of her death.

He had walked out of the surgery with the sensation that something painlessly amputated from him had made him clumsy and lopsided. There was a void and though, briefly, as he went about his daily chores, shopping and preparing meals for himself and stooping over the sink, he could forget about it, he was never for long unaware of it. His son came to call on him with his garrulous wife and the void was there; he played chess with the bedridden old man in the flat on the second floor and between moves – the old man was always slow – the void persisted.

But one day, where the void had been, there was suddenly this terrible pain, as though something molten had been poured into it to harden to an intolerable weight of lead. He lay on his bed and groaned and the cold sweat trickled down his cheeks. The pain came back and that second time it was as though some filament running along his left arm had leapt into incandescence. Eventually he went to see the impatient young man, his blond hair reaching to the collar of his jacket, who had taken the place of the patient old man, a refugee from Hitler's Germany, who had once been his doctor. The young man told him that he had angina; but it need not be serious, if he were careful he had many more years ahead of him, there was no reason why he should not live to be seventy. What the young man had not bothered to note – it was all there in a folder before him – was that his patient was already seventy-one.

So that was how he came to his decision: I've had enough. And he came to it gently and simply, with neither surprise nor shock. He went to see his solicitor and he made a new will, leaving less of his money to his son and daughter than would eventually please them and more to the RSPCA. He began to tidy up the flat, discarding whatever would be useless to anyone else and tearing up the duplicates of income-tax returns years and years old (he had been an accountant by profession), receipted bills, photographs, letters. He made a fire in the yard of all this detritus, once so important to him and now so trivial, and watched as the photographs curled and darkened (yes, that was him in that extraordinary bathing costume that had a skirt reaching almost to his knees and that was his daughter in her school blazer and straw hat), as the income-tax returns took flame and then subsided to a crimson glow, as the letters (written to him in the trenches by the hospital nurse whom he had eventually married) were reduced to a grey dust. There was a wind that summer morning and everything consumed so easily.

He already had the pills, prescribed not for him (he had never had difficulty in sleeping) but for his wife. Some time soon he would swallow them, when this succession of brilliant, beautiful summer days had ended and he had ceased to enjoy the sensation of glad accomplishment derived from the order that he had created out of a lifetime's disorder.

It was his custom every evening before supper to go for a brief walk along the tow-path. He had walked there with his children and his wife on his returns from work; and then, later, he had walked there with his daughter and the dog, a mongrel, that she had taken away with her to the New Forest, where it had soon been run over – ironically, in a country lane by a car crammed with tipsy trippers. Now he walked there alone, a man who looked much younger than his years and whose walk was determinedly sprightly even though that impatient young doctor had warned him never to over-exert himself or be in a hurry.

That evening, in the late sunlight, the river was particularly beautiful, uncoiling lazily like some vast, shimmering snake. Some boys, trousers rolled up to their knees, were wading in it, intent on dredging something out of its depths. Their arms were black with sludge, even their cheeks were daubed with it. Beyond them an eight skimmed by, the cox's voice falsetto as he shrilled, 'In, out . . . In, out . . .' A dog scampered past, trailing some nameless horror – it looked like a putrescent length of tripe – from its slavering jaws. A valedictory sadness came over him, as he passed into the shade of the four beech trees and then out again into the sunshine, where, on the other side of the sagging fence, flat white figures moved lethargically over the baize of the cricket ground. His boy had played there, before he had married and got portly and rich and self-important.

He walked on, still at a sprightly pace, even though he was experiencing that disagreeable but now familiar tightness of the chest that made him from time to time halt and gulp for breath. The sun was warm on his face; the breeze was warm in his hair.

There were four houses here, their railings removed during the war and never put back, with plateaux of mangy lawn outside front doors that, because of flooding, were raised some feet above the tow-path. Many years before a prostitute had lived in one of them, until outraged neighbours had managed to drive her out. She used to sit, broodingly monumental, in a skimpy cotton frock, her face painted like a clown's and her hair an immense orange beehive about it, out on her lawn, in a deck-chair, striped red and blue, on evenings such as this. He smiled to himself at the remembrance. His wife had joined the general outrage – so bad for the children to have to see that kind of thing going on under their noses. But if the children glanced at the huge, impassive woman, waiting for her custom on those waning summer evenings, it was only for a moment. She had never been of the slightest interest to them.

All at once he heard his cat miaow, and he halted, under a solitary beech tree smaller than the four that he had passed, that breathlessness now grown acute as he thought: 'This is some kind of hallucination.' He looked up, and there, high in the branches, she was gazing down at him, with a seemingly tranquil gaze out of her clear blue eyes, even though her miaowing, persistent now, reiterated over and over again on the same two notes, told him that she was terrified.

Then a voice said, from the other side of the tree, from the pock-marked plateau of grass on which the prostitute used to lie out in her deck-chair: 'I don't know how to get her down. I suppose I'd better send for the fire brigade, but they charge for that, don't they?'

'Is it – is it your cat then?' For he still believed it to be his.

'Yes. Silly little brute. She will go up there after birds and then she can't get down again. My husband used to climb up to fetch her. The other day I had to tip a boy to go up for me.'

She was a middle-aged woman, with the coarse straight blond hair, round, rosy-cheeked face and thick thighs and ankles of a Russian peasant woman. She had large white teeth, and he noticed, as she now smiled at him, that one of them, just at the corner of her mouth, was chipped.

'Is your husband not at home?'

'Oh, no.' She gave a loud, clear laugh, as though he had said something funny. 'He ran away months ago.'

The cat continued its plaintive miaowing; and now both of them peered up into the tree. Eventually he said:

'Perhaps I could get her down for you.'

'You?' Then, realizing that her incredulity might offend him, she said quickly: 'Oh, you wouldn't want to dirty your nice clothes.'

He was, in fact, wearing a pair of old grey flannels that had shrunk so that there was a gap between them and his canvas shoes, an open-necked shirt and the darned cardigan.

'I'll have a try,' he said.

'But do you think you ought to . . .?'

He grabbed a branch of the tree and swung himself up, hearing her gasp out in involuntary panic, 'Oh, do be careful!' It was all so easy; nothing to it. He did not feel the smallest breathlessness or discomfort. He began to climb, his feet unerringly finding one hold after another. Once he looked down and through the leaves, flickering in the evening sunlight, he saw her round, upturned face, the eyes screwed up, below him. It gave him an extraordinary surge of pleasure. It looked so beautiful, wholesome and kind and beautiful, glimmering up out of the swirling green. And I don't feel giddy, he thought. Not in the least.

'Don't let her scratch you!' she called out. 'Be careful!'

The cat did scratch him, in brief terror, as he put out a hand, pleading, 'Good puss; come, puss, come, come.' But he hardly noticed as the talons, cruel and sharp, lacerated the side of his neck. Then all at once the cat was purring as he clutched her against him. He began the slow descent, pausing from moment to moment to look either down at that glimmering upturned face or out, over the tow-path, to the lazy, snake-like coils of the river.

'Shall I take her from you?' She put up a hand and he noticed how coarse and rough its palm was. He imagined her peeling potatoes, scrubbing floors and digging the garden. He passed the totally passive cat down to her and she cradled it against her ample breast, almost as though to suckle it there.

'That was splendid of you, I'm so grateful,' she began. And then, as he jumped down off the lowest branch and began to wipe his hands on the handkerchief he had pulled from his trouser pocket: 'Oh, but look what she's done to your neck! Oh, the naughty thing!'

Touching the long scratch with his fingers, so that their tips became smeared with blood, and then pressing the handkerchief, already darkened with grime, to the wound, he said that it was nothing, nothing at all. But she replied that of course it wasn't nothing, it could easily go septic, she must wash the place at once and put some iodine on it.

So that was how he entered the dilapidated, untidy house, so unlike the flat that he had left in such scrupulous order behind him; how he came to be sitting on the broken lavatory seat while she first washed the scratch and then, telling him, 'This will hurt, I'm afraid,' dabbed with a piece of iodine-soaked cottonwool; how eventually, as the eight returned up the river, they sipped at glasses of a warm, too-sweet sherry together out on the pockmarked plateau of grass.

'It's funny I've never seen you before,' he said. 'I walk along here almost every evening.'

'I've seen you, often.'

'Once, many years ago . . .' He broke off; he had been going to

tell her of the statuesque prostitute sitting out on this same patch
of grass as now they were doing.

'Yes?'

'I used to come here with my children,' he said. 'And with our
dog. But that must have been long before you came to live here.'

'My husband insisted on buying this house. I never wanted it.
And then when he did his bunk it was all he left me. Nothing
else.'

'It must be valuable now. These houses facing the river . . .'

'Yes, I suppose it is. But it's damp and the rooms are too small
and the rats come in from the river. That's why I got the cat.
But she's no earthly use as a ratter.'

'Siamese never are. Mine felt she was far too grand to chase
after vermin.'

They revealed little of themselves to each other; for much of
the time they sat in silence, looking out at the peaceful river,
with its occasional swan or boat or flotsam. She offered him
another glass of sherry but he said that no, thank you, he should
really be getting home. She said, well, then, another time, and
he said yes, that would be nice, very nice, another time, of course.

He was awkward when he got up to go and the awkwardness
seemed to communicate itself to her, so that, a woman not
naturally shy, she became so for a moment. 'I do hope that
scratch doesn't go septic,' she said, and unaccountably her plain,
pleasant, round face began to redden.

'Oh, no. It's nothing.'

Out on the tow-path, he called over his shoulder: 'Next time I
pass, I'll look out for you.'

'Yes, please.'

He sketched a brief wave and she waved back. She had picked
up the cat again and once more she was cradling it against her
ample breast as though to suckle it. The setting sun glinted on
her thick, blonde hair. Though she must have been, oh, fifty or
fifty-five, she suddenly looked young.

He walked back home, full of a calm, spacious happiness. He
walked even more briskly than usual but he felt no breathlessness, no tightness, no pain. He thought of that round face

glimpsed through the shivering foliage, with the eyes screwed up and the mouth slightly parted to reveal those large, white teeth. He thought of the thick, sturdy thighs and ankles as she had lain out in the deck-chair with the glass of that sweet, tacky sherry resting on her slightly protuberant stomach. He thought of the walk that he would take the next evening and of how, perhaps, she would be out there on the plateau before her house.

He warmed up the stew that Mrs Crawford had prepared for him and for once he ate every morsel of one of her over-lavish meals instead of putting at least half of it down the waste-disposal unit. Then he poured himself a whisky and, glass in hand, wandered out into the dank, narrow yard, while from the open window of the flat above pop music blared out. But for once the din did not annoy him. He walked over to the elder tree, and then, on an impulse he could not explain, he tipped up the glass and let a few drops of the whisky trickle down on to the spot where the cat had sat, hunched up in that last vigil of hers, awaiting her death.

He went back into the flat and, though it was still early – the sun had hardly set – he began to take off his clothes and prepare for bed. He wanted the morrow to come quickly so that, once again, he could walk along the tow-path, past the dogs and the boys wading out into the sludge and the skimming eights, and then perhaps, beyond the four giant beech trees, once again could meet . . .

In his pyjamas he opened the drawer of the bedside table and took out the glass tube with the twelve white tablets within it. For a long time he considered them; then he went into the bath-room, pulled out the plastic stopper and emptied them into the lavatory basin and flushed them away. Still holding the tube, he went back into his bedroom, lay down on the bed, outside the sheet, and closed his eyes. Leaves swirled and rippled and among them a round, peasant face gleamed up at him. . . .

His son and his daughter, who had never greatly liked each other, had been dividing up the spoils. By an unspoken agreement the son had not brought his wife and the daughter had not brought her friend.

'When I first saw him like that – clutching that bottle – I felt sure he must have killed himself,' the son said. It was to him that Mrs Crawford, totally calm but for a faint exasperation at a disruption to her daily schedule, had telephoned.

'And Dr Hamilton must have had the same idea to have wanted a post-mortem, I suppose.'

'Oh, yes. He said as much.'

The son opened another drawer of the desk, as scrupulously tidy as the one before it. 'The way that everything has been put in perfect order . . .! Like someone who has made all his preparations for a long journey ahead of him. He must have had some kind of premonition.'

'Poor Father.' And for a brief moment the daughter felt it. 'It wouldn't have been really surprising if he *had* done himself in. He had so little to live for.'

'Well, it was a nice way to go.'

The daughter sighed, deciding that it was she who was going to have that Stubbs print over the chimney-piece, whatever her brother said.

The Fence

I

IN the premature autumn dusk the figure, glimpsed through trees, looked to Muriel like some piece of discarded clothing trailed across the fence. Far off, a voice was booming out over a megaphone that it was time to leave the park.

'Hans! Hans!' Muriel wailed, the mist like invisible cobwebs on her lips. But the dog, rustling in the sodden undergrowth, did not come. It was not her dog but the dog of an elderly neighbour, now shrivelling his already shrivelled body yet further on a beach in Agadir. Muriel, who hated dogs, above all dachshunds, and who had never kept one herself, none the less looked after this one far more solicitously than its doting owner ever did. She was a woman with a strong sense of responsibility.

'Hans!'

The clothing across the fence stirred, as though the sharp-nailed wind had plucked at it, and the dog, instead of answering Muriel's summons, now catapulted out of a saffron tunnel under dripping trees and raced in that direction.

'Hans!'

Wagging his tail and emitting a high-pitched yapping, he bounced around the tall, distant figure.

'Oh, shut up, you silly dog! *Shut up!*'

Across the forlorn undergrowth and across the forlorn years – how many? seven? eight? – that voice, reverberantly contralto, clanged like a muffled bell.

That was how the two women met again.

'Sybil! How extraordinary!'

'Oh, hello, Muriel.' To Sybil there was evidently nothing extraordinary in it. She turned back to the fence, large gauntleted

hands twisting rusty wire around a sagging post. Between effortful breaths she said, 'Those little bastards! From the Comprehensive. They swarm all over the place like locusts. Wreck
everything in sight. They've broken down this fence time and
time again. Can't be bothered to walk the few yards to the
entrance.'

For a moment Muriel wondered if Sybil, by some freak
circumstance, had been obliged to take a job in the park.

'Blast!' Sybil pulled off one of the gauntlets, holding it between her teeth, and again struggled with the wire. The bare
hand was purple, with a floury look around the cuticles.

'You've hardly changed,' Muriel said. 'I recognized you at
once.'

Again the voice crackled over the deserted park, asking them
to leave.

'The little brutes will have that down again in no time at all,'
Sybil said, surveying her handiwork. 'I've spoken to the keepers
but what can they do? I once saw seven or eight of them taunting
one of the gardeners – a boy who looked the same age as them.
He was bedding out some plants and they began to pelt him with
conker shells. He was terrified. Fled eventually.'

'Which way are you going?'

Sybil pointed vaguely into the mist.

'Why not come back with me for a cup of tea or a drink?' In
London Muriel often felt lonely, with Neville away all day at the
Museum and Rosie at secretarial college. She needed the support
of the identities of others and drooped, a creeper wrenched from
its stake, when that support was removed. 'We're in a maison-
ette in Hornton Street. It would be so nice to talk about old
times.' Old times were the days when Sybil had been their
lodger, reticent, self-effacing and yet oddly formidable, in the
enlarged cigar-box that was their house in Kyoto.

Sybil gave an abrupt little shake to her head – how well
Muriel remembered that shake, from the times when she and
Neville had tried to persuade their lodger to do something she
had no intention of doing, or not to do something on which she
had already set her heart. The carrot-red hair, sticking out in

wisps from under the woollen scarf, was now streaked with silver. 'Can't, I'm afraid. Another time. There's been this sale in Brighton and I told Keith I'd be at home to hear whether two or three bids we'd left had been successful or not.'

'Keith! Is he still around?' Muriel was amazed. He, too, had been part of the old times, though he had never been a lodger.

Sybil nodded. 'We're married,' she said laconically.

'*Married!*' Muriel's amazement now turned to stupefaction, her mouth falling open and her small eyes popping.

'Didn't you know?'

'I'd no idea. None at all. When we went back to Australia we lost touch with, oh, almost all the old crowd.'

'It was you who owed me a letter,' Sybil said, arching her shoulders backwards as though to relieve a muscular ache. 'Two, in fact.'

'Yes, I'm sure it was,' Muriel agreed, thinking how surprisingly elegant Sybil now looked. That was Keith, of course. Muriel could hear his clear, rather high-pitched voice exclaiming, 'Sybil, pet – if you don't mind my saying this – that purple jacket is frankly a mistake with that blouse!' But in those days Sybil did not listen to him. 'I'm dreadful about correspondence. And Neville is worse.'

The two women began to walk towards the gate, the dog trotting behind them.

'So you and Keith married!' Muriel exclaimed again, on that note of unflattering wonder.

'Why does it surprise you so much?'

'Oh, I don't know ... You were very good friends, of course. You always got on extremely well, had the same interests. What's he doing now? Is he still with the British Council?'

'Nothing.'

'Nothing?' Keith, son of a working-class family, had had no private means.

'Well, he has a host of interests. He's always busy. The collection takes up an awful lot of his time.'

'The collection?'

Sybil hesitated, obviously unwilling to go on and wishing she had never started. 'Our collection, the collection we've built up together.'

'You mean – the kind of things we all used to ferret around in the junk shops to find?'

Sybil gave a little smile, almost a smirk. 'Well – yes. In a sense. Japanese.'

'You both always had so much taste and knowledge.'

'Well, so did Neville.'

Muriel sighed. 'Yes. But, poor darling, it's always cost him so much to bring up a family that he's never been able to afford any of the things he'd have really liked to buy.'

'I go up here.' They were now in Holland Walk.

'I'd love to see you again. And Keith, of course. Well, fancy that!' Again Muriel reverted, involuntarily, to the surprisingness of it. 'You and Keith! Somehow I never imagined . . .' She had imagined other things – that Keith had had an affair, briefly, with the wife of a French consular official, that he had been keen on this or that Japanese girl, that he might even have been attracted by herself – but never that he would bring himself to marry dear old Sybil. 'Do give me your address and telephone number.'

'Well, we live in darkest Notting Hill,' Sybil said, with obvious reluctance. It took Muriel some time to get her to be more specific.

'I'll ring you,' Muriel said at the end, since it was obvious that Sybil would never ring. 'We must have a get-together. Rosie will be thrilled when I tell her.'

'Rosie?' It was as if Sybil had completely forgotten the eleven-year-old with whom she used to stay at home, playing Scrabble, while Muriel and Neville went out to dinner parties. 'Oh, *Rosie!* Yes, what's happened to her?'

'She's fine. At a secretarial college. She's going to make some-one a marvellous secretary. You know how efficient she always was, even then.'

'Was she? Yes, I suppose she was.'

Muriel eyed her friend up and down, taking in the expensive coat of a soft, smoke-blue wool, the expensive shoes on the long, narrow feet, the expensive solitaire on the same finger as the platinum wedding ring.

'Now look! Just look at that!' Sybil, whose eyes had been wandering away from Muriel, suddenly pointed with outstretched arm at a branch dangling rawly from the tree from which it had almost been amputated. 'Oh, those little brutes! Why can't they control them? Why don't they forbid them to come here? I'd really like to lay into them! I really would!'

2

'It's perfectly obvious that they just don't want to come,' Neville said wearily after the second of Muriel's invitations had been refused. 'Who can blame them? It's years and years. And in any case if we hadn't all been stranded in Kyoto together at that particular time we should probably never have become friends.'

But Muriel was not one to give up. She rang again and yet again, refusing to recognize the note of barely controlled exasperation that, by her third call, had crept into Sybil's voice.

'You'll be in to tea, won't you, darling?' she said to Rosie on the day when, at long last, the Seckers (as she must now think of them) had agreed to come.

'Oh, I don't know, Mother. I don't know.'

'They'll be so disappointed if you're not here. You know how fond they both were of you. Particularly Sybil.'

'*Was* she fond of me?'

'Well, of course she was. You used to play all those games of Scrabble together.'

'I've forgotten all about it.'

'You can't have, darling. How can you have?'

Keith, who had been in his early twenties in Japan – Sybil must be at least ten years older than he – now looked middle-aged, his shoulders bowed and that incredibly soft, almost silvery hair of his thinning and tarnished. It was as if some invisible dust had settled on him, dimming his bright-eyed eagerness and giving to his once fresh complexion a greyish, unhealthy sheen. When he talked now he barely opened his mouth or moved his lips, so that Muriel and Neville both found themselves sitting on the edges of their chairs, leaning forward, in order to catch what he said.

Neither he nor Sybil at all wished to talk of old times. Muriel would cry out, 'Oh, do you remember when . . .?' and they would gaze at her, on each face a curiously dazed, bewildered look, as she launched into some story involving them all. Neville and Rosie watched and listened in silence, seated uncomfortably on straight-backed chairs since there was only one arm-chair and a sofa in the inadequately furnished flat.

'When did you give up teaching?' Muriel at last asked Sybil. 'Was it when you married?'

'A little before that. My old aunt died – you remember the Worthing aunt? – and to my amazement she left me all her money. My cousins were far from pleased. I've no idea why I should have been her favourite. I saw so little of her, being so much abroad.'

Muriel knew now why Keith no longer worked; and she also thought that she knew why he had made so seemingly improbable a marriage.

'How lovely to be left money!' she cried. 'Was there lots and lots of it?'

'Enough,' Sybil said laconically. Keith looked displeased, with that familiar expression that made him suck in one corner of his mouth and peer down his long, delicate nose.

'We long to see your collection,' Muriel now said. 'Don't we, Neville?'

Neville nodded.

'We've been asked to put it on show at the V. and A.,' Keith murmured, stroking his knees with the palms of his hands.

Sybil darted an angry look at him. Evidently she had not wanted him to let this out.

'The V. and A.!' Muriel was as astounded as she had been when she had heard of their marriage. 'Then that must mean that . . . Your collection must be quite something out of the ordinary.'

'Well, we like to think it is.' Keith gave a small self-congratulatory smile, almost a smirk, peering again down his long nose. It was almost exactly the same smile-smirk that Sybil had given when talking of the collection in the park. 'We've worked hard enough at it. Haven't we, Sybil?'

Sybil nodded. 'Bringing up a family can't be as troublesome and exhausting as building up a collection like that, I'm sure.'

Rosie spoke, almost for the first time that afternoon: 'Then you haven't any children?'

'No. We haven't any children.' Sybil clamped her mouth shut. It was as though the girl had said something indecent. Then she resumed: 'We never wanted any. It was either the collection or . . .' Her voice trailed away.

'How terrible!'

Muriel was appalled by Rosie's comment; but Keith and Sybil seemed not to have heard it, though it was hard to see how they could have failed to do so. A silence followed, in which each of them avoided the gaze of everyone else, as though absorbed in a number of separate reveries.

Then Keith swivelled his long, narrow torso around in his chair and said to Rosie, almost behind him, 'Do you collect things?'

'Collect things? No!' She was a striking girl, with her wide-apart, pale grey eyes, her large mouth and her air of quietly triumphant conquest. 'I can't understand people who collect things. I don't want to possess things, anything at all. I hate the thought of it.'

'It's another generation,' Muriel said in apology for the brusqueness and uncompromisingness of this statement.

'Oh, she'll probably come to it in the end,' Neville interposed in his soft, deep, slurred voice, chewing on his pipe. With his leathery complexion and sand-coloured hair, growing thin on his head but thick on the backs of his hands, he looked as if he had been kippered for years in the smoke, thick and evil-smelling, that erupted from it.

'I don't think so.' Rosie was quietly emphatic. 'I don't see what satisfaction there can possibly be in just owning things – or people, for that matter. What's the point? If I want to look at works of art, then I can look at them in museums. And if I want books, then I can borrow them from libraries. And provided I have a room of my own – a comfortable bed – some chairs . . .'

'You like to own clothes,' Muriel reminded her. She turned to their guests. 'You've never seen so many clothes. And half of them she never wears. She buys them, she wears them once and then – that's the end of them.'

'Sounds extravagant,' Keith said. 'Oh, I was like Rosie in the old days – remember? I didn't want to be tied to anything or anyone. That room of mine in Kyoto – absolutely bare. You couldn't understand, any of you, how I could live in it. And when I found one of those pieces in a junk shop I had no interest in it once I had paid the bargain price.'

'You were always awfully generous with your finds. Wasn't he, Neville?'

Neville nodded, remembering all the things that Keith – whose eye was so much better than theirs – had insisted on giving to them.

After the Seckers had gone – more than once Muriel had caught Sybil surreptitiously examining her watch, her hands clasped round a knee – Rosie commented, 'What a creepy pair!'

'Creepy! What do you mean?'

'They're corpses, both of them.'

Rosie gave a small, fastidious shudder as she left the room.

'Neville, what *does* she mean by that?'

'I've no idea.'

3

Muriel did not allow the Seckers to forget their promise to show her and Neville their collection; but it took a lot of patience, persistence and the issuing of many further invitations, refused more times than accepted. Sybil would say in excuse that everything was in such a mess, the central heating had broken down, they were expecting one of Keith's more tiresome relatives for a stay of a week, they were so busy with their catalogue; at which, doggedly determined ('Oh, do leave them alone!' Neville would remonstrate), Muriel would repeat yet again how much she and Neville were longing, absolutely longing, to see all those lovely things.

Finally and ungraciously Sybil said, over a cup of coffee in Barkers, 'Well, I suppose you *could* come to tea next Sunday.'

'Oh, how exciting! Oh, Neville *will* be pleased! He'd have loved to collect things – I mean, really valuable things – himself. Sometimes I feel guilty that I married him and produced all those children for him. Perhaps he'd really have been happier without us.'

On the morning of that Sunday, however, Keith telephoned, his voice unaccountably high-pitched and tremulous, to say that there had been various, unspecified 'complications', which would make it necessary to put off the visit for a week. But next Sunday would be perfect, absolutely perfect. And they'd bring Rosie with them, wouldn't they?

'Oh, I don't know.' Muriel was disconcerted by this inclusion, since she had made up her mind that Rosie must have offended the Seckers. 'She leads very much her own life, you know. But if she's free, well, of course, I'm sure she'd love to come too.'

In the event, Rosie was free; and, surprisingly, agreed to join the party.

'Don't you think that perhaps you ought to change into something, well, a little more formal?' Muriel suggested before they set off. Rosie had appeared in navy-blue slacks and a shapeless red roll-necked sweater that had once belonged to Neville.

'No. Why?'

By now Muriel knew better than to say why. 'I just thought…' she murmured placatingly.

As the three of them trailed up one mean street into another yet meaner, Neville a little in front of the two women, his narrow shoulders hunched and the hood of his duffle coat obscuring most of his head, Muriel saw exactly what Sybil had meant when she had said that they lived in 'darkest Notting Hill'.

'How odd to choose a district like this if they have all that money!'

'*Have* they so much money?' Rosie asked.

'Oh, I should think so. Neither of them works. And if they've built up this marvellous collection . . .'

'I suppose the money's all hers.'

'Well, I imagine so. I don't really know for sure,' Muriel replied, knowing perfectly well.

The street was a narrow one, its grimy and dilapidated late-Victorian houses giving the strange illusion of leaning in towards each other. At one corner an abandoned two-seater convertible was rusting away, a tyre missing and its hood trailing in shreds; at another three black youths were leaning against railings, hands in pockets and eyes fixed in front of them, melancholy, detached, not menacing.

Muriel gave a little shudder. '*Can* this be the right address? Perhaps we've made some mistake.'

The gate hung askew on a single hinge; the steps up to the front door, its paint cracked and peeling, had a long diagonal fissure slicing through three of them. This house was larger than any others in the road, with high arched Italianate windows and a deep foss-like area around the front basement. The garden pressed in on either side, dank and sodden, with trailing fronds and rose-bushes that had grown to the height of Neville's shoulder.

After Muriel had rung the bell there was a long silence, during which she and Rosie looked at each other, both overcome with a wild desire to giggle. Then they could hear the sounds of bolts being eased back, a chain being removed, a key turning and turning again.

'Oh, hello.' Keith, a huge bunch of keys dangling from a hand, did not sound welcoming.

'We were not sure if this was the right house,' Muriel said over her shoulder, as she entered.

'A lot of people say that when they come here for the first time. We chose it for that reason.'

The dim hall was cluttered with objects down its whole un-carpeted length. It felt extremely cold.

'Shall I take your coat?'

'Oh, I think I'll keep it on for the moment, thank you.' Muriel suppressed a shudder.

Neville slipped off his duffle coat and handed it to Keith, who draped it over a bronze Kwannon, some three foot high, and then opened a door. 'Come in here. It's where we sit as a rule. It's easy to heat.'

A single-bar electric fire glowed in one corner of what once must have been the morning room. Muriel went straight over to it, holding out her hands. Books were piled everywhere; Keith was removing some from a sagging armchair. 'Sybil will be down in a second.'

Outside the window of the square, inelegant room, a back garden, all choked flower-beds and overgrown bushes, pressed up close.

'Do sit.'

Rosie lifted a file off a stool and perched on it. Muriel sank into one corner of a sofa, with a mewing of springs, and Neville into the other.

'We have a twin strategy,' Keith explained. 'First, all those bolts and bars and locks and chains – the ones you probably heard – and an elaborate system of burglar alarms. Secondly, camouflage.'

Rosie looked up, startled, from her scrutiny of a threadbare rose on the carpet at her feet. 'Camouflage?'

'We purposely do nothing to this house. We want it to look the poorest in the street. Not easy. But I think that we've succeeded.' He gave a fleeting smile. 'We do nothing to the garden, we never paint the outside, we see that the linings of our curtains are in tatters. That way no potential burglars can possibly feel the smallest encouragement. We entertain hardly at all – only old friends like yourselves, whom we can trust implicitly. We don't want any outsiders to get any inkling of what we have here.'

'It's like a fortress,' Muriel said, with wonder.

'Or a prison,' Rosie put in softly.

At that moment Sybil came in carrying a tray with nothing on it but tea-pot, tea-cups, sugar bowl, milk; Muriel hoped that neither she nor Keith had taken in Rosie's comment.

Soon, even before they had finished drinking the lukewarm tea, Keith started to bring out objects from his collection – tea bowls, scroll-paintings, netsuke, snuff bottles. All were beautifully boxed and in many cases also cocooned in layers of silk. 'Take care!' Sybil would caution as he unwrapped some treasured piece; but it was difficult to see how he could have taken more care than he was doing.

Muriel felt herself filled with both wonder and a wild, aggrieved envy. Neville would certainly be feeling the same wonder, she knew; but envy was an emotion alien to his sweet, placid nature. 'Well, that *is* something!' he would exclaim. 'That really *is* something!' And then Keith would peer down his long, delicate nose, with that near-smirk, and Sybil would draw a long, contented sigh.

Rosie soon got bored, hardly sparing a glance for each object that Neville passed on to her and that she, in turn, passed on to her mother. 'Take a look at that glaze!' Neville would tell her. 'Marvellous!' Or he would run a nicotine-kippered finger round the rim of a tea bowl. 'Feel that! Just feel it!' Rosie rarely carried out his instructions. Once a scroll-painting of a grinning tiger seemed to interest her; and on another occasion a lacquer box, the lid of which was decorated with a fish that Neville told her was a carp. But that was all.

Eventually she got up and wandered about the room, Sybil's eyes from time to time turning to her with a vague, wary hostility, but the others too immersed to pay her any attention. She pulled a book out of a bookcase and briefly flicked over its illustrations of temples, temples, temples, the enormous volume balanced on a knee. When she put it back horizontally on a shelf different from that from which she had taken it, Sybil's hostile glance sharpened.

Then Rosie crossed to the window and peered out into the rank, darkening garden. Its trailing briars and fronds, its overgrown bushes and its giant clumps of cow-parsley looked as if they would force apart the walls that enclosed them, perhaps even eventually push down the house.

All at once she saw a cat in the middle of a thorn tree, one branch of which almost scraped the window. The cat, a tabby, with disproportionately long, pointed ears, sat hunched, its paws tucked under it, as it gazed at her with unwinking amber eyes. She tapped on the pane with a knuckle; and the cat's mouth gaped and shut noiselessly. Again she tapped and again the cat entreated her with no sound.

She put her hand up to the catch, intending to open the window. But even before she touched it, so it seemed, there was a terrifying clangour.

'What's that!' Sybil, who had been involved in answering some question for Muriel about the Kano School, leapt to her feet.

'Christ!' Keith also now jumped up.

Then he saw Rosie. 'Oh, it was you!' he shouted crossly through the din. 'I'll turn it off. You mustn't touch the windows. None of them can be opened.'

He began to laugh apologetically for his previous anger, and Muriel and Neville laughed too. But Sybil, stiff and still outraged, her shoulders flung back and her eyes fixed remorselessly on the girl, did not do so.

'What would you do if it was really someone breaking in?' Rosie asked, looking straight at her.

Sybil turned away and gave no answer.

4

'Well, how did you get on?' Muriel asked a few days later.

Rosie began to pull off her gloves and then to unbutton the sheepskin coat that reached almost to her ankles. 'Well, it's a job.'

'Not much fun?'

'Oh, I don't know.' She gave a little shudder, gritting her teeth, and then extended her hands, stretching and clenching the fingers, over the old-fashioned gas fire. 'It's so *cold* in that house of theirs. And they're oh, so *weird*.'

'They never used to be like that. Keith was rather fun in the old days. Full of silly practical jokes, not caring about anyone or anything.'

'Oh, he cares all right now. About one thing. That collection of theirs. I suppose it *is* very valuable.'

'Daddy says it is. He says he can't think of any private collection to compare with it outside Japan or America. I mean – they have something of everything.'

'They were both cock-a-hoop because they'd got this tea bowl for, oh, fifty or sixty pounds in some auction in Ealing or Hounslow or somewhere like that. They kept asking me if I didn't think they'd got the most terrific bargain. And, honestly, I didn't know what to say. It was this kind of shit-colour and all irregular in shape. A child could have made it. *I* could have made it.'

'What did you have to do for them exactly?'

'The catalogue, of course. Deadly! Sybil had been typing it herself, using two fingers. They'd been too terrified to get in outside help until now. They seem to trust me. Or, at least, Keith does. I don't think *she*'s all that pleased to have me around.'

'I'm sure she is, darling. She was always devoted to you.'

'Not now. One senses these things.'

'It's just her manner.'

Rosie flung herself into a chair. 'She was always watching me. Never left me alone for more than a few minutes at a time. How was I getting on? she'd ask, breathing down my neck. I'd be sure to let them know if I had any problem? Eventually I said that I did have one problem and that was keeping warm.'

'Oh, Rosie! You didn't!'

Rosie nodded. 'She then brought in that one-bar electric fire. I sat so close over it that I managed to scorch my skirt.'

Muriel sighed. 'Anyway, they're paying you well.'

'Not well. But enough.' Rosie reached in a pocket for a crushed packet of Gauloise cigarettes. 'They didn't like my smoking. I could see that. *She* kept emptying the ashtray and *he* said more than once that I would take tremendous care about any fire risks, wouldn't I? Oh, and she remarked that French cigarettes smelled somehow *different*, didn't they?'

'Well, I suppose with all those wonderful things stacked in every corner . . .'

'He's not a bad old thing, not really. Without her, oh, I'm sure he'd be quite different.' Rosie sank deeper into the dilapidated armchair, hunching her shoulders. 'He's rather pathetic really. So under her thumb. And this thing about burglars – it's become a mania with him, with both of them. He's started to wonder if they ought to have agreed to put on the exhibition at all.'

'Why? What do you mean?'

'Well, it'll get lots and lots of publicity. And then everyone will know that there, in Notting Hill Gate, is that terrifically valuable collection. It's asking for trouble, he says.' She drew on her cigarette, staring at the flickering radiants on the fire before her. 'Perhaps it was a mistake to agree to work for them.'

'Oh, darling, surely it's much more fun doing that kind of job than working in an office.'

'I'm not so sure.'

'*Of course* it is!'

5

Three days later Muriel found herself stationed beside Sybil at the fish counter at Barkers.

'Hello, Sybil! I didn't know you came so far afield to shop.'

'Oh, hello.'

Muriel told herself that Sybil was probably harassed and impatient to be served and that this, not unfriendliness, explained the chilliness and abruptness of her greeting.

'I want some buckling, please. You have some buckling?' Sybil leant across the counter, paying no further attention to Muriel.

'You know, if you don't want to make the journey this far, I can always buy anything you need and send it along with Rosie. I come here almost every day. Just telephone and tell me.'

Sybil gave an odd sideways jerk of her head, as she took the fish from the assistant. 'Oh, I think domestic shopping is something one always has to do for oneself. Thank you all the same.' The thanks seemed to come as a reluctant afterthought. Sybil began to move away, a heavy basket on one arm.

But a rebuff, however brutal and whether from friend or lover, had always had the effect of bringing Muriel on rather than putting her off; so that now, abandoning the crowded counter, at which she had been waiting for several minutes, she at once scurried off in pursuit.

'I wanted to tell you . . . Oh, Sybil!'

'Yes?' The monosyllable was not encouraging and neither was the taut line into which the mouth was drawn after she had uttered it.

'Rosie *is* so enjoying working for you both.'

'Is she?'

'It was a wonderful idea. Just right for her. She'd have hated the routine of an ordinary office.'

'Well, I can see that routine is not something for which she has much fondness or aptitude.'

Muriel remembered, fleetingly, the occasions on which Rosie had set off late for work or had failed to complete work she had brought home with her over the weekend. 'I hope you're both pleased with her?'

'Oh, she's managing all right. It's her first job, isn't it? One can't expect too much. It's a pity she can't spell better. But then I find that few young people nowadays can spell at all.' Sybil peered over the cheese counter. 'Have you ever tried this Cheshire Blue?'

'Cheshire what?'

'Blue.' Sybil pointed. 'It's rather rare. This is one of the few places in London where one can find it. It's a favourite of Keith's. I'd better buy some.'

Obviously their conversation about Rosie had come to an end.

6

Muriel asked her usual question, 'How did your day go?', as she retrieved the coat that Rosie had flung across a chair in the hall and began to hang it up. But the girl merely hurried upstairs with a shrug. Muriel remained in the hall, head tilted upwards, as she listened to the sounds of drawers being tugged open and pushed shut, with an occasional 'Oh, hell!'

'Have you lost something?' she called up eventually.

'No. Why?'

'I just thought . . . I heard you . . .'

'Must you spy on me *all* the time?'

'I wasn't *spying*, darling. I just thought, just wondered . . .'

Muriel whispered to Neville in the sitting room, 'Something must have upset her.'

'Well, you'll only make her worse if you ask her what it is.'

There was crash, as of something like a suitcase falling to the floor, from the room above. 'What was that?' Muriel asked.

Neville shrugged and blew pipe-smoke across the top of the book that he was reading.

Eventually Rosie slouched in, hands deep in the pockets of her skirt. 'That woman!' she said. 'I've a good mind to pack it in.' She punched at the buttons of the television set, so that each channel flickered on and then off.

Neville said mildly, 'If you don't mind, Rosie. I'm trying to concentrate on something rather difficult.'

Rosie threw herself down on to the lumpy sofa, a forefinger busily enlarging a hole in the stretch cover.

'What happened?' Muriel asked.

'Nothing precise. Nothing that one can take up. But she makes it so clear that she just loathes my guts.'

'Oh, darling . . . I'm sure you're imagining that, you know.'

Rosie shook her head. 'Not on your life. She detests me. And she'd like to see me out.' She continued to work away at the hole with a relentless, absorbed expression. 'But she's not going to get me out. I'm not going to give her that satisfaction. Unless she actually dismisses me and he agrees.'

'It's just her manner,' Muriel ventured.

'Her manner's the least of it. Even he gets embarrassed at the way she speaks to me. But he's so pathetically weak . . .'

'Keith?'

'Yes. Hopeless. He can't bear a showdown. You should hear some of the things she says to *him*. Worse than anything you

ever say to Daddy. But he puts up with it, puts up with it all.'
Rosie got to her feet, stretching her arms above her as she
yawned. 'I feel so sorry for him. That's why I don't tell them to
stuff it. It's bad enough for him if I'm there. It would be far, far
worse if I wasn't. . . . Well, I suppose I'd better get myself some
bread and cheese or something before I go out.'

'Oh, are you going *out* this evening? I'd no idea.'

'Does it matter?'

'No, darling, of course not. It was just that I was looking forward . . . Oh, never mind.'

'*Must* you make one feel so guilty?'

'I've made a quiche for supper. You can have a slice of it now.
Where are you going?'

'Cinema.'

'With Bob?'

Rosie nodded.

'Oh, I *am* glad you're seeing him again. He's *such* a nice boy.
I was beginning to think that perhaps you and he . . .'

'He's a ghastly bore. And a prig. But, oh well, I felt I wanted
to go out tonight. I wanted to enjoy myself.'

Neville looked up from his book. He cleared his throat as he
ran spidery fingers through his sandy hair. 'If you're not enjoying that job – if Sybil is being such a trial – I should chuck it in,
if I were you.'

'Well, I might,' Rosie said with a sigh.

'There's no shortage of jobs for trained secretaries. Interesting
jobs.'

'Oh, I know that.'

Neville and Muriel listened as, whistling tonelessly, Rosie went
off down the passage to the kitchen. Then, guessing her to be out
of earshot, Muriel said, 'She won't give up that job. Not in a
hurry.'

'Why not?'

Muriel shrank from formulating even to herself her reasons
for that assessment. She shrugged: 'Oh, I don't know. It's just
something that I feel. A hunch.'

7

More than a week later Muriel was again in Holland Park, walking Hans. The dog's owner was by then back from his holiday in Morocco, but he had caught flu and had telephoned to Muriel, whom he knew he could always rely on, to ask her to look after both the dog and himself.

It was one of those January days when, briefly, the whole atmosphere glitters with an illusion of imminent spring. Muriel, who had been feeling tired and depressed – she herself had only just recovered from a long, nagging cold – now, suddenly and unaccountably, began to feel elated. Even the group of school-children who made wild barking noises at Hans, terrifying him out of his wits, and then all but pushed her off the path into a muddy gutter as they marched towards her, five and six abreast, could not wreck that mood. Where the sun shone down through the trees, thawing out the frost, the grass glistened, a tender green. Only the previous evening she had said to Neville, 'Oh, I'll be glad to get away from London and this flat!' and he, chewing on his pipe, had nodded, the two of them suddenly possessed by another of their wild, uncontrollable urges to migrate, they did not yet know where. But now, as the dog scampered across the lawn, leaving an erratic trail behind him, she thought: How beautiful all this is!

'Hans! Hans! Come here! Hans!'

She was standing exactly at the place where the dog had rushed off to find Sybil at that first encounter; and she now saw that two people – children, presumably, from the school – were scrambling over the same fence that Sybil had then been intent on repairing.

'Hans!'

As she called the name again, she realized to her amazement that the female figure was – *could* it be? – Rosie; and that the man into whose arms she had just that moment jumped was, yes, Keith.

Rosie put down a hand to the dog. 'Hans! Fancy seeing you here!'

'Rosie!'

'Hello, Mummy.'

Rosie obviously felt no embarrassment; Keith no less obviously did. He released the girl – he was still holding her arm – to brush away a dead leaf that was sticking to the hem of his overcoat. His face began to redden.

'It was such a lovely day that we felt we couldn't stay indoors a moment longer. Could we, Rosie?'

'Not with that dreary catalogue.'

'Sybil's at the dentist. Poor thing – she's been having a lot of trouble with her teeth recently. We shouldn't really have climbed the fence but it's such a long way round.'

'Everyone does it,' Rosie said. 'Look! There's quite a path through the undergrowth.'

Muriel felt dazzled and dazed, as though by some flashing light. The light, she suddenly realized, was the happiness reflecting back and forth between them. She looked from one to the other, her shoulders hunched and her hands deep in the pockets of her shapeless coat.

'Which way are you walking?' Keith asked politely.

'Oh, home now.' She knew they did not want her company. 'I'm feeling rather chilled.'

'Chilled! But it's so warm today! Gloriously warm!' Rosie turned her face up to the low sun, lips parted to reveal teeth on which the saliva glistened as the melted frost glistened on the grass. 'I want to show Keith the rose-walk.'

'There are no roses there now, darling. It's too late for them.'

'Never mind!' Rosie turned to Keith. 'Let's go and have a look in any case.'

She strode off and Keith, first murmuring something inaudible in excuse to Muriel, followed.

'Hans! Come here! Come *here*!'

It took Muriel a long time to get the dog away from the two retreating figures, who seemed to be totally unaware of his continuing presence. He would obviously – she felt it as a bitter betrayal – have preferred to be with them than with her.

8

Some ten days later Muriel was awaiting Rosie's return from the Seckers before she served up supper.

'I can't think what's happened to her. She's never been as late as this.' She looked again at her watch. 'It's nearly eight, you know.'

'She probably went on from work to meet some friend and forgot to warn you.'

'It's not like her to forget.'

'Oh, she often forgets. You know she does.'

Muriel sighed, went across to the window and stared down into the rain-swept street. 'I hope nothing's happened to her.'

'What could have happened to her?'

'I don't like her walking back along Holland Walk. It gets – sinister once the darkness falls.'

'Rosie's well able to look after herself.'

'No girl is well able to look after herself if a gang sets on her.'

'Why should a gang set on her?'

'You know it happens. Every day.'

Muriel had a foreboding of disaster, she could not have said why.

Neville looked up at her over his book. 'Dish up. Don't wait for her. You can put her food in the oven.'

'It gets so dry.'

'Well, that's her look-out. If she can't be on time . . .'

'Perhaps I ought to ring up . . .'

'Ring up? Ring up where?'

'Keith and Sybil. They may have kept her late. Or asked her to stay on to eat with them.'

'It seems unlikely.'

'I don't see anything unlikely about it.'

Muriel listened to the telephone receiver, tense body pressed against the wall, as it rang on and on. She imagined its clangour reverberating through the empty house like the clangour of the burglar-alarm that Rosie had inadvertently startled into life by placing her hand on the window-catch. Neville stared at her briefly and then murmured with vague exasperation, 'Obviously out.' But still she listened.

Then, at long last, the eerie buzz-buzz-buzz ceased. Some hand must have removed the receiver from its cradle. But when Muriel cried, 'Hello, hello, hello!' with increasing urgency, no one answered. 'Hello!' she shouted yet again.

Finally, she put back the receiver; Neville was now gazing at her from his chair by the fire. She chewed her lower lip, brows puckered. 'That's odd.' An icy tremor suddenly slithered over her arms and down between her breasts. 'That's very odd.'

Pensively, she dialled again. The number was engaged.

She rang up the operator and was told, after what seemed many minutes, that the receiver must have been left off the hook.

'That's odd. That's very odd.' She stared at the dial.

'What's odd?' Neville demanded.

Muriel told him.

'Nothing odd about that. They just don't want to be disturbed.'

But Muriel went out into the hall and hurried into her coat. 'I'm going out,' she called, her voice unnaturally shrill and tense.

'Going out? Where?'

'I'll only be a moment.'

'What about supper?'

She slammed the front door on the question.

She and Neville were the kind of people who seldom took taxis, just as they seldom ate out, drank in pubs or went to concerts and theatres. But now she unhesitatingly flagged down the first one that she saw.

Curiously, since her memory for such things was usually remarkable, it was some time before she could recollect the Seckers' number and street. But at last she thought that she had got them right and the taxi began to slither northwards through the rain.

It was from the far end of the road that she became aware of the burglar-alarm, at first little more than a faint trilling in the ears, then a distant jangling, and finally, as the taxi began to slow, with the driver peering out at the high, narrow houses in search of the number, a frenzied clangour.

'There's some sort of crowd over there,' he shouted over his shoulder as he swerved towards the kerb on the opposite side of the road.

'A crowd? What crowd? Why a crowd?'

But she felt no real astonishment; somehow she seemed to have experienced all this already.

'Search me! But there's a burglar-alarm going off. Maybe they've found someone breaking in.'

Muriel jumped out of the taxi and pushed some coins at him. Two or three slithered through her fingers and rolled into the darkness; she did not bother to attempt to retrieve them. From behind her she could now hear a siren adding its wail to the din.

She pushed through the crowd curdled around the gate. More people were crammed into the garden, pressing against the overgrown bushes and even trampling them underfoot.

'What's happened? What is it?' she asked a huge Negress in a turban and a coat trimmed, improbably in that weather, with what looked like feathers.

White teeth glistened in the moonlight. 'Someone's fallen into that area. Out of there.' She pointed high up the face of the house, craning back her neck, to where one of the narrow, arched Italianate windows showed a jagged, tacky-seeming scar.

'Through the *glass*?'

'Seems so.'

Muriel tried to push closer, imagining that from somewhere down in that foss-like area she could hear muffled, disconnected groans. Then a rough hand was thrusting her to one side.

'Make way! Make way, please! Just clear this garden! Everyone! Make way!'

9

Muriel had been to the hospital.

'Well, how was he?'

'He *looks* ghastly. And he seems very low. Desperate.'

'Poor chap.' Neville, who had an irrational terror of illness and hospitals, had not offered to accompany her.

'An arm and a leg are both on – well – kind of pulleys.' Neville repressed a shudder and averted his eyes from her, as though she were the patient. 'I suppose he broke them. And one can hardly see his face for the bandages.'

'Was *she* there?' Neville's voice trembled.

'She arrived as I was leaving. Hardly seemed to know me.'

'Shock?'

'Perhaps.' What Muriel had really meant was that Sybil had hardly seemed to want to know her.

'Did she give you any idea of how it happened?'

'Well, she wasn't awfully keen to talk at all . . . I asked her, of course. And she then said something about his having had some kind of giddy turn – he'd had one or two before . . .'

'Seems unlikely.'

Muriel shrugged. It was not merely unlikely, she had decided; it was impossible. Keith had been the casualty in some battle, even though the nature of that battle was something at which, for the moment, she could do no more than guess. Rosie, she knew obscurely, had been somehow involved; but she shrank from questioning her about it and the girl would not, of herself, volunteer anything whatsoever.

Coming back from her visits, Muriel would give the latest bulletin; Rosie would withhold all comment. Muriel would suggest that perhaps she might like to accompany her to the hospital the next time she went there or, at the very least, send a get-well card; Rosie would shrug irritably and do neither. When Muriel said that perhaps they ought to invite Sybil over to lunch or dinner – surely she must be lonely – Rosie replied, stonily emphatic, 'No, I'm sure she wouldn't want to come. It's the last thing she'd want. Don't trouble her,' and Neville, clearing his throat, surprisingly put in, 'Rosie's right, you know. You'd better leave her.'

For once, subdued by something commanding in both their manners, Muriel did what they told her.

10

'He's back at home. He still can't walk, his arm's in plaster. And the scars on his face . . .' Muriel gave a little shudder, hugging herself as she hunched her plump shoulders and drew her small, pointed chin down on to her breastbone. 'I could hardly bear to look at them.'

Rosie went on with some clumsy darning, saying nothing.

'Are you going to start work with them again?'

A spasm passed briefly across Rosie's face, as though she had stabbed herself with the needle over which she was bowed. She shook her head.

Muriel could no longer subdue the curiosity that, through all these days, had been throbbing like an abscess deep within her. 'Don't they want you to return? Surely they do!'

'I've no idea.' Rosie's lips barely moved.

'Oughtn't you to ask them?'

'No.'

There was a long silence as Rosie jabbed her needle into the tights that lay across her knees and Muriel stared at her, her small eyes yet smaller in their puckerings of flesh and her well-meaning face flushed and damp.

Then the girl said, 'I don't want to go back. I've no desire to go back. It's the last thing I want. I think – I think I want to work abroad.' It was as if that idea had come to her only at that moment. 'Italy. Or Greece. Or France even.'

'A reference would be useful, darling. They won't give you a reference if you don't even bother to –'

'They can keep their reference!'

'What have you got against them?'

'Nothing. Nothing at all. I just – just don't want to start up there again. That's all. Is that so odd?' Head lowered, she gnawed at the thread as though she were about to devour the tights held up before her.

'N-no.' Muriel sounded doubtful. Then suddenly (that abscess deep within her bursting) she found herself asking the one question that, she now realized, she had been wanting to ask ever since she had heard those horrible muffled, disjointed groans from the foss-like area deep beneath the house. 'Why do you think he did it?'

'He had a giddy turn, didn't he?'

'You don't believe that? I don't. He must have – must have wanted to do something decisive.'

'That was his trouble,' Rosie said. 'That he *couldn't* do anything decisive.' She stared bleakly at her mother.

'What do you mean?'

'She'd – filleted him.' She gave a little smile, almost a smirk, that reminded Muriel of that smile-smirk of both Sybil and Keith when they had talked of the collection. Rosie might almost have been copying it. 'That's what she'd done. And it was typical – pathetically typical – that when he did at last make that gesture of defiance, it shouldn't have succeeded.'

'Shouldn't have succeeded?'

'Well, he didn't die, did he?'

The question was so brutal that it halted Muriel. She had wanted to ask: Was there anything between you both? Did she give him some kind of ultimatum – the collection or his freedom? Did he decide that he must have both those things and could not go on living if she allowed him only one? But the prying words refused to come.

Rosie got to her feet and began to fold the tights, her eyes, suddenly guilty and pain-racked, fixed on her mother. Her lips were almost white; her eyelids fluttered as though in a dust-laden wind.

Then Muriel decided that it was no longer necessary to put any of the questions that she had wanted to put. She knew, she knew it all.

II

Many weeks later – Rosie was by now working as governess to the children of a rich industrialist in Milan – Muriel and Neville walked with Hans through the park in the chill sunshine of a March afternoon. They were talking of a job for which Neville had applied in Canada, their arms linked and their faces averted from the razor-sharp wind that sliced at them down an avenue of leafless trees, when suddenly Muriel tightened her grip and halted.

Hans was racing off to where, almost knee-deep in the saffron undergrowth, Sybil was once again attempting to repair the fence.

'What's the matter?'

'Nothing.' Muriel began to hurry on. 'Hans. He's gone off to make friends with someone.'

'Where?' Now Neville halted, looking around him with his pale, weak eyes.

'Never mind.' Muriel jerked at him, propelling him along the path. 'It's too cold to stand about. He'll catch up. He always does. He won't get lost.'

In a remote corner of her vision gauntleted hands went on with their futile task of attempting to make the fence secure.

Hard Feelings

'HAS my – ahm – nephew got here before me?'

Sometimes, as now, Adrian would describe Mike as his nephew or even as his son; but more often – since he was a snob in spite of his repeated protestation 'I can truthfully say that I haven't an ounce of snobbery in my make-up' – he would describe him as his secretary. Though he was never conscious of it, his choosing of one of these designations or the other depended on whether Mike was at that moment in favour or not. Mike was very much in favour that weekend, after a long period of being out of it.

'Your nephew, sir? No, sir, no one has asked for you.'

There had been a time when Adrian would take pains to mention to any desk-clerk that the reason why he and Mike shared a room was that he had this dicky heart and his doctor had told him that he must always have help within call. But in recent years he had come to realize that whether he and Mike had adjoining rooms or shared a room was a matter of total indifference to the staffs of the anonymous London caravanserais in which on such occasions, forsaking Brown's or Bailey's, he would always put up.

'When he arrives, send him up, would you? Say that I'm waiting for him.'

'Very good, sir.' The desk-clerk, who was not used to receiving tips from customers when they checked in, or indeed at any time, blushed as Adrian pushed a fifty-pence piece towards him. 'Er – thank you, sir.'

'Is that a Rifle Brigade tie you're wearing?' There was a variation of this worn ploy, in which Adrian asked if the tie were an Old Etonian one.

'This, sir? Oh, no, sir.' The young man fingered it delicately.

'Well, it may be, but if it is, I didn't know it. I bought it at Simpsons.'

'It gives you a vaguely military air. Which suits you. I like to be welcomed by a young man who's clean and well dressed and has hair that's a reasonable length. And polite. I stopped going to the rival establishment up the street after being cheeked by a night-porter whom one could only describe as a hippie. Perhaps he was one of these revolting students out on strike.' When Adrian laughed, the clerk decided that he must join in too. 'Well, anyone can see that you're going to go places in this organization. I have a friend in the hotel business – one of the biggest men – and he tells me that the right kind of personnel are worth their weight in gold. Well, it stands to reason. We've built all these hotels but we've done damn little about finding the right people to staff them.'

The clerk was flattered by Adrian's attention, as simple people were usually flattered by his policy of what he called 'building-up'. The opposite of building-up was, of course, pulling-down – a process that Adrian confined only to those people not present to defend themselves against it. 'Yes, I make it my policy to build up. That's the way to get the best out of others.' Getting the best out of others meant getting out of them what was best for Adrian.

The diminutive page with the bags whistled in the lift and continued to whistle as he conducted Adrian down the corridor to his room. Adrian, who was unmusical, did not realize that the boy was whistling flat; but he was none the less irritated by the sound, regarding it as yet another indication of a decline in the quality of service in English hotels.

However, true to his building-up policy, he jingled the change in the pocket of his greatcoat, produced a ten-pence piece and held it out: 'There you are, my lad . . . And how old would you be?'

The boy had just heaved Adrian's suitcase on to the luggage rack, an exertion that had left him surprisingly breathless. 'Sixteen, sir,' he said, in an adenoidal voice so high-pitched that Adrian assumed it had still to break. 'Thank you, sir.' He palmed the coin with none of the embarrassed hesitation of the desk-clerk.

Adrian noticed with distaste that the boy's shoes were scuffed and his fingernails grubby and bitten, but he resolved to persevere. 'Sixteen! You're very tall for sixteen, aren't you? I should guess from your accent that you're a Geordie like myself.'

'No, sir. I'm a Scouse.'

There were times when Adrian, whose family had come from Northumberland, also claimed to be a Scouse, but it was too late to do so now. 'And how do you like it in the south?'

'It's not so bad.'

'But you don't get the same kind of folk. Not the same matiness. That's what I miss. The matiness. Give me the North Country' – he pronounced 'Country' as a stage Yorkshireman would – 'every time.'

When the boy had gone, Adrian began to unpack the suitcase that his sister Pamela had packed for him. Though he was to be away from Tunbridge Wells only for the night, she had put in three of everything: three pairs of shoes; three of the shirts, one of them silk, that she herself washed and ironed for him, since he was adamant that they should never be sent to the laundry; three of the silk-and-wool vests and pants that he always bought from Harrods, because wool alone chafed his skin; three pairs of socks and three sets of cuff-links and three ties. The cuff-links were larger and more ornate and the ties brighter and wider than one would expect this military-looking middle-aged man, with his neat, bristling white moustache and his brogue shoes and his conservatively cut tweed suit, to wear. Drat the woman! Adrian searched everywhere but there was no sign of his Floris Malmaison toilet-water. She always contrived to forget something on these trips.

Although his shirt was spotless after the journey – he had put it on for the first time that morning – he none the less decided to change it for another. He would wear the purple tie, he decided, with the matching purple handkerchief peeping out of the breast-pocket of his jacket. Mike had given them to him, with some subtle prompting, as a birthday present only a few days before the trouble had broken. Adrian had never worn them since. But now all that was behind them at last and it was some-how symbolic of the change to have decided to take them out of the drawer again and to put them to use. Mike should be pleased.

Adrian, who was obsessive about cleanliness – in the early years it had been difficult to persuade Mike to have a bath at least once a day, to change his underclothes regularly and to wash his hands before meals – went into the bathroom in his pants and vest, to soap his neck and forearms and armpits and splash water over his face. Then he brushed his teeth vigorously and gargled with Listerine, throwing back his head and rolling his protuberant blue eyes from side to side. If only he had that toilet-water! But at least he had the deodorant spray. It was the only brand of deodorant that he found he could use; every other kind brought him out into a rash.

He deliberated whether to squat on the lavatory; but he had already tried twice on the train, to no effect. It was odd how some people complained that excitement made them loose; with him it had precisely the opposite effect. He had better make sure that Pamela had remembered to pack the fruit-salts.

Turning over the various medicaments in the suède leather pouch with which he always travelled, he was so absorbed that he did not hear the first knock at the door. At the second he felt a curious leap of panic, even though he had been telling himself for days how much he was looking forward to this reunion.

'Come in!'

The door opened and Mike entered, his suitcase in his hand. It was odd, Adrian had often reflected, how at these hotels there was always a page at hand to help him with his bags but Mike was usually left to lug his up himself.

'Hello, Adrian!'

'Mike! Marvellous to see you.'

Adrian pulled on his blue silk dressing-gown, and then hurried over. 'Let me look at you!' He gripped Mike's shoulders, holding him at arm's length. 'You look wonderful, Mike. Wonderful. Not a day older. God, it's good to see you again. Here, give me that case of yours.' But though he extended an arm, Adrian made no attempt to pick the case up. 'No, I shouldn't put it on the bed, if I were you. There's a rack-contraption for it over there. Tell me all about yourself. You got my letter saying that I thought it best if we met here? You know what it's like getting across London. Otherwise I'd have met your train at the station.'

'That's OK, Adrian,' Mike said in a hoarse, subdued voice that seemed to belong to someone totally different from the exuberant Mike that Adrian had once known. 'I got a taxi. No time at all.'

'Oh, Mike! Extravagant as ever!'

'Well, I'm just getting over this flu. Don't seem I can shake it off. I told you in my letter. I've got no energy.'

Illness frightened Adrian. If he himself were ill, he rushed at once to the doctor; if others were ill, he would either rush away, ignore the fact, or say that it was 'only nerves'. 'Well, you look in terrific health.'

'I wish I felt it.'

Adrian hoped that Mike was not going to be in one of his 'down' moods. They could last for several days, and no exhortations to 'snap out of it' or to 'look on the bright side, for God's sake' were of any avail.

'Poor Mike!'

Mike was about to stretch himself out on Adrian's bed, his shoes still on; but Adrian was quick enough to stop him just in time: 'Actually I thought I'd take that bed, as it's nearest to the door to the loo and you know how I often have to get up in the night. Do you mind?'

'All the same to me.'

Mike stretched himself out on the other bed, putting his hands behind his head and emitting a couple of yawns so wide that Adrian could see his uvula.

'Don't tell me you're tired.'

'Like I said – I'm recovering from this flu.'

'Because I've planned an exciting evening for us,' Adrian went on, ignoring all mention of the flu. 'Two seats in the third row of the stalls for *No Sex Please – We're British*. Pamela saw it and said that Evelyn Laye was terrific – didn't look a day over forty. And then I've booked a table – guess where?'

'Veeraswamy's?'

'You know I can't eat Indian food since I had that tummy trouble. No. I'm going to take you to Chez Pierre. Remember it?'

Mike remembered it. 'Yep,' he said without enthusiasm.

'You look terrific, Mike.'

Adrian always imagined that if one said a thing often enough and with enough conviction, it would eventually be true. In fact, Mike looked so far from terrific that his appearance after these five years had given Adrian a disagreeable pang, instead of the uplift he had promised himself. Drink sometimes had the same kind of effect on him these days: he would sip at a glass of brandy and find that, instead of his spirits rising, all that rose was a recalcitrant heartburn.

'Well, that's nice to know.'

'As handsome as ever. I bet you've been breaking hearts galore in Sheffield.'

In the past Mike had liked Adrian to flatter him about the good looks and the physical strength which he had possessed so conspicuously and, even more, about the business acumen in which he had been wholly deficient. But now he merely turned his head to one side on the pillow, emitting a long sigh.

For a moment Adrian was appalled as he looked at him. God, how he had aged. His face had fallen in – could it be that he was wearing false teeth? – and instead of that marvellous ruddy colour, recalling the boyhood spent on a farm near Taunton, his complexion had a greyish sheen, as of lard. The hair had not merely thinned, retreating on either side of the widow's peak so that the forehead looked disproportionately high for the features beneath it, but it had lost all that rich, oily, blue-black vitality that Adrian had once found so exciting. Mike had always spent an inordinate amount of time caring for two things: his hands and his figure. But the hands now looked raw and rubbed, many of the fingernails broken, with a nicotine stain on the right one that made it appear as if he had spilled iodine over forefinger and middle finger; and his figure had, quite literally, gone to pot, the abdominal muscles which he used to exercise each morning with innumerable press-ups now sagging to give him a little paunch.

But he was still good-looking, Adrian hurriedly assured himself; and those violet bruise-like shadows under the brown eyes – how odd that the eyes no longer sparkled – were probably only the result of that old trouble of *overdoing things* (the euphemism that Adrian had always used). None of us got any younger; one had to remember that five years had passed and Mike was now – what was it? – well, at least thirty-one.

'It's marvellous to see you again. As though it was not five years but only five days. Yet what a lot has happened.'

'It certainly has.'

Adrian went over to the bed and sat down on it, one hand cupping Mike's knee, while with the other he reached for his hand. (Yes, those nails certainly were ugly; but he had probably broken them at his work.) Mike did not move, one hand still behind his head, the other limply in Adrian's, and his eyes searching the ceiling.

'I think what you've done is a marvellous thing,' Adrian said. 'I always knew you would. Not many people would work their way back like that. I don't mind saying that I'm proud of you, Mike. Damned proud. You're a free man again. That's how I look at it. Because all these years you were like someone in prison, weren't you?'

'I don't want to talk about it.'

'No, of course, you don't. And we're not going to talk about it. But I just wanted to say how – how *proud* I am of you.' Adrian squeezed the kneecap. 'You realize – don't you, Mike – that I did it all for your own good? It wasn't revenge. You realize that, don't you? But I had to make you get back your self-respect. That was the important thing. If a man loses his self-respect – well – he's done for. Finished. Isn't he?'

'I don't want to talk about it, Adrian.'

Adrian leapt off the bed. 'Now not another word. It'll all be as if none of it had ever happened. We had such good times together before – before that nightmare. And we're going to have lots and lots of good times now. You'd better get off that bed and start getting ready, or we're going to be late.'

Mike sat up, rubbing at the inflamed lids of his eyes; but he did not rise to his feet. Again he gave a huge yawn. 'I'm ready,' he said.

'But wouldn't you like a shower?' Adrian persisted. 'Or a bath. I asked for both.' He noticed that Mike's shirt was grey around the collar and hurried on: 'And why don't you wear this shirt I have here?' He pulled open a drawer and held up a pale green silk shirt. 'I got it in the sales – at Austin Reed – only last week. Pamela thinks it too young for me, but we know how conservative she is! You can borrow it now and, if it really suits you, perhaps I'll give it to you.'

For the first time Mike showed some animation as he examined the shirt. 'It's a beauty,' he said. 'Real silk. I thought at first it was one of those terylene jobs. You know how terylene makes me sweat. Can I really borrow it?'

'Of course. But why not have a shower first?'

'I had a bath this morning.'

'After that long train journey it'll freshen you up. Go on. You'll find a cake of Chanel "Gentleman's Soap" in there. I brought it specially. I remembered how you liked it.'

'So it's the life of luxury again,' Mike said, more as a question than a statement, as he stripped off first shirt and then vest. The sight, after all these years, of the dark pelt on his chest, narrowing to a line that ran down his navel and then again widened, filled Adrian with a sudden longing and sadness. Poor Mike! He was really a good boy, a very good boy! It was that Danish *au pair* slut and that whole Bayswater crowd that had really been responsible. He was weak, that was the trouble with him. A country boy, who couldn't resist the temptations that others put in his path.

'Dear Mike. Dear, *dear* Mike.'

Naked, Mike came over and stood beside Adrian. Then with a nervous, tentative gesture, like someone making up his mind to stroke a dog that has the reputation of biting, he put out one of

H.F.—C

his hands and laid two fingers on the back of Adrian's neck. 'I've missed you,' he said.

'Have you really? Have you really, Mike?'

'Yep.' He looked down at Adrian, with a small, melancholy-bitter smile that Adrian could not remember ever having seen before. 'Sheffield was very different from Tunbridge Wells. And the factory was very different from the shop.'

Adrian sighed. 'There were often moments when I relented, Mike. I hated to think of you going through all that. But then I said to myself, "No, it's for his own good." And it was, Mike. Wasn't it?'

The younger man did not answer for several seconds. Then he seemed to shake himself: 'Yes, I guess it was, Mike. Yes, I'm grateful to you.'

He went into the bathroom and as Adrian continued to sit there on the bed, listening to the sounds of splashing water, there came back to him, he did not know why, Mike's voice telling him about his father: '. . . He was a right old bastard. Hardly a day passed when he didn't take the strap to me. But I suppose I should be grateful to him. He made me what I am. There's many a kid nowadays who needs that kind of treatment – just as I needed it – and who'll spoil for want of it.' They had been lying side by side – in Amsterdam, was it? – and Mike had been a little drunk as he talked up at the ceiling with Adrian's arm across his chest, pinioning him affectionately to the vast double bed.

'Yep, this is a super shirt, Adrian.'

Naked, Mike had returned to the bedroom, rubbing briskly at his hair with a towel, and peering down at the shirt.

'Oh, Mike! You silly boy! That's not the hotel towel, that's mine! Why on earth didn't you ask?' But then Adrian relented; it was a pity to spoil things at a time like this. 'But it doesn't matter. Go on! Use it! Use it!'

In the darkened theatre Adrian found himself stealing surreptitious glances at the face beside him. Occasionally Mike would laugh at some joke on the stage, but for most of the time his expression remained unhappy, even despairing, the eyes dull and the corners of the mouth – there was a small cold sore on one side – turned slightly down. In the interval he did not want a drink – 'No, don't let's bother,' he said, shaking his head when Adrian suggested one – though in the old days he always liked his double gin-and-tonic and the opportunity to quiz the audience.

'Not feeling too good?'

Mike shook his head. 'I'm feeling fine.'

'We've so much to talk about. Over dinner, not here. I've all kinds of ideas for the future.'

Mike stared emptily ahead of him, the knee that had been restless throughout the performance now once again beginning to jerk up and down.

In the restaurant Adrian said, 'I know exactly what you'll like,' and proceeded to order for Mike exactly what he liked himself. 'This is a celebration and only the very best will do,' he summed up, as he handed the menu back to the waiter. 'We must fatten you up, Mike. I don't think they feed you properly in those digs of yours.'

'Oh, the grub's not too bad. Plenty of it. But like I said, I've had this flu and I don't seem to be able to shake it off.'

'What shall we have to drink? Champagne? Yes, it must be champagne.'

After Adrian had dealt with the wine waiter at length, Mike leant forward, one large, raw hand supporting his chin, to ask, 'How's Pamela?'

'Pamela?' They had not yet talked of her. 'She's aged a bit, you know. But she keeps pretty fit and active. I wish *I* had her health and stamina, I can tell you that.' Although Adrian's sister had undergone a hysterectomy only a few months before, it was convenient for him to maintain the fiction that her health remained far superior to his own. 'She sent her love. And hopes to see you soon.'

'Thanks.'

Something in the intonation of the monosyllable made Adrian protest, 'You mustn't think that she doesn't like you, old chap.

There was a time, I know, when she was – well – jealous. And of course all that business upset her a lot, it was bound to. Especially the loss of Aunt Bea's silver. But she shares my admiration for you now. It was an extraordinary achievement, paying us back through all these years. Quite extraordinary. I can't think of many other people who would have done it.'

Mike did not answer; he raised a *grissino* to his mouth and gnawed intently at the end with a dry, splintering sound, as though it were made of wood.

'I know you think that maybe I'd have been a bit more – ahm – lenient, if it hadn't been for Pam. But you're wrong, you know, I'd have behaved just the same even if she hadn't had anything to do with it. I didn't *want* to put you through it. And the money wasn't *all* that important – or the other things. I've never been one who bothered much about possessions. Now have I? But I felt that you must get your self-respect back, like I said. Otherwise – well, how could things ever be right between us?'

'Yep, Adrian. I see that, of course I see that.'

Mike's tone was still apathetic and he did not look at Adrian as he spoke.

'This smoked salmon is superb, really superb. My God, they do you well here.' Adrian gulped a mouthful, and then, fork and knife poised, ruminated, his eyes fixed on the third button of the shimmering, pale green shirt opposite to him.

He had first met Mike, then a marine, in one of the pubs in Portsmouth to which, telling Pamela that he was going to attend a sale in that part of the world, he would make intermittent visits in search of what he called 'a teeny adventure'. Adrian was experienced enough to know that Mike, like every other of his past pick-ups in that pub, was interested only in making money; but he had also sensed in the boy something unusual – a deep-seated and totally unconscious craving for affection and admiration. A visit to Tunbridge Wells, when Pamela was on a cruise, was followed by weekends in London and weekends in Paris and Amsterdam and then three weeks in Torremolinos in the house of a rich and idle homosexual who was probably Adrian's closest friend. When Mike had eventually come to the end of his term of

service it had seemed natural enough to ask him if he would like
to work in the antique shop which Adrian and Pamela shared.
'What does he know about antiques?' Pamela had demanded,
and Adrian had replied acidly, 'He doesn't have to *know* about
antiques. What we need is someone strong enough to do all the
fetching and carrying that we can't do.' But Mike, though strong,
had a dislike of manual labour and the part-time helpers with
whom Adrian had hoped to dispense were soon back again.
What Mike, with his charm and air of openness, could do to
surprising perfection was to sell.

'He's changed my whole life,' Adrian would gush. 'Who'd
have thought that he'd make such a marvellous assistant? A
totally uneducated boy like that. It's a miracle. A real miracle.'

Adrian set about 'civilizing' Mike – that was the word that he
used to his friends and sometimes even to Mike himself – and in
this mission he was generally far more successful than he had
ever dared to hope. True, Mike never learned to hold a knife
other than as if it were a pen and there were certain vowel sounds
that no instruction could eradicate; but Adrian was soon able to
boast to all and sundry, 'You know, I can take him absolutely
anywhere without a moment of embarrassment.'

Of course Mike could be a wee bit naughty. He would drink
too heavily and what he drank was often whisky for which
Adrian and Pamela had paid. Then there were the 'sluts' (Adrian's
word) on whom he would spend far more money than he could
possibly afford and whom, when Pamela and Adrian were away,
he would even bring back to the house, though emphatically and
repeatedly told not to do so. 'He's not really interested in girls,'
Adrian would say. 'But he must have at least one in tow if he's
to keep his self-respect.' In this Adrian, so wrong about so many
things that concerned Mike, probably was right.

When the netsuke disappeared – Adrian had picked it up for
ten shillings in a junk shop in Battersea and, delighted with his
cleverness, had assured Mike, with some exaggeration, that it
was worth at least a hundred times that sum – it was natural
enough to accept Mike's explanation that some customer must
have pocketed it when his back was turned: after all, every

dealer suffered that kind of loss from time to time. When, a few weeks later, the shop was burgled, Adrian again suspected nothing, though there were some odd features of the break-in that made one of the two detectives in charge of the case speculate that perhaps it might have been an inside job. Less than a month afterwards it was the turn of the house – among the things taken was all Aunt Bea's Georgian silver, left to Pamela alone, since the old woman had never cared for Adrian; and this time, too, the same detective talked of an inside job and questioned Adrian about everyone in his employment. Adrian admitted that he had never been entirely happy about an Irish knocker with whom he sometimes traded; and when the police revealed that this man had had a conviction for receiving stolen goods, Adrian went round saying that the police knew the identity of the culprit but just could not get enough evidence against him.

It was Pamela who finally trapped Mike. From time to time she had been complaining that small sums of money had been missing from her bag, but Adrian had pooh-poohed the idea of any theft – the trouble was, he told her, that she just splashed money around and forgot where she had done so. But Pamela, without telling Adrian, marked some five-pound notes; and one of these she found in Mike's wallet, which she searched one night while he was having a bath.

Adrian still would not have believed Mike to be dishonest – he had a rare faculty for disbelieving anything that he did not wish to believe – had it not been that Mike himself poured out his confession. Seated tearfully in nothing but a dressing-gown on the edge of his bed, with an implacable Pamela on one side of him and a horrified Adrian on the other, he admitted to everything. 'Christ, I hate myself!' he kept exclaiming, between one nauseating detail and another. 'You trusted me, Adrian, you did all this for me, and this is how I have to pay you back. I'm a shit, Adrian. You've got to face the fact that I'm nothing but a shit.'

Eventually he broke into gulping sobs, that sounded like an effortful kind of retching, his large hands clasped between his bare knees and a thread of saliva running down his open mouth on to his chin and then to one lapel of the dressing-gown. Adrian, strangely moved as he had not been moved since the occasion, many years ago, of his mother's death, would have liked to have touched him in comfort, but he was too frightened of Pamela to do so.

'You'd better call the police,' Mike said at last.

Adrian looked at Pamela. Then he said, 'You know I couldn't do that.'

'But Christ, you've *got* to, Adrian! I mean to say! I deserve all that's coming to me.'

'I couldn't do that to an old friend like you.'

What Adrian really meant was that he could not do that to himself. He had a terror of scandal.

'But look how I've treated you! The one person who ever took any real trouble with me in the whole of my life. You've got to call the police.'

It was as though his desire for punishment was as intense as Pamela's desire to see punishment inflicted on him.

Adrian and Pamela stayed up late that evening discussing what course of action they must take. Meanwhile Mike lay on top of the bed in his room, still in nothing but the dressing-gown but indifferent to the cold that made his large hands grow clumsy and stiff, his teeth chatter and his body shake. Pamela had always really hated Mike, though she had pretended to like him; and like so many people who pass over the threshold of middle age in the bitter knowledge that they have never known a recipro- cated love, she regarded her possessions as extensions of her own being, so that what Mike had, in effect, done in making off with Aunt Bea's silver was to amputate a limb from her.

Eventually brother and sister managed to reach a verdict and together they went into Mike's room – it was significant that, for the first time since he had come to stay with them, neither of them knocked or asked if they might enter – and told him what it was. They would take no legal steps against him; but he would have to sign a confession of all that he had told them and over the next five years, week by week, he would have to pay back their losses.

'But you can't do that, Adrian!' Mike had cried out; and at first Adrian thought that he was protesting because the terms were too harsh. But then he went on, 'You ought to hand me over to the police. That's what I deserve. I'll take my punishment.'

Adrian shook his head. 'Pamela and I have decided that we just couldn't bring ourselves to do that.'

Mike's face was pulled out of shape, like a child's when it is about to give way to a storm of tears. Head lowered, he staggered off the bed, approached Adrian and then threw his arms around him, his head on his shoulder.

'Christ! What have I done to deserve a friend like you!'

The next day Mike went north to exile and five years of hard labour; and now the five years were over and the total restitution had been made.

Adrian raised his glass. 'We must drink to the future, Mike. To our future together.'

Hesitantly Mike raised his glass. 'To our future together?'

'Why not? You'll come back to the shop, won't you?'

'Well. I – I don't know.'

Mike put the rim of the glass to his lower lip but did not sip.

Adrian felt an upsurge of irritation that his offer should have evoked, not the expected joy, but a response so ambiguous.

'Wouldn't you *like* to come back?'

'I'd like to come back. 'Course I would, Adrian. But would it – I mean would it – would it *work*?'

'Why shouldn't it work?'

'There's Pam.'

'So what?'

Mike shrugged unhappily.

'Pam and I have discussed it all.' The discussions had, in fact, been prolonged and acrimonious; but as usual Adrian had finally got his way. 'She's in full agreement with me. A hundred per cent. We both want you back.'

'Well, I'll have to think about it, won't I, Adrian?'

'Surely you don't want to go on in those frightful digs, doing that frightful job?'

Mike shook his head, again holding the glass against his lower lip without sipping it.

'Well then?' Adrian put out a hand and covered the raw hand that was clutching the stem of the glass. 'It can be as it used to be in the old days, Mike. It needn't be any different.'

Mike gave a sudden, choking laugh, not of mirth but hysteria. 'It's *got* to be different. You wouldn't want all that to happen again, would you?'

'It won't happen again.'

In the taxi on the way back to the hotel Adrian felt tender and relaxed. He slipped an arm round Mike's shoulder: 'Oh, it's good, it's damned good to have you back, Mike. All those years. I don't know how I got through them. Perhaps it was silly of me, perhaps I ought to have forgotten the whole affair and told you to return. But it wouldn't have been fair to you, would it? Would it, Mike?' Mike did not answer, his face expressionless as he stared out of the window at the lights that whisked past. 'Dear Mike.' Now Adrian had a hand on his knee. 'You know, you're the only person I've ever loved. Yes, honestly.' Adrian had said this to other people but now, in a moment of devastating clarity, he saw that it was true. He had never loved anyone else, because he had never been capable of loving; but somehow Mike had given him that capacity. Then he thought, with a piercing jab of excitement, of the hotel bedroom that awaited them.

There seemed to be an ineluctable weariness in all Mike's movements as he stripped off his clothes, dropping them unfolded, one by one, on a chair. Naked at last, he sprang into one of the beds – the one that Adrian had assigned him – and tugged sheet and blankets up to his chin. He was shivering; his jaw was trembling.

'One moment, Mike.' Adrian suddenly felt that his bowels, obstinately closed all day, now wished to open. 'Hang on.'

His dressing-gown swished as he hurried into the bathroom. Then he came back; went awkwardly to the chair over which his jacket was draped; bent over; got something out, which he stuffed into his dressing-gown pocket; and disappeared again.

Soon he re-emerged, beaming: 'There we are! Now I feel much comfier.'

The dressing-gown was placed on a hanger on the door; the key was turned. Adrian was wearing only a pair of Y-fronted pants. It was his modest habit to wait to remove these until he was under the bedclothes.

'Dear Mike.'

But when he put his lips to the cheek on the pillow beside him, he was astonished to taste something damp and salt.

'Mike! What's the matter?'

'What did you get from your jacket?'

'When?'

'Just now. When you went to the toilet.'

'Only some Kleenex. You know how I hate tough lavatory paper.'

'You took your wallet.'

'What are you talking about?'

'You had all your money in your wallet. And you took it in case I should pinch it.'

'Nonsense!' But there was no conviction in Adrian's voice.

'Then let me look in your dressing-gown pocket. It must be there now. Or did you hide it in the toilet?'

'Well, yes, Mike, I did take my wallet. But that was because I didn't want – didn't want to put any temptation in your way. Was that so bad of me?'

'You were right not to trust me. Perhaps I would have taken it.'

'Don't say such silly things. All that's behind you. We both know you've learned your lesson.'

Again Adrian tried to take Mike in his arms; but the younger man remained obstinately on his back, his arms behind his head and his eyes staring upwards.

'Mike! . . . You're not angry, Mike?'

A long silence.

'Mike?'

Mike then said in that hoarse, subdued voice so unlike the voice that Adrian had known, 'It wouldn't do, Adrian.'

'What wouldn't do? What *is* all this?'

'My coming back.'

'But I *want* you back.'

Mike shook his head. Then he said in the same hoarse, subdued voice: 'Will I get into the other bed or will you?'

'For God's sake, Mike!'

But Mike climbed slowly, shivering, out of the bed, his arms crossed over his thin, hairy chest and his shoulders hunched, to enter the other bed with a creak and a long, trembling sigh.

'I just don't know what all the fuss is about!' Adrian raised himself on an elbow and peered at the outstretched shape in the bed beside him. 'You really are incredibly touchy.' When, after several seconds, Mike had still not said a word, Adrian conceded, 'Oh, very well then! If that's how you want it! But I'm – ahm – I'm sorry, Mike.'

Still there was no answer; and when Adrian held out a hand across the space between the two beds, Mike did not stir.

'No hard feelings?' Adrian said.

Again there was silence.

Subject and Object

WHEN, returning from Matins, Mrs Randel-Elder found the object right in the middle of the top step of her dear little house off Chelsea Green, she decided at once that that Alsatian, belonging to that common couple in the basement flat opposite, must have left it there. It was not the kind of thing that one enjoyed clearing up at the best of times, still less before settling down to the Sunday joint. If Nanny were still with her, instead of in St Luke's recovering from a stroke, she would have asked her to be an angel and do something about it. But as it was, it was she herself who had to fetch the shovel and later the bucket of disinfectant and the mop. It was both disagreeable and humiliating to have to do something like that and she only hoped that the neighbours were too much occupied with getting and eating their Sunday lunches to see what she was up to.

It was only after her own Sunday lunch that she suddenly wondered how the Alsatian dog had managed to enter the front garden. She had shut the gate when she had gone to church, she was sure of that, and it had still been shut on her return. The wall was too high even for a dog so large and agile to leap or climb. Oh, but she knew what had happened, she knew all right! That couple must have let in the dog on purpose, just to pay her out for what she had felt obliged to say to them the other day.

When her daughter Ruth came round for tea Mrs Randel-Elder told her all about the object, while Ruth's American husband was down in the cellar collecting some bottles of claret that were the real but undeclared reason for their visit; and Ruth then said, 'Well, of course, Mother, if you *will* pick quarrels with people of that class, what can you expect?' and Mrs Randel-

Elder replied that she had not *picked* a quarrel, but if a dog repeatedly cocked a leg against your gate, you could hardly be expected to take that kind of thing lying down, now could you?

It was some ten days later that she came on the second of the objects. This time she almost stepped on it as she was about to clamber up on to the high bed that she and her dead husband had once shared together, that darling Mummy and Daddy had shared before that, and that now so often seemed so terribly large, chilly and empty. Ugh! How on earth could it have got there? As, breathing heavily, she scrubbed and scrubbed at the thick pile of the carpet, she wondered whether at any time that day she had left a window or door open. Unless, of course, that dreadful couple had either picked the lock or got themselves a key. The thought also came to her that perhaps the daily, Mrs Moon, outwardly so friendly and cheerful, might have let in the dog to pay off some secret score of her own. But that hardly seemed possible. She had often said that Mrs Moon, who lived on the nearby Peabody estate and whose husband had been a Guardsman and was now a bank commissionaire, was the salt of the earth. She decided to say nothing to Mrs Moon. It would be too embarrassing and, well, somehow *infra dig*.

After that, the objects arrived more and more frequently and she began to develop a dread of coming on them. She had never expected that one day she would feel relief at walking out of her home and apprehension at returning to it. One never knew where one might not find one of the disgusting things next: by the bath, in the cupboard under the splendid new double sink, in a dark corner of the dining room, once even on top of that darling Chippendale chair inherited from Auntie Ida. It seemed now as if she were perpetually shovelling, mopping and scrubbing with soap and disinfectant. Mrs Moon began to remark on the disinfectant smell – Mrs Randel-Elder had, for some reason that puzzled her, still not been able to brace herself to tell her about the objects, and they never appeared while she was there, almost as though the dog (if it *was* that beastly dog) or whoever was the culprit was somehow kept at bay by her stolid, no-nonsense presence. 'It smells like a hospital in here,' Mrs Moon would comment. Or, like a teetotaller reproaching an alcoholic, 'You've been at that disinfectant bottle again.'

Ruth came back with her husband and their three children from the holiday in the Bahamas for which Mrs Randel-Elder had paid; and Mrs Randel-Elder at last ventured to speak to her again about the objects – with her, too, she had experienced a reluctance to refer to the matter, though she could not have said why. Ruth stared at her mother out of those large, watery, slightly protuberant blue eyes of hers, and said, 'But it sounds *most* extraordinary!' and then, 'Are you absolutely sure you're not . . . ?' She broke off. Mrs Randel-Elder retorted, 'No, I am *not* imagining it! Not at all. Oh, I knew you'd say that! Typical.' Ruth nibbled at a biscuit with her tiny rabbit teeth and then said meditatively, 'Ed and I think that you shouldn't be living alone. Apart from your heart, London is no longer a place for a woman of your age to be living alone.' Mrs Randel-Elder knew that Ruth was again going to suggest that she should move into that convent where they took in wealthy old women; and she also knew that her daughter and that feckless husband of hers had their eyes on the house. She decided never to mention the objects again.

It was when Mrs Moon said, 'You don't look at all well, ma'am, if you don't mind my saying so,' that Mrs Randel-Elder decided that she would have to tell the police, embarrassing and humiliating though that would be. In the event, it proved even more difficult than she had expected to explain to the two rather oafish young men, the apparently senior of whom had thick blond hair almost down to the collar of his tunic, and while she was doing so, she did not at all care for the way in which they alternately stared at her and exchanged glances with each other. 'If you could *show* us . . .' the blond one said, in his disagreeable North Country accent, when she had finished. 'Show you!' Mrs Randel-Elder cried out. 'I'd hardly leave an object like that lying about the house.' The policeman shrugged and again he and his colleague exchanged those slightly smirking glances. 'In that case, madam . . .' Well, one just had to accept the fact that now-adays a totally different type of man was going into the force.

She had been foolish to imagine that she would get any help from that quarter. As they departed, the policeman, who had left his colleague to do most of the talking, now turned to say, 'Perhaps next time one of these – these *objects* appears, you'd ring us, madam, before you clear it up.' He seemed to put the word 'objects' into insulting inverted commas. She did not like that at all, not at all.

After that life became a nightmare of coming on the objects and endlessly shovelling, mopping and scrubbing. When Mrs Moon again remarked that her mistress seemed to be off-colour, Mrs Randel-Elder told her hysterically that she was never, ever to say that again to her, and Mrs Moon then shook her head to herself as she turned back to her task of cleaning out the oven and mumbled that she was sorry, she was sure, she knew better than to put her nose into what was no concern of hers. Ruth asked more than once, 'Are you sure you're all right, Mother?', until Mrs Randel-Elder was goaded to answer that it would be a long time before she decided to die and Ruth inherited the house. Ruth looked shocked and angry at that, biting her thin lower lip. Later she told her husband that Mother was really becoming awfully *odd*. Mrs Randel-Elder wondered whether to go away for a while: to dear, boring old Kitty in that draughty house near East Grinstead, or to one of those ghastly health-farm places, or even on a cruise. But she was not going to be beaten by whoever it was that was playing this peculiarly nasty trick on her. *They* were obviously intent on getting her out of the house (it was then that she first began to suspect Ruth, Ed and perhaps even the children of being responsible) and she was not going to play their game, oh no.

All the worry and dread and the ceaseless effort of cleaning up – the objects were now turning up three and four times a day – began to have a bad effect on her failing heart. When she went to see the doctor he asked if anything were on her mind, and reluctantly she blurted out the whole story about the objects. He stared at her over his glasses, much as the policeman had stared, with a kind of pitying incredulity, and then he said that perhaps he'd better have a word with her daughter and meantime he would prescribe a tranquillizer in addition to the heart pills. Mrs Randel-Elder told him that she would be grateful if he would say nothing, nothing whatsoever, to her daughter, who had enough troubles of her own already. The doctor sighed. He had known Mrs Randel-Elder for many, many years and was in the habit of referring to her as a tough old bird.

A few nights later Mrs Randel-Elder was aroused from sleep by a noise from downstairs. She sat up in bed, put on the light beside her and listened. The noise, a kind of shuffle, was not repeated. She was not afraid, not at all. She was glad that at last *They* had made Their presence known by something other than those filthy objects and that at last she might be able to catch Them at it. She got out of bed, slipped her arms through her wrap and began to creep down the stairs, an old woman with yellow, horny feet and hair that looked as if it were made of fine, silver wire. The noise had come from the sitting room, immediately below her bedroom, and it was into it that she tiptoed. But when she switched on the light there was no one to be seen. She began to sob silently to herself in a fury of frustration; and as she did so, twisting her arthritic hands in each other, she suddenly saw the object just beside the grand piano, on which darling Mummy used to play so many years ago and which now stood, untouched and untuned, under the French windows into the garden. She approached the object and looked down at it; and slowly, like viscous floodwater seeping under a door closed in panic against it, a memory began to break in on her . . .

She was a child of seven and Mummy was gazing down and saying, 'But it's disgusting, absolutely disgusting,' and the boy – he looked only about fourteen, though later they had learned that he was nearly twenty – had pleaded with her and Daddy to let him go, he hadn't meant any harm, he'd never been in any kind of trouble before, he was only looking for one or two small things to see himself back to Wales. 'But how could you?' Mummy had demanded. 'How could you? How could *anyone*?' And the boy, his pale skin almost transparent now with fright, had run a desperate hand through his tangled red hair and had half-sobbed that he was sorry, truly he was, he only wanted

another chance, another chance, that was all. Daddy had intervened at that point to say nervously that people did things like
that when they were really scared (he had, after all, been through
the Boer War and he knew about such things) but Mummy said,
what nonsense, nothing so disgusting, so utterly disgusting, had
ever happened to her before, there was absolutely no excuse for
it. And so the boy – whom they had come on when they had
returned from a Boxing Day pantomime – had been eventually
led away by two policemen . . .

Again Mrs Randel-Elder stared down at the object; and yes,
it was exactly the same object, in exactly the same place, at which
the terrified, disgusted little girl in her pale blue taffeta frock had
stared down, until Mummy had cried, 'Oh, for heaven's sake
get the child out of here!' and Nanny – who had just then
appeared in dressing-gown and curlers – had led her away. It
was the same, exactly the same. And at the realization she felt
a terrible pain somewhere deep inside her, as though a root long
buried were being wrenched away . . .

She heard a little whimper; and turning with a start, she found,
so near to her that she could have put out a hand and touched his
trembling, transparent cheek, that boy of, oh, more than seventy
years ago. His mouth opened, the lips loose and wet, just as they
had been then, and even before he said the words, she knew
what they would be: 'Another chance . . . Another chance . . .'

She gave a shrill scream. The root was being dragged out of
her, agonizing jerk by jerk. She put her hands to her breasts.
Then she felt some object shift and slide within her, with a
terrible twist of the bowels, and she suffered that final humiliation
that fear inflicts on the living and life inflicts on the dying.

To the Camp and Back

In recollection, it seemed to Christine as if it had snowed every day of that winter at Oxford. Certainly it was snowing that Saturday afternoon, the large flakes drifting down languorously as she trudged towards the camp to meet the German prisoner whom her Quaker cousin, a don at one of the colleges, had trapped her into meeting. 'But I don't really like Germans,' she had protested when, arriving for a cup of tea at his rooms, she had been told of the other visitor who was coming, and Michael had answered, 'Forget that Thomas is a German. The important thing is that Thomas is Thomas.' She had never been able to forget that Thomas was a German, neither then nor on the two subsequent occasions they had met in Michael's rooms. How could she, when her fiancé had been shot down by the same Luftwaffe of which Thomas had been a member? And yet here she was, on her way to meet him, having promised to take him out to Blenheim.

Christine saw him, long before he saw her, in conversation with two other prisoners: they were all laughing as they passed under the railway bridge, and then one of his friends punched Thomas in the ribs in play. She felt a momentary resentment that they should be so light-hearted when, for days past, she had been in a mood of depression.

Thomas at last saw her, waved, grinned and began to hobble up the hill. She had forgotten about his leg, the knee shattered when he had been shot down; the injury had not been noticeable in Michael's rooms, but now she wanted to cry out, as he hurried towards her, 'Take care! We've plenty of time!'

'Christine!' It was Michael, not Christine, who had told him to call her that. 'You could have waited for me in Michael's room. I did not expect you to walk up here to meet me in this snow.'

'Oh, I wanted some exercise after a morning in the Bodleian – the university library.'

As he hastened to hold out a hand – this German habit of always shaking hands was something that embarrassed her – she saw that, ungloved, it was raw and swollen with chilblains.

'Your hand!' she could not help exclaiming, even at the moment she could feel it icy in her own.

'Yes.' He gave a small, bitter smile. 'Unfortunately one of my comrades must have borrowed my gloves.'

'Perhaps I could find you a used pair. Or Michael could.'

'That is very kind of you. But I am afraid that they too might be *borrowed*. Then you would never see them again.'

'That wouldn't matter.'

They began to trudge back to the town in silence, the flakes settling on their bowed heads and shoulders and from time to time touching a cheek or eyebrow, feather-soft and icy.

'Is your influenza really over now?' Christine asked at last. She, too, had had influenza, and she thought that perhaps she had given it to him, since she had gone out with it to Michael's on that occasion of their first meeting, instead of retreating to bed.

'I cannot make it last any longer.' Again he gave the small, bitter smile, with which she had become increasingly familiar since she had come to know him. 'Tomorrow I must go back to work.'

'And how do you feel about that?'

'Bad.' He laughed. 'No, not all bad. I shall get some money. But in this weather!' He gave a shiver, hunching himself deep in his cumbersome camp-issue greatcoat, and then laughed. 'I am not tough enough for a prisoner. I dislike the cold and I get too easily tired. I am not used to working nine or ten hours a day in the fields.'

'What job will you be doing?'

'Tomorrow we shall pick brussels sprouts. Do you like brussels sprouts?' Christine pulled a face. 'No, I do not like brussels sprouts either. And I like them less and less now that I must pick them. Where we were working last month, there were some land-girls and I have seen them cry with the cold. The sprouts are frozen and your hands get frozen and there is nothing you can do about it.'

'When will you get back home?'

Hands deep in pockets, he raised his shoulders in a gesture of hopelessness. 'In any case I have no home. Bombed. The Russian zone. My parents are dead and my sister does not write to me. Perhaps she also is dead? Perhaps, after all, it is better for me here. For the others it is often different – they have mother and father or wives and children waiting. But otherwise – what is there?'

'Things will get better. After all, it's only since Christmas that you've been allowed out. There'll be other concessions.'

'Oh, yes, slowly things will be better.' But he said it without confidence: no doubt he had heard that said, and said it himself, often enough before.

For the rest of the walk she talked to him about music; before the war he had been studying the clarinet – 'But all that is now in the past,' he said with the hopelessness that got on her nerves. 'I shall always listen to music but it is now too late to hope to play it for others.'

Because Blenheim was outside the five-mile limit for the prisoners, Michael had proposed that Thomas should disguise himself in some of his clothes.

'Isn't that forbidden?'

'Of course.'

'Then you could get into trouble?'

'I suppose I might. If he gets caught. But he won't be the first prisoner to whom I've lent clothes, not by a long chalk, and so far I've got away with it.'

'Oh, Michael, you're an idiot.' But she admired him for a recklessness of which she knew herself to be incapable.

In the rooms, so hot after the cold outside that Christine flung off first her overcoat and then the jacket and cardigan under it, there was a note, propped up against a vase, waiting for them:

'Have to deputize for an ailing colleague. A seminar on Swift – know nothing about him! Clothes in bedroom. May see you later?'

Michael's clothes fitted Thomas well; his chest and shoulders were a little too broad for the jacket and he had to wear the trousers low on his hips, but otherwise it would be impossible to guess that the suit had not been tailored expressly for his figure. He looked like any ex-service graduate and if one stared at him – Christine was staring now, as he stood before her – it would not be because one suspected him of being an impostor, but merely because of his stature and good looks.

'Why are you looking at me like that?'

'You seem so – different.'

'Of course! Now you can pretend that I am also a professor like your cousin.'

Still she stared; and the depression that had weighed on her for the last weeks – ever since she had met him, had she thought about it – shifted uneasily, and then, in a sudden rush, slithered away from her, just as outside the oriel window of the college, now that the wind had veered, huge cakes of snow kept disintegrating to plunge downwards into the quad.

'One would not recognize you,' she said in a tone of wonder.

'Let us hope that no one does.'

When they reached Blenheim the sun was already sinking. Momentarily, the palace caught its rays and brimmed with fire; each window became a peep-hole into the conflagration, so that it seemed as if, even while they watched, the flames would burst through, the roof would collapse and the whole great edifice would tumble, subside, disrupt in a million particles of light. But in a few seconds it was all over. The sun descended into mist; the fire ebbed; the windows became windows. Everything was bare, moist and chill.

Now it was thawing fast, and as they tramped through the solitary park, the slush wet their feet and the trees wet their clothes. Noises of invisible dripping were all around them. Far off, they could hear a roar of water descending into 'Capability' Brown's artificial lake. Yet for all the melancholy and the damp-

ness, the place had its beauty; the lake, stretching on into the
mist, the faint, barely perceptible outline of the trees, the
dimming light and, beyond, the fantastically uncertain silhouette
of the palace – in all this, Christine's former depression seemed
to have taken on an external form, so that, viewing it, she felt
strangely comforted.

How it happened then she did not know. Sometimes, thinking
about it later, she decided that she had willed it to happen. But
was it possible to simulate a fall so neatly? – the foot touching
the ice, slipping, the hand flung out, the whirl around, each
intricate movement timed precisely as in a ballet until his arm
came across her.

Then they were clutching each other, her face first against his
coat and then raised questingly upwards to his. She could
hear him mutter something in German, incomprehensible to
her.

'What are you saying?'

'I am asking – why am I so lucky?'

His saliva tasted bitter as his mouth closed on hers, but
strangely that did not disgust her, she only felt a deep pang of
pity for him, knowing about the wretched diet on which the
prisoners had to live.

'Is that right?' he asked.

'Is what right?'

'For me to love you. What future can there be for us?'

'Oh, don't talk about the future!'

Suddenly she felt fretful and frightened.

'But some day we shall have to talk about the future.'

'But not now.'

'Ah, Christine, you must understand that I am –'

'No, not now. Not now.'

Again she raised her mouth up to his, tasting the saliva
that seemed to have in it all the accumulated bitterness of his
captivity.

'I live only for the present,' she said, slipping an arm through
his. 'You must learn the same. Only for the present.'

'Only for the present. I will try.'

He said it on a note of weariness that made her feel anxious and ashamed.

'This way?' He pointed. Arm in arm, so close that from time to time they had stumbled over each other, they had neither of them cared in which direction they were going. Now they had lost themselves. 'Yes, I think so,' he answered himself.

'But surely the village is over there?' Christine pointed to the left.

'No. Over there, I think.'

She laughed. 'Does it matter anyway?'

'A little. You forget that we have a bus to catch. And I must be back at the camp in time.'

'Heavens! How prosaic you are!'

'Prosaic?'

'Unromantic.'

'It is not good for a prisoner to be too romantic. Is it? See what has happened to me.'

Again she felt an obscure twinge of shame and guilt.

'Poor Thomas!'

'Do you know when I first realized?'

'Realized what?'

'That I loved you, of course.'

'*Do* you love me?'

'Of course.'

She had put the answer playfully; now the calm reply brought her not exhilaration but a foreboding chill.

'Well, it was the first time I saw you,' he went on. 'Do you remember how I stammered and went red and could say nothing?' Yes, she remembered. In his coarse, cumbersome prisoner's clothing, he too had then struck her as coarse and cumbersome, in no way attractive. 'I think that was the first time that I fully realized what it meant to be a P O W. I ran away from the room ashamed of my uniform, my heavy boots and my greasy cap, my clumsiness, my embarrassment, everything. You looked so — so clean.' He laughed, pressing her close against his body as he did so. 'Yes, that is a funny thing to tell a girl. But nothing at the camp, no one, seems really clean. One scrubs the floor and one scrubs one's clothes and one scrubs oneself. But there is always something, an atmosphere, a smell, like the sweat-stains one can't get off one's uniform.' He broke off. 'Now we really are lost!' He halted, peering through the mist, while one of his hands felt for her breast through the constriction of her winter clothing.

'No, we're not. Listen. I can hear the traffic on the main road. Beyond those fields there.'

'That is no traffic.'

'Don't be silly! Of course it is. We've only to walk across the fields, we can slip through the barbed wire here.'

He looked unconvinced.

'You don't believe me?' He smiled and shook his head.

'I bet you five bob. Do you take me on?'

'If you win, I shall not be able to pay you.' All at once a look of humiliation had come over his face. 'You are with a man who is not even able to pay for his own bus fares.'

'I wish you wouldn't talk like that. Naturally you can't pay for things. That's understood.'

'Still –' He made a gesture of resignation. Then he burst out: 'Perhaps it is stupid of me, but I do not like always to eat other people's food, always to spend other people's money. First it was Michael, now it is you.'

Shouts came to them through the mist, vague figures emerged only to disappear again; a football materialized in mid-air and thudded to the ground with a whisk of slush. Three boys, with bare, red knees, red faces and cropped hair, collided together as they ran towards it; then they saw Christine and Thomas and skidded to a halt.

Christine approached. 'I wonder if you could tell us – is the main road over there?'

'It is. But you can't go through this way.' The tallest of the three boys, who must have been ten or eleven, had picked up the football and placed it under his arm. His raw face, its short, saddle-back nose covered in freckles, expressed an overweening hostility.

'Oh, why not?'

'Because this is private land, that's why. Didn't you see the barbed wire? All this land belongs to my father. It's his farm.'

'But surely he wouldn't mind –? You see, we've been lost. And we're afraid we may miss our bus if we don't get to Woodstock soon.'

The boy put his hands on his hips, dropping the ball to the ground. 'You can't go through,' he repeated.

'But that's absurd. We can't turn back. We don't even know the way. It'll be dark quite soon.'

'That's your look-out. Shouldn't have come through in the first place.'

The other two boys, their stockings rucked about their ankles and their shorts pinched at the waist by identical snake-belts, had so far only scowled at the intruders. But at this point one of them chimed in, in a shrilly girlish voice: 'Serves you right for trespassing.'

'We're not trespassing,' Christine snapped back. 'We've done no harm.'

'Well, you're jolly well not going a step further. That's flat. Otherwise I'll go and tell my father. He'll see you off. And damn quick too!'

Thomas, who had so far refrained from joining in the argument, touched Christine's elbow. 'We'd better turn back.'

'Certainly not! And let these little wretches boss us around? Come on. Don't let's take any notice of them.' Thomas hesitated. 'Come on!'

'We don't wish to get into trouble. While I'm in these clothes,' he added in a low voice, 'and more than five miles from the camp.'

'What trouble *can* we get into?'

Christine had said this loud enough for the boys to hear. 'You'll soon see,' the oldest threatened. The three of them had clustered into a tight, menacing group.

Christine strode forward and Thomas followed. As she moved, the boy sprang out to bar her path, but she pushed him aside. He raised one hand, presumably to strike her, but then thought better of it. 'I'll tell my father,' he screamed. 'You attacked me! Daddy! Daddy! Daddy!'

'Oh, go to hell!' Thomas called back over his shoulder.

'Go to hell yourself,' one of the boys yelled, and another: 'Bloody foreigner!'

As Christine and Thomas hurried over the mist-blanketed field, they could hear the boys behind them, jabbering excitedly among themselves or raising their voices to shout an occasional insult. Something splashed a few feet from them. 'What was that?' Christine asked. Again there was a splash: a ball of snow exploded at her feet, drenching her shoes and stockings. 'That'll teach you!' an invisible voice jeered.

Looking over her shoulder, Christine had a momentary glimpse of a barbarically triumphant face before Thomas's – or rather Michael's – hat was knocked off. As Thomas picked it up, attempting to brush away the granules of coffee-coloured ice with the sleeve of his coat, he swore in German under his breath. Then he said, 'Wait for me. I shall go back to them.' He stuffed the hat into a pocket.

'What can you do? What's the good? I suppose we're in the wrong. In any case we don't want a row. Oh, come on!'

Again and again they were hit by snowballs. Their clothes were soaked; the chill, muddy slush stung their faces and melted in their hair. At last they saw the roadway glimmering ahead of them. 'The beasts! The filthy little beasts!' Christine gasped over and over again. At the rim of the field Thomas held the barbed wire up for her as she attempted to get through; but such were her exasperation and haste that the hem of her dress caught, she tugged and a large rent appeared. At the same moment slush spattered outwards from the hard surface of the road.

As they hurried off, the boys leaned over the barbed wire to bay at them: 'Go on! Get out of it! Beat it!'

'Oh, Thomas, Thomas, Thomas!' As soon as they had turned the corner of the road and could no longer hear the shrill voices of their persecutors, Christine clung to him, sobbing with hatred and humiliation. His own face was pinched and grey, as he gasped again and again for breath. 'How cruel, how needlessly cruel! You with your leg! And I'm drenched, drenched to the skin!'

'I wish you had let me go back.'

'To do what?'

'To – to punish them.' He spoke with a cold fury.

'Oh, what would have been the good? It would probably have ended in the police-court and you, being a prisoner, in civilian clothes . . . Oh, how unjust it all is!'

'I am afraid Michael's suit will need cleaning. How shall I explain it to him?'

'Tell him what happened. He'll understand.' Thomas shook his head. 'Why not?'

'Because . . .' He hesitated. 'No, I shall tell him something else.'

'But why? Why?'

'You will not understand this. I feel ashamed. That those three children – !'

'Ashamed?'

He nodded. 'Look what they have done to you. And I – I could do nothing, nothing at all. We ran away.'

'But what else could we do?'

'I do not know.'

'Then what's the point of talking about it?' she demanded, suddenly exasperated.

'No.' He drew away from her, the arm that had been around her shoulder falling limply to his side. 'You have not understood me.'

They trudged on in silence until they came to the bus-stop and there, still in silence, hunched deep into their clothes, waited until they saw the blurred lights of the bus moving slowly down from the crest of the hill.

Michael was not in his rooms.

'I need a drink,' Christine said. 'What about you?'

'Ought you to take a drink if Michael is not here?'

Christine laughed. 'Michael doesn't mind. I always help myself. And he helps himself in my rooms – if I have anything drinkable, that is.'

'He is a good man,' Thomas said.

'Yes, I suppose he is.'

Christine poured herself some brandy. 'Have some,' she said, raising her glass to the light. 'Just what we need to make us warm.'

Thomas shook his head.

'Michael won't mind. Really. Don't you believe me?'

'I believe you. But I don't want anything.'

His mood of moroseness had not lifted.

When she had swallowed the brandy in three burning gulps, Christine refilled her glass and then went into the bedroom where Thomas was changing. She seated herself on the narrow iron bedstead while, self-consciously, his back to her, he began to strip.

She shuddered. 'God, it's cold in here!'

'It will be colder at the camp.'

'Oh, the camp!' Suddenly she was bored with the camp. Her glass to her lips, she examined his stooping form as he unknotted the laces of a shoe. Then, when he was in nothing but the rough khaki vest and pants with which all prisoners were equipped, she rose from the bed, set down the glass and went up to him. She put her arms round him from behind; then she turned him to her. She had expected to catch fire; but the touch of his flesh, in its embarrassment and awkwardness, all at once filled her with melancholy. Again she shuddered; she felt a sudden impulse to burst into tears. She clung yet tighter to him in an attempt to regain the exhilaration of the time before they had been chivied by the three boys.

His hand, still stiff and icy, passed roughly over her face once and then again. She put her mouth up to his, her eyes closed. His lips felt dry and chapped.

'Oh, Thomas.' As they kissed, she pulled him in towards her and then down on to the narrow bed.

For a few moments they lay there awkwardly, their hands running over each other's bodies. Then he disentangled himself and got to his feet.

'What's the matter?' she asked, still lying across the bed.

'Not here,' he said, pulling on his prison trousers, his back to her.

'If not here, then where?'

He sighed, then shrugged. Turning, he said, as he did up the trouser buttons, 'Michael might come in.'

'Oh, Michael! He wouldn't mind. He might even enjoy the sight.'

She had shocked him, she could see.

'You are joking,' he said slowly, as though he were not sure if she were joking or not but hoped that she was.

'No. I'm not joking.'

She jumped off the bed and began to do up the buttons of his jacket for him. As she did so, she looked into his face; but he would not meet her gaze, his eyes turned obstinately sideways and down.

Christine accompanied him back to the camp, even though he protested that it was foolish for her to get cold and wet again. In almost total silence they trudged up the endless gravel-strewn track, its surface scarred with cracks and holes now brimming with slush, past disused lots where bits of machinery rusted deep in grass, past sodden front gardens of mean, red-brick houses, past an occasional field enclosed in a jumble of sagging wooden stakes and trails of barbed wire. 'God, how depressing this all is!' Christine exclaimed at one point. 'Why don't they *do* something about it?'

Thomas halted and turned to her: 'Christine, go back. It is too long a walk for you.'

'No, I want to go all the way. I've never seen the camp.'

'You will have to return alone. That is not good. Let us say good-bye now.'

But she would not be dissuaded.

From time to time, other Germans, muffled in long, dark-blue greatcoats, would hurry past them, momentarily turning to stare at the well-dressed English girl splashing through the puddles on the arm of one of their fellows. Sometimes these Germans would themselves have women with them, young girls for the most part, with mud-stained stockings and frizzed hair on which the damp coruscated. When they peered at Christine, she imagined that their faces assumed an air of disdain, to match the disdain that she felt for them, though she knew it to be ungenerous. These same little chits, or other little chits like them, could be found round any camp where American troops were stationed.

Eventually one particularly noisy group passed them, composed of at least half a dozen prisoners and even more girls. One of the girls was enormously fat and as she waddled along, her face almost wholly concealed by a scarlet pixie hood, a prisoner, far slighter than her and a little taller, suddenly scooped her up in his arms and ran ahead with her. She kicked; giggled shrilly; eventually emitted one piercing scream after another.

'All the juvenile delinquents in Oxford must come out here on a Saturday evening,' Christine said, when this straggling group had passed.

'Yes, it is horrible.' He spoke with a puritanical distaste. 'You will hear men boasting of making love with girls of fourteen and fifteen. Then they imagine that all English women are like that. I would rather go without.'

'But what can the girls hope for in return?'

'A baby!' He gave a contemptuous laugh. 'Oh, they do not want much. A ring made out of a spoon, a brooch made out of an old sardine tin . . .' Again he gave the same contemptuous laugh: 'You see, it is not very romantic.'

'You're awfully priggish about them.' She pressed his arm to take away any sting from the reproof.

'If I speak so strongly, it is probably because I have often myself felt the temptation to take one of those girls. Being a woman, you cannot perhaps understand that. Perhaps I shock you?'

'No, of course not.'

So far from shocking her, the shamefaced admission had caused her a sudden flutter of excitement.

'It is not so much that you want to lie with a woman,' he went on doggedly. 'But you want to have a woman, any woman near you – to look at her, to talk to her. . . . Would you prefer that I did not tell you this?'

'Of course not. I want to know everything about your life.'

'The horrible thing is that, however a prisoner decides this problem, the solution is always *ersatz* – always a substitute. All of us know that. That makes us ashamed.'

'Am I also *ersatz*?'

'*You?*' He was deeply shocked and pained. 'You are not one of these prostitute girls. Please do not talk like that.'

'Is there so much difference?'

'Do not talk like that, Christine.'

She laughed; but he refused to take it as a joke.

They were now on the last and steepest curve of the road before it reached the camp. 'I'd never realized how far it was. How on earth did you manage when your leg was bad?'

'I thought of the punishment if I came back late. That is how I managed.' He put a hand on her arm and again seeing how raw and swollen it was, she cursed herself for having forgotten to find him the promised pair of gloves. 'Let us say good-bye here. We do not want the guards to see us.'

'The other girls have gone as far as the gate,' she said, in a sudden impulse to taunt him.

'You are not like the other girls. I have told you, Christine.'

As he took her clumsily in his arms and kissed her, first on the cheek and then on the mouth, she was all the time conscious of nothing but the sweaty smell of the shapeless greatcoat in which he was muffled.

'Until next Saturday?' he said.

She nodded, her eyes suddenly making out the shapes of two other figures, a prisoner and a girl, clutching each other under a tree further down the slope. Did she and Thomas look as ugly and graceless as they did?

'Do not walk out here. I do not wish you to come out here again. I will meet you in Michael's rooms. All right?'

Again she nodded.

With a final kiss and a wave of the hand he left her; and then she experienced a baffling feeling of relief. Standing under the dripping tree, she watched him while he trudged up the remaining few yards that took him to the bend at the top of the hill. Then she turned, that relief surging into a no less baffling exhilaration, and began to walk back.

The two lovers further down the road had separated and the German was thrusting towards her with long, impatient strides. A farm labourer, she decided, as he came close; and therefore far better able to endure this kind of life than poor, educated Thomas. He passed her without even glancing in her direction, his wide face tensed into the exasperated concentration of a child worrying over a lesson he cannot master. His girl was already running down the hill away from him, trailed by a thin, shaggy mongrel dog. But soon her headlong pace slowed; she halted to pick up a stick to throw to the dog, and when she moved on again it was not at the run but with draggingly indecisive footsteps that brought Christine closer and closer to her with each stride.

They were now both on a footpath crossing a triangle of waste land covered in brambles, strips of old clothing, rusty tins and sodden newspapers. A brook, swollen with the melted snow, raced alongside, washing clean the roots of the stunted thorn trees that lined its banks. Eventually this brook thrust beneath a bridge, where the girl stopped, gazing down into the frothy, mud-stained waters; the dog sat leaning against her legs. Hanging over the rickety balustrade, her bosom pressed up against her thin arms, she struck Christine as being no more than fourteen or fifteen. Her hair had evidently once been elaborately curled, but the damp now made it hang in wispy ringlets to her hunched shoulders. She wore a man's burberry, stained with grease, a fur beret and a pair of improbable platform-heeled shoes with straps across the instep.

She turned from her contemplation of the brook just as Christine passed her: 'Excuse me, dear!'

'Yes?'

'You couldn't spare a fag, could you? I'm clean out.'

Christine hunted for her cigarette case in the pocket of her coat; then as she held it out she suffered a moment of irrational panic – supposing this child were to snatch it and make off? It had been the last gift of her dead fiancé.

'Ta. Got a light?'

Christine was already pulling out some matches.

The girl sucked greedily at the cigarette as Christine did up her coat and pulled on her gloves. 'I could do with that. Just what I needed.' As Christine began to walk on, the girl called: 'Say! Who was the one you was with? Was that Thomas?'

Doggedly Christine hurried forward, head lowered, while the voice pursued her: 'Say! Wait a moment! There was something I wanted to ask you.'

In her haste she splashed into a puddle and the icy water spurted up a leg; but she hardly noticed. To herself she was saying all the things that she had wanted to shout back at the girl but had not dared to. *Get away. Don't talk to me. Don't call me dear! I'm not one of you. I want no part of you.*

Michael stretched his long legs out towards the fire and then ran a hand through his tousled hair with a sharp, tugging motion.

'I'm sorry I missed Thomas. How did the afternoon go?'

'The weather was foul. We got soaked out at Blenheim – you've probably already realized that from the state of your clothes. And then I was a fool and walked with him all the way back to the camp and got soaked again.'

'He's an interesting sort. I think the most interesting to come my way. Though one wishes he'd been blessed with some sense of humour.'

Christine suddenly wished to talk about any topic other than German prisoners.

'How did the seminar go off?'

'Fortunately there was a very loquacious American present, who knew far more about Swift than I've ever known.' He tugged at his hair . . . 'Yes, if only Thomas could be persuaded to take life a little more *lightly*. Though I know it must be difficult in those circumstances, poor devil.' He kicked out at a lump of coal and sparks whirled up the chimney. 'Going to see him again?'

Christine stared into the heart of the blaze. 'Oh, I don't know,' she said. 'I might, I suppose.' She leant forward still staring into the fire. Then, with sudden finality: 'Probably not.'

A Scent of Mimosa

It was long past midnight when the municipal Citroën dumped the four of them outside the Menton hotel. Tom, the youngest and most assertive of the Katherine Mansfield Prize judges, grabbed Lenore's arm and helped her up the steps. It was Lenore, thirtyish and thinnish, who had that year won the prize, given by the municipality. Though they had never met until the start of their journey out to the South of France together, he was always touching her, as though to communicate to her some assurance, at the nature of which she could still only guess. As they followed behind, Theo and Lucy, the other two judges, maintained a cautious distance from each other. There had been some acrimony, many years before, about an unsigned review in *The Times Literary Supplement*. Lenore could no longer even remember which of the two had written it and which had felt aggrieved.

In the hall they all stared at each other, like bewildered strangers wondering what they were doing in each other's company so late at night, in an unknown hotel, in a foreign town.

Tom broke the silence, swaying back and forth on his tiny feet: 'Well, what's the programme for tomorrow? Christ, I'm tired!'

Lucy hunted for one of three or four minuscule, lace-fringed handkerchiefs in the crocodile bag that dangled from her wrist. When travelling with her stockbroker husband she was used to more luxurious hotels, more powerful cars and more amusing company. 'Apparently we're going to be taken up into the mountains for another banquet.' She held the handkerchief to the tip of her sharp nose and gave a little sniff.

Theo, who was almost as drunk as Tom, wailed, 'Oh God! Altitude and hairpin bends always make me sick.'

'Well, there'll be plenty of both tomorrow,' Lucy replied, with some relish.

Lenore gazed down at the key that she was balancing on her palm. 'The Ambassador told me that he would be placing a wreath on some local war-memorial. Tomorrow's armistice day, isn't it?'

Lucy, who had been affronted that the prizewinner and not she had been seated on the New Zealand Ambassador's right, exclaimed, 'What a dreadfully boring man! Nice, but oh so boring!'

'Oh, I thought him rather interesting.' Lenore was still secretly both frightened and envious of Lucy, who was older, much more successful and much richer than herself. 'Some young New Zealander's going to meet us up there, the Ambassador told me. In the village. He's coming specially for the Katherine Mansfield celebrations.'

'I suppose if your country's produced only one writer of any note, you're bound to make a fuss of her,' Tom commented.

'Well, we'd better get some sleep. If we can.' Lucy began to walk towards the lift. 'The beds here are horribly hard and lumpy.'

Tom again held Lenore by the arm, as he shepherded her towards the small, gilded cage. So close, she could smell the alcohol heavy on his breath.

Lucy got out first, since on their arrival together she had managed to secure for herself the only room on the first floor with a balcony over the bay. Bowing to Lenore, she sang out, '*Bonne nuit, Madame la Lauréate!*'

Lenore gave a small, embarrassed laugh. 'Good night, Lucy!'

Theo got out at the next floor, tripping and all but falling flat, with only Tom's arm to save him. He began to waddle off down the corridor; then turned as the lift-gates were closing. '*Bonne nuit, Madame la Lauréate!*'

Lenore and Tom walked down their corridor, his hand again

at her elbow, as though once more to assure her and perhaps also himself of something that he could not or dared not put into words. They came to her door.

'Well . . .' He released her and clumsily she stooped and inserted the key. 'Tomorrow we'll drive up into the mountains and watch poor Theo being car-sick and meet the Ambassador's young New Zealander. And, of course, hear lots and lots of speeches.'

She opened the door; and at once, as though frightened that she would ask him in, he backed away.

'Well, *bonne nuit, Madame la Lauréate*!'

'*Bonne nuit, Monsieur le Juge!*'

She shut the door and leant against it, feeling the wood hard against her shoulder-blades. Her head was throbbing from too much food and drink, too much noise and too much French, and her mouth felt dry and sour. What would each of the others be doing now that they had separated? She began to speculate. Well, Lucy would no doubt be taking great care of each garment as she removed it; and then she would take equal care of her face, patting and smoothing, smoothing and patting. Theo, drunken and dishevelled, his tiny eyes bleary and his tie askew, would perch himself on a straight-backed chair – he always seemed masochistically determined to inflict the maximum of discomfort on himself – and would then start work on the pile of postcards that he had rushed out to buy as soon as they had been shown into their rooms. The postcards would, of course, arrive in England long after his return. Someone had told Lenore that he had a wife much older than himself and a horde of children and stepchildren – six? seven? eight? – to all of whom he was sentimentally devoted. And Tom? Tom, she decided after some deliberation, would walk along to his room, wait there for a few minutes, and then take the lift downstairs again and go out into the night, wandering the autumnal streets in search of a – well, what? She did not know, not yet; any more than she knew the nature of the assurance that that constant touching was designed to convey.

The bed was soft, not hard and lumpy at all as Lucy had complained, too soft, so that its swaying was almost nauseating. Perhaps poor Theo would be bed-sick and would have to take to the floor. . . . She shut her eyes and yawned and yawned again. . . . She was asleep.

When she awoke, it seemed as if many hours had passed, even though the dark of the room was still impenetrable. Her body was on fire, the sweat pouring off it, her head was throbbing and she had an excruciating pain, just under her right ribs, as though a knife had been inserted there and was now being twisted round and round. The central heating was always turned too high in these continental hotels; and after having eaten and drunk so much, she ought not to be surprised at an attack of acute indigestion. She threw back the sheet and duvet and then, after lying for a while uncovered with none of the expected coolness, she switched on the bedside lamp and dragged herself off the bed. For a long time she struggled with the regulator of the radiator that ran the whole length of the window; but the effort only made her sweat the more, it would not budge. She would have to open the window instead. Again she struggled; and at last the square of glass screeched along its groove and she felt the icy air enfolding her body.

From her suitcase she fetched a tube of Alka-Seltzer and padded into the bathroom. It was as she was dropping two of the tablets into a tumbler of water, the only light coming through the half-open door behind her, that suddenly she felt a strange tickling at the back of her throat, as though a feather had lodged there, coughed, coughed again, and then effortlessly began spitting, spitting, spitting.

Giddy and feeling sick, the sweat now chill on her forehead and bare arms, she stared down at the blood that had spattered the porcelain of the basin and was even dripping from one of the taps. She felt that she was about to faint and staggered back into the bedroom, to fall diagonally across the bed, her cheek pressed against the thrown-back duvet. Oh God, oh God . . . She must have had some kind of haemorrhage.

She lay there, shivering, for a while. She would have to see a doctor. But how could she call one at this hour? The best thing

would be to go along to the room of one of the others. But she
shrank from appealing to either Lucy or Tom. It would have to
be Theo.

She got off the bed, still feeling giddy, sick and weak, and
went back into the bathroom to wash away the blood. This
time she turned on the light. The two tablets of Alka-Seltzer
were now dissolved; but, with an extraordinary hyperaesthesia,
she could hear the water fizzing even when she was still far away
from it. She approached the basin slowly, fearful of what she
would find in it: the trails and spatters of blood on the glistening
porcelain and over the tap. But when she was above the basin
and forced her eyes down, there was, amazingly, nothing there,
nothing there at all. Porcelain and tap were both as clean as she
had left them after brushing her teeth.

It was cold and damp by the mountain war-memorial, a lichen-
covered obelisk, one end sunk into the turf, with a stone shield
attached, bearing names that for the most part were Italian, not
French. The Mayor, cheeks scarlet from the many toasts at the
banquet and medals dangling from his scuffed blue-serge suit,
stood before it and bellowed out an oration to which Lenore did
not listen, her gaze tracking back and forth among the faces,
mostly middle-aged and brooding, of the handful of villagers
huddled about her. Lucy had retreated into the back of the
municipal Citroën, saying that she was certainly not going to
risk a cold just before she and her husband were due to set off
for the Caribbean on a holiday. Theo was holding a handkerchief to his chin, as though he had an attack of toothache, his
tiny eyes rheumy and bloodshot. Tom, who had been chatting
to their dapper young chauffeur in his excellent French, now
stood beside the man, faintly smirking.

At last the oration ended and the Ambassador, grizzled, grey-
faced and grave, walked forward with his wreath, stooped and
placed it against the tilted obelisk. An improbable girl bugler,
in white boots and a mini-skirt that revealed plump knees at the
gap between them, stepped proudly forward and the valedictory
notes volleyed back and forth among the mountains. Again

Lenore felt that tickling at the back of her throat; but now it was tears. She always cried easily.

Suddenly she was aware of a smell, bitter and pungent, about her; and she wondered, in surprise, what could be its source. It was too late in the year for the smell to come from any flower at this altitude; and it seemed unlikely that any of the village women – with the possible exception of the girl bugler – would use a perfume so strange and strong. She peered around; and then, turning, saw the tall young man with the mousy, close-cropped hair and the sunburned face, his cheekbones and his nose prominent, who was standing a little apart from the rest of the gathering. A khaki rucksack was propped against one leg. Their eyes met and he smiled and gave a little nod, as though they already knew each other.

The ceremony was over. In twos and threes the people began to drift away, for the most part silent, and silent not so much in grief as in the attempt to recapture its elusive memory. The young man, his rucksack now on his back, was beside her.

'Hello.' The voice was unmistakably antipodean.

'Hello.'

'You won the prize.' It was not a question.

'By some marvellous fluke. I've never had any luck in my life before. Everything I've achieved, I've had to struggle for.' She gave an involuntary shudder, feeling the cold and damp insinuate themselves through the thickness of her topcoat. 'You must be the New Zealander.'

'*The* New Zealander? Well, *a* New Zealander.'

'We heard that you were coming.'

'I always try to come.'

The Ambassador was approaching, still grey-faced and grave. 'Your New Zealander has arrived,' Lenore called out to him.

'*My* New Zealander?' He looked at the young man, who held out his hand. The Ambassador took it. 'So you're from back home?'

The young man nodded, at once friendly and remote. 'Wellington.'

'What brings you here?'

'I wanted to be present at the ceremonies. I was telling Miss Marlow, I always have been.'

'Then you're a fan of K M?'

'Oh, yes.'

Lenore was becoming increasingly bewildered. She turned to the Ambassador. 'But didn't you say . . .? Didn't you tell me last night – at the banquet – that you were expecting a New Zealander?'

'I?'

'Yes, surely . . .'

'But I'd no idea that this young man would turn up, none at all.'

'But I'm sure . . . Didn't you . . .?'

'We've never set eyes on each other. And we know nothing about each other. Do we?' He appealed to the other man.

'Nothing at all.'

'Anyway' – cold and tired, the Ambassador began to move away – 'it's been nice to meet you. What's your name?'

'Leslie.' It might have been either surname or Christian name.

'We'll be seeing you again?'

'Oh, yes. I'll be at the prize-giving ceremony tomorrow. As I said, I've been at every one.'

Lenore and the young man were now alone by the lop-sided war-memorial. Far down the road she could make out Theo, shapeless in his ancient overcoat, a cap pulled down over his bulging forehead, as he urinated against a tree that soared up into the gathering mist and darkness. Tom was climbing into the car beside Lucy; Lenore could hear his laugh, strangely loud.

'How are you going to get down to Menton? Would you like me to ask if we can give you a lift?'

'Oh, that's very kind of you. But I think I'd like to stay here a little longer.'

'Here?' She could not imagine why anyone should wish to stay on in this cramped, craggy village, with all the inhabitants drifting back into their homes and nothing to see in the coagulating mist and dark and nothing to do.

He nodded. 'She came up here. She was driven up here by Connie and Jennie.'

'Oh, yes, they were the ones who let her the Villa Isola Bella, weren't they? Connie was the aunt.'

'Well, cousin really.'

'I didn't know she'd ever been in this village. I know the journals and the letters pretty well but obviously not as well as you.' Suddenly she did not wish to let him go; this imminent parting from a total stranger had become like the resurgence of some deep-seated, long-forgotten sorrow. 'Can't we really give you a lift? We can squeeze you into our car.'

He shook his head. 'I want to stay here a little. But I'll be down. We'll meet again?'

'Perhaps this evening you might join us for dinner? We have the evening free and we thought that we might all go to a fish restaurant in Monte Carlo. Lucy – she's one of the judges – says that Somerset Maugham once took her there and it was absolutely fabulous.' 'Fabulous' was not Lenore's kind of word; it was Lucy's. 'Do try to join us.'

'Perhaps.'

'Please! We'll be leaving the hotel at about eight-thirty. So just come there before that. It's the Hôtel du Parc. Do you know where it is?'

He nodded.

'How will you get down to Menton? There can't be a bus now.'

'Oh, I'll manage.'

'Lenore! Time we started back!' It was Tom's peremptory voice.

'I must go. They're getting impatient. Please come this evening.'

He raised his hand as she hurried away from him, in what was half a wave and half a salute. Then he remained standing motionless beside the war-memorial.

Lucy said fretfully, 'We want to get down the mountain before this mist really thickens.'

'I'm sorry. But that was . . . He was from New Zealand.'

'Is that the one you told us about last night?' Theo asked, wiping with a soiled handkerchief at eyes still streaming from the cold.

Lenore nodded. 'Yes, I did tell you about him, didn't I?' She all but added, 'But the funny thing is that the Ambassador pretended that he'd said nothing to me at all about his coming.' Then something made her check herself.

It was as though, walking over sunlit fields, she had all at once unexpectedly found ahead of her a dark and dense wood; had hesitated whether to enter it or not; and had then turned and in panic retraced her steps.

'Well, he's obviously not coming.' Lucy drew her chinchilla coat up over her shoulders and got to her feet. The two men also rose.

Lenore sighed. 'No, I suppose not.'

'He probably decided there were more amusing things for a young man to do on the Côte,' Theo said.

'I can think of less amusing things too,' Lucy retorted tartly. 'Perhaps he hadn't got the money for a slap-up meal.'

Of course, of course! Tom was right. Lenore saw it now. What she should have said was, 'You must be my guest, because I want to spend some of my prize-money in celebration,' or something of that kind. She had spoken of the 'fabulous' restaurant to which Lucy had been taken by Maugham – enough to put off anyone who was travelling on a slender budget. Of course!

Once again Tom tried to take her arm as they emerged into the soft November air; but this time she pulled free with a sharp, impatient jerk.

The next morning they were driven out to Isola Bella, the villa on the steep hill where Katherine Mansfield had lived for nine months in a fever of illness and activity. The villa itself was occupied; but the municipality had made over a room on the lowest of its three levels into a shrine. A bearded French critic, who was regarded as an authority on the English writer, explained to Lenore that an outhouse had been converted into a lavatory and shower, in the hope that some other English writer might soon be installed in what was, in effect, a tiny apartment.

'But Katherine Mansfield herself never lived here?'

He hesitated between truth and his loyalty to his hosts. Then: 'Well, no,' he agreed in his excellent English. 'Katherine lived above.' (He invariably referred to the writer merely by her Christian name.)

'And probably she never even came down here?'

Again he hesitated. 'Possibly not.'

Lenore wandered away from the rest of the party, up the hill to the rusty gates that led to the main part of the house. Ahead of her, as she peered through the curlicues of wrought iron, stretched the terrace on which the invalid would lie out for most of the day on a chaise-longue spread with a kaross made of flying-squirrel skins brought home from Africa by her father. Oh, and there were the mimosa trees, like elongated ferns – Katherine Mansfield had described how she would lie awake at break of day and watch the shafts of the rising sun shimmer through them. All at once, Lenore could smell the tiny yellow flowers still hanging from the fragile racemes. Though infinitely fainter, a mere ghost, it was none the less that same odour, pungent and bitter, that had enveloped her up in the mountains. But surely, so high up in the mountains, no mimosa could grow or, if it did, could come to bloom in November? As she breathed in the scent, deeper and deeper until her lungs began to ache with it as they had done that first night in the hotel, she thought once again of the New Zealander and wondered what had happened to him. She had hoped to see him in the town early that morning as she had wandered alone about it, pretending that she was in quest of presents but in reality in quest of him; but he had been nowhere. And now he had not turned up at the villa, as she had also hoped that he would do. Perhaps he had already moved on, with his exiguous rucksack, farther up the coast; perhaps she would never see him again.

Suddenly she wanted a spray of the mimosa. She rattled the gate and the rusty padlock swung from side to side, with a dry sound of scraping against the bars. The occupiers of the house must be away. But she tugged at the bell, hearing it tinkle from somewhere out of sight. No one came. She thought, If he were here, he could climb over for me. He'd find some way. She hoisted herself up with both hands, feeling the flaking metal graze a palm. But it was useless.

'Can I help Madame?'

It was the French critic, stroking his beard with a narrow, nicotine-stained hand.

Lenore explained what she wanted; and then he too tugged at the bell-pull and even shouted out in French. No one came. Oddly, she could no longer smell that pungent, bitter odour, not since he had come.

He shrugged. 'I'm afraid that I am too old and too fat to climb over for you. Perhaps if you come tomorrow, the owners will be here.'

'We're leaving tomorrow morning.'

'Then . . .' Again he shrugged. When he had first seen her, he had thought her a dowdy, insignificant little woman, and had hardly bothered to speak to her. But now he experienced a sudden pull, as though a boat in which he had long been be-calmed had all at once felt the tug and sweep of the tide. Now he too grabbed her arm just above the elbow, as Tom had kept on doing until that rebuff of the previous night. 'Let me assist you down the hill.' How thin the arm was, how pathetically thin and fragile – the arm of a child or invalid. He felt excited at the contact.

'I have given most of my life to Katherine,' he told her, as they began to descend. It was not strictly true, since he had given much of his life to other things: to the editing of a maga-zine, to the collection of Chinese works of art, to women, to eating and drinking. But at that moment, when his fingers felt the delicate bone inside its envelope of flesh, he not only wished that it had been so but believed that it had been so. 'In a strange way you remind me of her, you know.'

In the Town Hall the audience for the prize-giving ceremony

was composed almost entirely of elderly men in dark suits and elderly women in hats. Lenore had been told that she would have to make a small speech of thanks in French after Lucy had spoken, also in French, on behalf of the judges. Lenore had never made a speech in her life, let alone a speech in French, and she dreaded the ordeal. The hall was stuffy, its radiators too hot even on this autumn day. She felt headachy, sweaty and vaguely sick, as she listened, in a kind of trance, first to the orotund platitudes of the Mayor, then to the clipped phrases of the Ambassador and finally to Lucy's few witty, lucid comments. In rising panic she thought, If he were here, if only he were here! In one hand she was clutching the typescript, the French of which Lucy had corrected for her.

She heard her name and then one of the French officials was giving her a little push from behind, his hand to her shoulder. She rose and, as she did so, she felt the room revolve first gently and then faster and faster around her. She clutched the back of her chair, staring up at the face of the Mayor on the dais above her. All at once she could smell, far stronger than ever before, that pungent, bitter odour of mimosa. It was all around her, an enveloping cloud. She moved forward and then up the steps, the French critic putting out one of those long, narrow hands of his to help her.

She was handed an envelope, cold and dry on her hot and damp palm, and then she was handed a red-leather box, open, with a bronze medallion embedded in it. Whose head was that? But of course – it was Katherine Mansfield's, jagged prongs of fringe across a wide forehead. She looked down and read: 'Menton c'est le Paradis d'une aube à l'autre.'

The Mayor was prompting her in a sibilant whisper, perhaps she would wish to say a few words?

She turned to face the audience; and it was then, as she moistened her lips with her tongue and raised the sheet of type-script, that all at once she saw him, standing by himself at the far end of the hall, one shoulder against the jamb of a closed door and his eyes fixed on her.

She began to read, at first all but inaudibly but then in a

stronger and stronger voice. Her French was all but perfect; she felt wholly calm.

In the premature dusk, they talked outside the Town Hall, pacing the terrace among the stunted oleanders.

'You saved my life,' she said. She felt the euphoria that precedes a bout of fever. 'I can't explain it but I was, oh, petrified, I felt sure I could not say a word, and then suddenly I saw you and all at once . . .'

'I like that story of yours. Very much.'

'Oh, have you read it?' She was amazed. The story had appeared in a little magazine that, after three issues, had folded and vanished.

'Yes. It was – *right*. For her, I mean. It's the only story that she herself might have written, of all the ones that have ever won the prize.'

'That's a terrific compliment.'

'I mean it.'

'I'd hoped that perhaps you'd have joined us last night.'

'Well, I wanted to,' he said, with no further excuse.

'And then I thought that I might see you at the villa.'

'I've been there many times.'

'But not this time?'

He did not answer; and then she began to tell him about the mimosa on the terrace – how she remembered reading about it in the journals and the letters and how she had wanted a spray, just one spray, but there had been no one at the house and the gate was padlocked. 'If you'd been there, perhaps you could have climbed over. But none of our party looked capable of doing so.'

'I'll get you a spray.'

'Will you? Can you?'

'Of course.' He smiled. His teeth were very white in the long, sunburned face.

'But we leave early tomorrow.'

'What time?'

'We must leave the hotel at ten for the airport.'

'Oh, that'll give me time. Don't worry.'

Boldly she said, 'Oh, I wish there were no banquet this evening! I wish we could just have dinner alone together.'

'There'll be other times,' he said quietly. 'Anyway, I won't forget the mimosa.'

'Promise?'

'Promise.'

After that Tom was again calling and the cars were starting up and people were shaking her hand and saying how glad they were for her and that soon she must come back to Menton again.

When she looked round for the New Zealander, she found that he had vanished.

Lenore was back in her dark, two-roomed Fulham flat. At the airport Lucy had been whisked off by her husband in a chauffeur-driven Daimler, barely bothering to say good-bye. Theo had explained that it would be impossible to fit any more passengers into his battered station-wagon, already packed with his wife, a number of children, a dog and a folding bicycle. Tom had said that it looked as if the friend who was supposed to meet him must have got held up and he'd wait around for a while. So Lenore had travelled alone on the bus. She had felt chilled and there was again that pain, dull now, under her right ribs.

She shivered as she stooped to light the gas. Then she remained kneeling before it, staring at the radiants as the blue light flickering up from them steadied to an orange glow. He had failed to keep his promise and she had no idea of where he might be or even of what he was called – other than either his surname or his Christian name was Leslie. It was hopeless. She got up, with a small, dry cough, and went into the bedroom. There she hauled her suitcase up on to the bed and began to unpack it, hurriedly, throwing things into drawers or jerking them on to hangers, as though she did not have a whole empty evening ahead of her and a number of empty days after that. At the bottom of the suitcase she came on the typescript of her speech – she crumpled it into a ball and threw it into the waste-paper basket – and the red-leather box, containing her trophy.

She pressed the stud of the lid and lifted it upwards with a thumb; and, as she did so, it was as if she were releasing from it the smell, pungent and bitter, that soon was all around her. She gave a little gasp; the pain in her chest sharpened. Looking down, she saw the spray of mimosa that lay across the medallion.

She took the spray in her hand; but it was dry, dry and faded and old as though it had lain there not for a few hours but for many, many years. 'Leslie.' She said the name aloud to herself and then, with no shock and no alarm but with the relieved recognition of someone lost who all at once sights a familiar landmark, she remembered that yes, of course, Leslie had been the name of the beloved brother killed in the war, whom Katherine Mansfield had always called 'Chummie'.

She touched the arid, dead raceme and some of the small, yellowish-grey blossoms, hard as berries, fell to the carpet at her feet. They might have been beads, scattering hither and thither. Three or four rolled back and forth in her palm. She felt a tickle at the back of her throat; it must be pollen, she decided wrongly.

Then suddenly the concluding lines of Kathleen Mansfield's sonnet on the death of her brother, read long ago and forgotten, forced themselves up within her, like the spurs of a plant, buried for years, all at once thrusting up into the light of day,

> By the remembered stream my brother stands
> Waiting for me with berries in his hands . . .
> 'These are my body. Sister, take and eat.'

She gave another little dry cough, and tasted something thick and salt on her tongue. The scent of mimosa was already fading as those blooms had long since faded. But she knew that it would come back and that he would come back with it.

School Crossing

THESE days it seemed as if his glasses were never clean. Yearning, importunate or mischievous, the small hands would reach out, soiling and smearing; and it was as if they soiled and smeared everything at which he looked. The garden at which he had laboured for many years, the house filled with the antiques inherited from his first and now dead wife, even the youthful face of his second wife: all seemed to have lost their pristine bloom. 'Don't!' he would ward off the hands. But the twins would think this some kind of game and, laughing hysterically, twisting and lunging, they would hurl themselves upon him. Sometimes he would be rough with them, repelling them with all his force, and then a bewilderment would suddenly freeze their half-formed features and he would see the same bewilderment on the face of their mother, as though he had all at once changed into someone else. He was always wiping the glasses. On a handkerchief. On the end of his tie. On a paper tissue or a table napkin or a sheet of lavatory paper. But the imprints of those two pairs of hands perpetually renewed themselves, just as the imprint of those twin lives now perpetually marked each hour of his existence.

It must have been the glasses: the obvious explanation. The glasses and some freak of light as the late sun filtered down through a jagged line of conifers on that late summer afternoon. It was the old drive that he knew so well, up the hill from the town. He had passed the Smugglers' Rest, with its faked creosoted beams, its plastic chairs and tables set out in the hope that some hardy travellers might be tempted to eat or drink outside, its neat hedges, neat flower-beds, neat paths; then the low line of red-brick council houses; then the notice, glinting briefly in the setting sun, SCHOOL CROSSING. School, his school. Or what he had thought of as being his school until they had taken it from him. Teaching English part-time to foreigners now, he tried not to think of that brutal dispossession. Never went near the school. Never wished to see any of his former colleagues, unless a little furtive, a little guilty, a little shamefaced, they themselves sought him out. Never spoke about it, not even to Clare, the young science teacher whom he had married.

SCHOOL CROSSING. The Aston Martin, which he could no longer afford to run, leapt effortlessly up the hill; and suddenly, for a moment, there they were, boys and girls straggling across the road. Faces turned at the sound of the engine. Some drew back, others scuttled over to the further side, jostling, ungainly, undignified. But why should they be out of school as early as this? School holiday? No. He had braked to a halt. And then, to his amazement, he had seen that there was no one there at all. The late sun glinted on the crown of the road; the conifers soared up on either side, their green encrusted here and there near their summits with rust; somewhere far off an owl hooted. Odd. He could have sworn. But it was the glasses, of course. He took them off, fumbled in his pocket for a handkerchief, found he had none and then, as so often, used the end of his tie. The tie seemed only to make them worse, leaving a halo over the left lens where before there had only been a streak. The sun sank with a strange abruptness, as though that patch of fire on the crown of the road had been doused with an invisible pail of water. Behind him a van was hooting. He looked in the mirror and saw that the driver looked like that Mason boy, son of a butcher, who had been one of the ringleaders ... But he wasn't going to think of the school, never, ever.

He engaged the gears and the car leapt forward, like some beast suddenly unleashed to seize its prey. Odd.

2

He did not tell Clare. One of the twins, the boy, had grazed his knee in a fall; and the other twin, the girl, had somehow contrived to break a Crown Derby cup. He had to hear about both accidents and he had to pretend that he cared more about the knee than the cup. Would he have mentioned what had happened on the hill if he had come home to peace instead of turmoil? He did not know. Probably not. There was a lot that he never mentioned to Clare: a whole secret life of hurt feelings, humiliation, disappointment and resentment. She herself was so candid, telling him all her most intimate thoughts and feelings, that she could not guess at the depth of his lack of candour.

'A good day, Mark?'

'Oh, not too bad. Not too bad.'

He had picked up *The Times*; but as he was opening it, the boy twin began to scramble up on to his knees. One hand went out, crushing the paper. A shoe kicked his shin. Then the other hand was at his glasses. The child crowed with pleasure. Mark wanted to fling him from him. But instead he forced himself to laugh as he held the child's arms, one in either hand, and asked him:

'Well, how is that knee of yours?'

Again the child tried to lunge; but his father held him firm. Then the girl came up from behind and her greasy fingers . . . He looked across at Clare and he could hardly see her face. The smears seemed to be across it, not on his glasses.

'Oh, do take the children upstairs or into the kitchen or somewhere.'

She got up silently and again he fumbled for the handkerchief that he had not got and again he raised the end of his tie.

3

Several days passed before it happened again. Now it was dark and he was returning from a farewell party given by a group of jolly, noisy students from Norway. They had kept filling his glass even though he told them, Look I've got to drive home. I don't want to be breathalysed, now do I? He felt old and tired; a sour envy had invaded him, like the aftertaste of the acid Spanish wine, for the youth not merely of the students but also of his colleagues. He wondered how soon he could decently make his escape. A plump coquettish girl, with a downy moon-face and eyes of an Arctic blankness and blueness – she had always sat just under his desk, arriving at class long before any-one else in order to secure that place – had swayed up to him and enquired tipsily: 'You do not dance, Professor?'

'My dancing days are over.'

'But you will dance with me? A last dance?'

He shook his head. He forced himself to smile. 'Neither a last dance nor a first dance. Not after all these years. Not even with you, my dear.'

Surprisingly she had seemed not to be angered but delighted by the rebuff. It was what she must have expected. She laughed, throwing back her head and showing large, white, even teeth. Then she told the others: 'Professor Clark says that his dancing days are over! He will not dance with me!'

'Shame!' cried one of Mark's colleagues, a spotty boy whom he particularly disliked.

'Oh, come along, Mark!' another colleague, a girl, cajoled him, taking him by an arm and attempting to drag him among the dancers. He had never asked her to call him Mark and he always tried to avoid calling her by any name, surname or Christian name. Some of the students began to clap her as she tugged and tugged at him, her face growing red under its swaying fringe of jet hair. But he would not yield. 'No, I'm not going to dance. But you can give me something more to drink.'

A Norwegian boy splashed some more of the vinegary white wine into his glass.

Well, it could have been that wine. Because he had been a little drunk as he had walked out, long before any other of the teachers, into the frosty December air. He had dropped the car keys and he had felt uncomfortably top-heavy as he had searched over the asphalt of the yard for them, the tips of his fingers grazing themselves on its uneven surfaces. It must have been that wine and not his glasses, because as soon as he had got into the car, he took off the glasses and wiped them on a corner of a handkerchief that was still neatly folded in the trouser-pocket in which he had put it before setting out. Yes, it must have been that wine. What else could it have been?

It was misty as he drove up the hill and he passed only one car, crawling beetle-like ahead of him. He liked that surge of power as the Aston Martin devoured the little Fiat or whatever it was. It gave him a feeling of exhilaration; it never failed to do so. Which was why he had kept the car while at the same time urging on Clare a number of economies. The daily, holidays abroad, drinks before dinner, the laundry for his shirts: all must go before that car would go. Now that his joints so often ached and were stiff with rheumatism in the mornings, now that he found himself out of breath at the top of a hill or even of the stairs, now that one set of tennis, one swim, one orgasm, was enough for him, he found a compensation in the undiminished ferocity and pounce of that engine.

He could not see the crests of the conifers because of that pervading mist; at times he could hardly see the sides of the road as it curved up to the brow of the hill. The trees seemed to have merged into huddled, opaque masses as the fierce headlights picked them out. SCHOOL CROSSING. The cat's-eyes winked at him and then died as he raced past. Slam on the brakes. Their terrified faces. Some began to run. Others frozen. The tyres screeched. The car all but went out of control. He peered into the mist, the car door half-open and one leg hanging through it into the icy air. He had been about to rush out and shout at them. You bloody clots! Couldn't you hear my engine? Didn't you see my lights? And what are you all doing at an hour like this? Don't tell me that you're coming home from school! You might have got yourselves killed! But there was no one there, no one there at all; no target at which to direct his near-hysterical shock and rage.

He heard a chug-chug-chug behind him and the little beetle crawled up past the sign, slowed, all but stopped and then passed on. The driver was probably saying to himself, Strange. Why should he have stopped there? Alone too. But he seems all right. Better not to get mixed up in whatever it is. Perhaps he

just wants a piss. The silence closed round the coughing of the
little engine as it disappeared from view.

He raised the end of his tie; took off his glasses. But of course
it had been the wine, it must have been the wine.

4

After that he began to dread having to pass the notice. But there
was no other way to drive up from the town to the house: not,
that is, unless he made an enormous detour. Enormous and
costly too – that car devoured petrol with the same greed that it
devoured the distance between itself and any other car. It was
some silly kind of optical illusion. The trees with the sun low
behind them or with the headlights thrust against them. Some
trick of shadow. And the fact that he was tired, the glasses, the
wine. Nothing odd about it really. As a child, waking up and
seeing what seemed to be a stranger seated in the chair beside his
bed, a dark, humped stranger, with a white luminous face, he
had screamed and screamed and screamed; but all it was (his
mother rushing in) was his own clothes with the moonlight on
them . . . Silly. She had said that to him. Silly, silly boy. Why,
it's *nothing*!

It was nothing. But still the dread remained. As the Aston
Martin climbed effortlessly up the hill, he would feel his mouth
go dry, his heart would start to thump and he would peer ahead,
wondering . . . would it happen again this time? But days passed
and it did not happen and soon that tension of both the body
and the brain no longer gripped him. He had still not spoken
of what had happened to Clare or anyone else; and now he would
not do so, since obviously it was not going to happen again.

5

Going into the town one Saturday to shop, they left the two
children for a moment in the locked car while they changed
their books at the library. It had been a day of nagging rain; and
when they returned they found that the seats of the car, its sides

and even its roof were imprinted with the marks of small muddy shoes. He could understand how, without meaning it, they might have soiled the seats by scrambling over them or even the sides by kicking out; but to reach the roof they must have made a deliberate, malicious effort. 'Christ! What the hell have you been doing? Look at this! Look! Look!' He pointed here and here and here and the twins cowered and giggled, while Clare, in an effort to placate him, her face suddenly pinched and grey with apprehension, pulled a tiny, pathetic wad of a handkerchief out of her handbag and began to make ineffectual efforts to wipe away the mess.

'You'll only smear it! Leave it! I'll see to it when I get home.'

'It'll all come out. You'll see . . .' As so often, her fear of him made her turn on the twins. 'Oh, stop that silly sniggering!'

'Why can't you control these bloody brats?'

'They're your brats too.'

But somehow, deep inside himself, he never thought of them as his brats at all. They had come too late; and they had come unwanted.

Clare took the girl on her lap, leaving the boy in the back of the car. The boy was her favourite and so it was the girl to whom she gave this kind of preferential treatment. 'Look, pet. I've got this lovely book for you. Look. That's a dog like the one that Anna has got, isn't it? A big dog, with a big bushy tail. And big teeth. But a friendly dog. Like Anna's dog. A dog with long, *long* ears.' From time to time she would glance sideways at him with wary apprehension, wondering whether he would forget about the stains all over the interior of the car or whether they would make him difficult for the whole weekend. He drove thinking, Christ, what inanities!

The car seemed even smoother and even more powerful than ever; and that began to soothe him, as he pushed it up the steeper and steeper gradient, passing one car after another. Everyone seemed to have been shopping; every car was laden with children and baskets and carrier-bags and dogs and toys. SCHOOL CROSSING. There was a ramshackle saloon ahead of him, just beyond the notice; and then, as he pressed the accelerator to catch it up too and leave it in his conquering wake, suddenly, without any warning, the children began to stream across the road. In twos and threes. Shouting to each other. Laughing. One boy pushing another boy into a tall, solitary girl.

The impact of the braking threw the boy twin forward so that he struck his forehead on the seat in front. Fortunately Mark and Clare had both fastened their safety-belts, and the girl was secure in Clare's hands. The boy began to whimper, rubbing his forehead with a look of bewilderment on a face that was rapidly puckering. Cars passed, the cars that they themselves had passed. Faces looked round. What a bloody silly place to stop! That's one way to cause an accident. Idiot. Someone hooted.

'Are you all right, darling?' The child began to wail. Clare touched the spot with blunt, cool fingers. 'Does it hurt?' The child wailed louder.

'He's not hurt. You know how he always makes a fuss over the smallest things.'

'He could have been hurt. Badly. What on earth did you stop like that for?'

'Didn't you see . . .?' He broke off.

'See? See what?'

He thought quickly. 'The hedgehog.'

'Hedgehog?'

'In the middle of the road. I was afraid I'd run it over.'

'I saw nothing.'

'I saw it, Mummy! I saw it!' the girl began to shout. 'I saw it! Big, big hedgehog!'

The boy was sobbing now. Clare said to the girl: 'You'd better climb over to the back and change places.'

'Why?'

'Because he's hurt his forehead.'

'No!'

'Now, Sally, do what I tell you.'

'It's my turn to sit in front!'

'You sat in front last time.'

'Didn't!'

'Did.'

Oh Christ! It was with a cold, murderous rage that he engaged the gears and once more resumed the journey home. Would they never allow him any peace? Such was his fury against them that he hardly thought of those phantoms suddenly emerging out into the road. It was only later that he began to worry.

6

Bill Edmonds – 'Big' Bill as he was known all over the town to differentiate him from his partner, also Bill, who was small and fox-like – had once been Mark's closest friend as well as his doctor. Perhaps he still imagined that he was Mark's closest friend, since he was not particularly perceptive; but Mark had never felt the same towards Bill since that whole school business. Bill had not been loyal; or at least not loyal enough to say 'my friend, right or wrong'. His view that Mark had been partly wrong he had never concealed from him, even though he had conceded that Mark had also been partly right. 'You can't run a comprehensive as though it were a small and select grammar school. You know exactly what you're doing and a lot of that staff of yours have no idea what they're doing at all. But that doesn't mean that you can ride roughshod over them.' Later, when the affair had smashed Mark's career and smashed so much else, it had also smashed the peculiar intimacy that had joined the two men. They went on seeing each other; Bill went on prescribing drugs for Mark's blood pressure, his insomnia and hay-fever; Mark went on tutoring Bill's bored, backward daughter in mathematics during the vacations; the two couples went on entertaining each other to dinner and going on holidays together and playing tennis with each other. But, as far as Mark at least was concerned, the friendship had ended.

Now Bill said, 'Well, I'm damned if I can find anything wrong with you. The blood pressure's a little lower, in fact. The heart is fine.'

'I must have imagined it.' A statement more than a question.

Bill shrugged. 'Some trick of the light,' he said.

'I've thought of that. But it's happened at different times of the day. I mean, if it was a trick of the light, then if the light then changed, if it was coming from a different direction or a different source . . .'

'Your guess is as good as mine.'

'I suppose one might call it a hallucination.'

'Well . . .' Bill laughed, one massive buttock perched on the edge of the desk while he scratched at the other. He was always scratching himself.

Mark stared down at his linked hands and then darted an upward look. 'You don't think . . . Well, this isn't the beginning of a – a breakdown, is it?'

'Christ no! I'd be much more worried if you were hallucinating all over the place at all times of the day. The fact that it's just that one particular spot and just that one particular hallucination . . . But, in any case,' he added hurriedly, 'hallucination is not really the word for something so trivial.'

'Then what is?'

Bill did not answer that. 'You've been through a difficult time. Months ago, I know. But the after-effects of that kind of traumatic experience are often delayed. I should guess that you're a bit run-down. Liable to get depressed. Tired.'

'Well, those children certainly never let me sleep after six or seven!'

'Let me give you a tranquillizer.'

When Mark's first wife had been dying, Bill had also given her a tranquillizer, since there was nothing else to give her. 'A happiness pill' he had called it to Mark; and certainly whether because of her faith or because of that pill, she had died reasonably happy, when not in pain.

'Oh, I don't think . . .'

'Now come on! Half my patients are on tranquillizers. Nothing to it.'

Mark had the prescription made up; but he pushed the bottle into the back of a drawer and forgot about it.

7

The hallucination (if it was an hallucination) now came more and more frequently until it was happening almost every day. As he stepped into the car, sometimes even during his class, he would ask himself, I wonder if I'll see them today. They even appeared when he was giving another of the teachers, whose motor-cycle had broken down, a lift up the hill. There they were ahead of him (he had purposely slowed the car, just in case), straggling out over the road with their briefcases, trailing scarves, knee-high boots and loads of books. He could hear their loud immature voices and hear their loud immature laughter over the purr of the engine. He stopped and watched them, oblivious of his passenger, as they crossed over from the footpath to the lane on the other side. Some of the faces he had never seen before; they had come to the school since his day. Others he recognized and those he hated.

'Anything the matter?'

'What?' The last of them had gone. He attempted to pull himself together. 'I was – was looking at that owl in the tree over there. He's often there at this hour.'

'You must have the most fantastic sight. I can hardly see a thing.'

'It's as though he waited for me. Every evening.'

'Well, imagine that!'

Mark released the hand-brake. Suddenly he felt the sweat icy on his forehead, on his neck and in the small of his back.

8

He and the famous ophthalmologist had been at the same Oxford college together; but there had always been a faint condescension even then from the spectacularly gifted man to the one far less gifted, and now it had grown more marked. The ophthalmologist, thin and sharply handsome, with his modish clothes and his modish haircut, might have been at least ten years younger than the schoolmaster.

'Fancy deciding to start a family so late in life! I'd no idea. It's as though I'd suddenly decided to get married.'

'Well, we didn't really *decide* to start a family. It just happened.'

'Still it must be fun.'

'Up to a point.'

'I don't really care for children myself. Or animals.'

Mark nearly said, 'Neither do I.' But some impulse of loyalty to Clare, not to the twins, restrained him from doing so.

'Which must mean that I have a shocking character,' the ophthalmologist went on, obviously not believing anything of the kind.

When he had finished his examination he said, 'Well, *I* can't find anything amiss.' (Mark did not care for the emphasis on the pronoun. Who did he think could find anything? A psychiatrist?) 'The eyes are perfectly normal for a man of your age. In fact, I don't think I'd have even prescribed those glasses for you. You could easily do without them.'

'Then what . . .?'

The other man shrugged. 'You might have floaters. People with short sight often do. They're maddening things and, if you start to think about them – to become too conscious of them – they can cause you a lot of misery. I had a patient once, a woman, who even advertised in *The Times* for a cure for them. But there isn't one, of course. As I'd told her.'

'I've had floaters. I know what you mean. But they could hardly account for my seeing a number of schoolchildren and seeing them in detail . . . Could it?'

The ophthalmologist, who wanted to get home before going on to Covent Garden, sighed and shrugged. 'You might be haemorrhaging slightly from the eyes from time to time. Though I see no evidence of it. I've often thought that that's all that Joan of Arc's visions amounted to. She never menstruated, you know. But she might have bled instead from the tissue of the eye. It's not unknown. Not at all. I had a woman patient who did precisely that.'

'You don't suggest that I'm menstruating from my eyes?'

The two men laughed; but Mark's laughter was nervous and strained.

'Good God no! And in any case, you'd have reached the menopause by now and the bleeding would be over.'

Again they both laughed.

The ophthalmologist put his arm around Mark's shoulder. It was as a patient that he thought of him now, not as a friend, and the gesture was a purely professional one. 'I should guess you need a holiday. You look rather strained. You've aged a bit since that last Gaudy. Why not go away for a holiday?'

'I might do that.'

'I should ignore the whole thing. Drive through your vision! Why not? Prove to yourself that there's nothing there at all.'

'Yes.'

The ophthalmologist realized that, so far from encouraging his patient, he had only discouraged him further.

9

Mark had left his car in the station car park. When he went to reclaim it there he found two schoolboys examining it carefully. These schoolboys were not from the comprehensive but from the posh preparatory school a few miles outside the town. Mark knew that from their caps.

'That's a lovely job you've got there.'

'Super.'

'Fantastic.'

Mark put his key in the door, smiling at them, saying nothing. He felt that somehow he must appease them.

'Must cost a fortune to run.'

'What's the fastest you've done?'

'Oh, I've no idea. But she's fast.'

'I bet she is!'

They hung around; probably they wanted him to offer them a ride. But he did not do so. He slammed the door and thought, You're like those others. Just like those others. Except that you wear those caps and you sleep in dormitories instead of at home and you have that disdainful upper-class drawl. I hate the lot of you. It was you who smashed me. Smashed me.

He drove off, not even bothering to look at them again.

It was a beautiful December afternoon and he ought to have been happy at the thought of going home after a day in a London that seemed to him, with each visit, to become more and more noisy, more and more crowded, more and more squalid. But he was not happy. He thought of that lucky ophthalmologist, who had been wise enough not to burden himself with a wife and children; who had visited the Caribbean for his last holiday and was going to visit East Africa for his next; who had been about to go to Covent Garden to see *Traviata*. Back home, Clare would complain that the dishwasher had broken down again or that a bulb needed replacing; the children would have broken something or lost something or soiled something; the ink-stain would still be in the centre of the sitting-room carpet; the seat of the chair on the left of the fireplace would still be sagging; he would still be able to see where Clare had stuck that Crown Derby cup inexpertly together.

The Aston Martin began to leap up the hill. Would they be there, waiting for him among the trees? In a curious way, he felt that his fragile, failing body was now somehow fused with the strong, ever-powerful one of the car. I should ignore the whole thing. Drive through your vision, why not? Prove to yourself that there's nothing there at all. What's the fastest you've done in it? Well, I'm doing over seventy now and on a gradient like this. Lovely job. Super. Fantastic. His heart was now the throbbing heart of the engine; his nerves trilled with each of the explosions that sent it hurtling onwards.

SCHOOL CROSSING.

I should ignore the whole thing.

The impact was terrible. The car ploughed on and on. Then at last it jolted to a stop. Staring out ahead of him, he thought, This must be what is meant by seeing red. The whole windscreen was smeared with blood.

The Love Game

HE was wearing gym-shoes, dyed orange from the tennis court, with an ungainly knot where one of the laces had snapped. The hair, thick on his bare muscular legs and arms, was almost exactly the same colour as the shoes. He had unbuttoned his shirt and the same hair, moist with sweat – he had been sitting for a long time in the sun in that corner of the garden – covered his chest like a pelt. The khaki shorts were rucked up tight over the bulging crotch; they were stained with oil from the car, at which he had been tinkering earlier that Sunday. He was squinting down at one of the colour supplements, his lower lip drawn in under teeth that were so large, white and regular that when Anna had first met him, she a nurse and he a medical student, she had asked him, jokingly, if they were false. His nose had been broken, not in a rugger match as everyone assumed, but in a bicycle accident as a schoolboy.

A year ago, seeing him sit out in the sun in that physically arrogant posture, legs thrust out before him, she would probably have gone over to him to run a hand through his thinning hair, down his cheek and on to his chest. But now she merely said, standing several yards away: 'Oughtn't you to change?'

'Change? Why?' Bill spoke in a husky voice that always suggested he was recovering from a cold.

'Twenty to one. He'll be here at any moment.'

'So what?'

'You can't greet him like that. In those filthy shorts and gym-shoes.'

'I don't see why not. This is Sunday, after all.'

'He's sure to be in a suit.'

'I've no doubt. But I'm certainly not going to get into one, not on your nelly.'

She frowned, as she tugged a dead head off one of the rose-bushes beside her and then gave an 'Ow!' as a thorn ripped the ball of her thumb.

'Now what have you done?'

'Scratched myself on this bloody rose.'

He threw down the newspaper and got to his feet. 'Let's see.'

'There's nothing *to* see.' She sucked the thumb, looking fragile and childish in her blue gingham frock, with her long, straight blonde hair tied at the nape of her neck with a length of darker blue ribbon.

'It's a bore, his coming.'

'He kept saying how much he wanted to see the house. And he might be useful to you.'

'I doubt it. He's not exactly generous to his subordinates. Leaves us to get on with most of his NHS work but no, not exactly generous. Well, it stands to reason.' He flung himself back into the canvas chair. 'No one cares to hear the sound of the younger generation knocking at the door.'

'He hasn't much to fear. Not yet.'

'My dear girl, he's slipping. Everyone knows that. Slowly slipping. Ever since his wife died and he had the coronary and his boy got into trouble.' He enumerated these misfortunes with quiet malice. 'If he was wise, he'd retire. He must have salted away a fortune.'

'Retire!' Anna had now thrown herself on to a blanket on the grass beside him, from time to time still sucking at the thumb although it had long since ceased to bleed. 'Why on earth should he retire? He's got years and years ahead of him.'

'Years and years?'

'Well, at least ten years. He's only sixty-two.'

'I suppose he wants to hang on until he gets a knighthood. Some hope.'

'It's on the cards.'

'Well, I daresay all these foreign jaunts of his might bear some fruit.' He raised a hand and scratched lazily under an armpit.

H.F.—E

'Corneal transplants. Cataracts. Not all that impressive over here these days. But in the African bush . . .'

'He's late.'

Bill looked at his watch. 'Perhaps he's lost the way. Or forgotten.'

Anna laughed. 'You'd like him to forget.'

'Well, it *would* be a more peaceful Sunday without him. Wouldn't it? Not that I've really got anything against him. We hit it off all right. Being patronized never really worries me.' He began to move his left shoulder up and down, frowning as he did so.

'What's the matter? Shoulder painful?'

'Hm. Must have pulled it when I tried to swallow-dive.' Now he was massaging the shoulder with one of the hands that often seemed to apprehensive patients to be too large and clumsy for a surgeon. 'Has he brought up the Ethiopian jaunt again?'

'Not since last week. He told me to think about it.'

'Well, you're bloody well not going.'

'It's a change,' Anna said coolly. 'What other chance would I ever get to visit Ethiopia?'

'There are lots of theatre sisters from whom he can choose. Why doesn't he take that Connors bag? She's as tough as any man.'

'He loathes her.'

'And how the hell am I supposed to make out while you're gadding around?'

'Only five weeks. And mother says that she'll come and look after you. You were away for almost as long on your rugby tour. . . . Well, let's think about it.'

She got to her feet and walked slowly behind his chair. Leaning over him, she put her cheek against his, feeling its moisture and its roughness. The smell of healthy sweat, which once used to fill her with excitement when he returned from the cricket field or rugby field, now repelled her. Why did he always have to sweat so much? It was not as though he had been *doing* anything, just sitting in the sun. 'When you're a famous consultant, then *you* can take me as one of your team.'

'That'll be the day.'

She knew that he knew that he would never now become a famous consultant; and that knowledge, though it had lain secret and unspoken between them for many months, suddenly pierced her with desolation. She caught him tightly against her: 'You'll make it,' she said. 'Of course you'll make it. Think of all the people who *do* make it.'

Beyond the rose-bushes and the straggling hedge of privet they heard the engine of a car.

'That must be his lordship's Bentley.'

'I wish to God that he'd drop that bedside manner with us.'

Lunch was over and Maurice was in the hall, enquiring over the telephone about one of his private patients, the wife of a Cabinet Minister, whose cataract he had removed the day before.

'You wouldn't catch him ringing up the hospital about a simple cataract patient in a public ward.'

'He has the reputation of being very good with his NHS people. Always addresses them by their names for one thing.'

'That's just a trick. It *means* nothing. How naïve can you be!'

Anna frowned as she poured out the coffee. She had forgotten to buy any beans and wondered if Maurice would guess that she had had to resort to Nescafé. The lunch had gone off well; or was it simply that the 'bedside manner' of which Bill complained had persuaded her it had? Their guest had been enthusiastic about the *lasagne* – 'I've seldom eaten better in Italy' – and had had a large second helping of the *coq au vin* even though he confessed that he had recently resolved 'to get rid of this awful paunch'. Of the paunch Anna could see no sign. Erect and slim, he was so far from being overweight that he had that slightly wrinkled, dried-out appearance of the middle-aged when they become too stringent about their diet. He had talked amusingly but without malice, telling stories of famous colleagues or famous patients, or of his experiences in the Western Desert during the war.

More than once Bill had either said something that Anna knew to be deliberately snide, or had used a tone of faintly insolent self-depreciation when referring to himself, to Anna or to anything that concerned them. When, for example, Maurice had talked of a motoring holiday he was planning in Turkey, Bill had said, 'That's a very *in* kind of trip. I'm afraid that we members of the Hoi Polloi are going to have to content ourselves with a package deal to Malta.' Later, when Maurice had spoken in flattering terms about a new assistant matron, Bill had countered, 'Well, of course, she puts herself out for a celebrity like yourself. But I can assure you she's much less accommodating with the rank and file. No, she certainly wouldn't do anything more than the minimum required of her for yours truly.' Maurice was a subtle and perceptive man and the feelings of envy and animosity behind such comments could not have escaped him; but evidently he had decided to ignore them. It was almost as though, Anna thought, he was trying to *woo* Bill, now adroitly praising him by implication, now asking for his advice and now sympathizing with him for the lack of promotion that should have long since come his way.

Maurice returned. 'Well, she seems all right. Complaining about the food but otherwise all right. I restrained myself from telling Robinson to pass on to her all the details of the splendid meal we'd just eaten. That would have been needlessly cruel. Thank you, my dear.'

As he took the coffee-cup from her, she marvelled, as she had often marvelled, at the beauty of his hands. They were waxen in their whiteness and malleability and the nails must have been meticulously buffed to give them that pinkish glow. 'Would you mind if I took off my jacket?'

'Of course not. With Bill in those filthy shorts, we could hardly object.'

'I'm sure that Maurice would agree that these days it's not at all the thing to be *endimanché*. Suits for Sunday went out with church-going.'

Maurice smiled as he removed his lavender-grey jacket and then adjusted his cuffs, fingering the heavy gold cuff-links as though to assure himself they were still there. He said nothing.

'Have you had any success at the sales recently?' Anna asked.

More than once they had run into each other at local auctions.

'Well, let me see . . . Yes . . .'

He began to tell her about the acquisition of a small Bonington drawing, unidentified in the catalogue, at a country house near Lewes, while Bill sank deeper and deeper into his chair and thrust his bare legs farther and farther out into the centre of the drawing room. Anna was afraid that he was about to fall asleep.

'Collecting has become my chief recreation. That and music.'

'Bill used to play the drums in a jazz group when he was a student. Did you know that?'

'Hardly Maurice's kind of music, darling. In fact, I doubt if he'd regard it as music at all.' Bill followed this comment with an enormous yawn, rubbing his hands up and down his cheeks.

'On the contrary. I'm a great jazz enthusiast. When you visit me – as I hope you will soon – I'll show you my collection.'

Bill straightened himself in the chair, frowning down at his grubby plimsolls: 'Is it true that you do this wonderful needlework?'

'I don't know about its being *wonderful*. Yes, I find it soothing to the nerves.'

'I shouldn't have thought *your* nerves needed much soothing.'

'You'd be surprised. Yes, I first took it up when I was convalescing in the war. Everyone thought it rather a joke – as I expect they do now. My wife's idea. Still, it was better than sitting round doing nothing, like a lot of my fellow patients.'

'I'd like to see some of it,' Anna said.

'If you're a very good girl and do your stuff properly in Ethiopia I might honour you with a gift.' He smiled again: 'That's a threat, not a promise.'

Bill was about to say something, then checked himself. Instead he asked, 'Would you like to take a look at the garden?' This was a ploy he often used to get rid of a guest who had overstayed his welcome.

'Why not?'

Bill and Anna tended the garden between them, with some help from the old man, a retired railwayman, who lived in a cottage at the end of their lane. The previous owner of the house had laid out and planted the flower-beds; Bill and Anna merely weeded them. The old man cut the grass.

'Ah – that must be a Vivien Leigh over there. I know it's vulgar to have a taste for hybrids – my wife wouldn't hear of them – but I must say I love that kind of bloom. Now what would that be?' He raised a rose between forefinger and middle finger, stooping to inspect it. Neither Anna nor Bill had any idea. 'No scent, unfortunately. But a marvellous shade of red.' It was evidently going to be a long tour and Anna knew that Bill must already be wishing that he had never proposed it.

'Good heavens! You have a tennis court. Several tennis courts.'

'Not ours, I'm afraid. They belong to the College – you know, the College of Education,' Anna explained. 'But they let us use them. They feel they have to, because we allowed them to cut down some of the trees that grew along that fence.'

'They blocked the light,' Bill took up. 'Do you play tennis?'

'I used to play. It's the only game at which I've ever been any use. In fact – I once played at Wimbledon.'

'Really?'

'Don't sound so astonished, young lady. Of course it was a long, long time ago. When there was much more finesse and far less power to the game. Yes, I took a set off Bunny Austin. But you're far too young even to know who Bunny Austin was. Both of you play?'

'Bill won't play with me. He says I'm too awful. Bill's rather good. As you might expect.'

'Oh, darling, it's never really been my game. You know that.'

'You beat the captain of the college tennis team.'

'Yes, that was rather funny.'

Bill began to describe how, watching two people from the college playing a game on the other side of the fence, he had not been able to resist calling out to one of them to tell him that he was repeatedly slicing the ball too high on his backhand. 'Perhaps you'd like a game?' the young man had replied sarcastically. 'Since you seem to know so much.' 'Right,' said Bill, who ever since his schooldays had made a practice of issuing and taking up such challenges. 'Why not? Ten shillings to the winner.'

'Of course you won,' said Maurice at the end of the story.

'Of course,' said Anna.

Suddenly Bill turned to Maurice: 'How about a game?' he said.

'A game?'

'Yes.'

'Now?'

'Why not?'

'Maurice is hardly dressed for a game of tennis,' Anna put in.

'I can lend him some togs.'

'You're not exactly the same build.'

'With shorts and an open-necked shirt that doesn't really matter,' Bill persisted. He turned again to Maurice: 'How about it?'

Calmly the older man deliberated, his hands deep in the pockets of his jacket as he surveyed the garden from one end to another. 'Only one set,' he said at last. 'But I don't think I'll be able to put up much of a show after that huge meal.'

'What shall we have on the game? Fifty pee? A pound? A fiver?'

'Whatever you say.'

'Then let's make it a fiver. We might as well play for high stakes – or at least what paupers like ourselves consider to be high stakes. Done?'

'Done.'

Anna was worried. As they returned to the house, Bill striding purposefully ahead of them she ventured to Maurice: 'Is it really wise?'

'Is what really wise?'

'Well, playing Bill.'

'Why not?'

'After your coronary, I mean.'

He laughed. 'Bill has obviously not been keeping you abreast with the latest pronouncements in that field. Exercise is essential – or so the experts all now tell me. No, I never think about my heart now. I play a round of golf most weeks, I even dig in the garden. And I'm a great walker.'

While the two men were changing upstairs, Anna began to clear first the drawing room and then the dining room, the sweat beginning to bead her upper lip and her forehead from the exertion of carrying trays back and forth from room to room.

'Not too bad a fit!' Maurice appeared, with Bill behind him. 'A bit baggy in the seat. But the shoes are exactly my size. Couldn't be better. They might be my own.'

Your own certainly wouldn't be so dirty, Anna thought. The unwashed white shorts no doubt still had clinging to them that animal odour that exuded from Bill even an hour or two after he had had a bath or shower; she wondered how Maurice, who smelled of nothing but expensive toilet soap, could bear to wear them.

Bill's eagerness now at the prospect of the match contrasted startlingly with the air of increasing boredom that had enveloped him after lunch. He made a number of practice shots as the three of them strolled through the garden and then lashed out at the long grass on the bank up which they had to climb in order to reach the courts.

'I hope that racket will be all right for you?' Anna said. She had noticed that Bill had, typically, appropriated the better of the two.

'Oh, yes. Fine. I'm not fussy about these things.' He smiled at her, his pale grey eyes resting on her face. 'It's not often one sees women with parasols these days.'

'That's because of these awful freckles of mine.'

'They're not awful. They're rather fetching.'

No one else was playing on the courts; usually the students came out later on Sunday afternoons, when they had digested their mid-morning drinks and two-o'clock lunches. Anna seated herself on a bench, careful to avoid the places where it was spattered with bird-droppings.

'Shall we have a knock-up first?'

'Fine.'

Bill's body contorted itself into a knot and then unwound to propel the ball into the net with a loud thud.

'My goodness! What a service! I'd no idea what I was letting myself in for.'

It was impossible to tell if Maurice were being ironic or not. As he spoke, he was adjusting the straps on either side of the baggy, stained shorts.

Even during the knock-up Bill played with the teeth-gritting, frowning ferocity that he brought to every game, however trivial its outcome. Maurice moved lazily about the court, his returns gentle and his concentration such that from time to time he would address some remark to Anna, usually with no relevance to the game in hand or even to tennis. Bill hated people not to take a game as seriously as himself – once he had refused to continue a rubber of friendly bridge when Anna had confessed that she had made a preposterous bid 'just for the hell of it' – and Anna therefore guessed that Maurice's nonchalance must already be riling him.

'Shall we begin?'

'Whenever you like,' Maurice called back. He looked over to Anna: 'You must remind me to tell you about the new Osborne play. I went over to Brighton last night to catch it.'

Bill won the first three games without any trouble. His play was forceful but ugly, with a number of smashes that landed in the net, but a number more that Maurice evidently regarded as irretrievable, since he made no move to retrieve them. For much of the time, Bill's face had on it that curious grimace, as of someone in acute pain, that Anna had long since got used to seeing whenever he was making a physical effort. Curiously, exactly the same expression appeared at the climax of their love-making. But she also noticed that, as he stooped to pick up a ball, he would often give a fleeting, private smile to himself. Already his shirt was sticking to his muscular back and there were dark patches under each armpit.

From time to time Maurice would call out 'Good shot!' or 'Well played!' but to such praise Bill made neither response nor reciprocation.

It was only during the fourth game that Anna realized that Maurice was not going to be trounced as she had at first supposed. He ran little and for that reason many of Bill's returns were winners, when with a more energetic opponent they would not have been. But his anticipation was adroit – even before Bill's racket had met the ball, Maurice seemed already to be ambling gently in the direction of where it would land – and no less adroit was his mixing of lobs and shots so sharply angled that Bill was always either racing back to the base-line or careering from one side of the court to the other. Once, such was the fury with which he propelled himself in pursuit of the ball that he crashed into the wire netting that divided the courts from the garden. 'Hurt yourself?' Maurice enquired, again fiddling with a strap at the side of his shorts.

'Hell, no,' said Bill, who had in fact grazed a hand.

The score crept up in Maurice's favour, even though he would still often throw away a point by leaving a ball that with a minimum of running he could certainly have saved. Now point after point went to him, until the score was three-all. Then the older man was in the lead and the score was four-three. Anna who, until that moment, had wanted Maurice to win, suddenly felt a pang of pity for Bill. To Maurice to win or lose was a matter of indifference, she was certain; but to Bill to lose any game was to lose yet another trick in the game of life. Often, after he had played on the losing side in a rugby match, he would sit brooding in front of the television set, refusing to eat, much less to go out that evening. As he now hurtled about the court, she could guess at his increasing fury and desperation.

In the next game, after the advantage had gone to Maurice, the older man managed to put the ball away neatly into the corner of the court farthest from Bill.

'Out!' his opponent called at once.

Anna, who was seated only a yard or two away, was certain that the ball had been in; and she was no less certain that Bill knew that it had been in.

'Out?' Maurice queried mildly.

'By about two inches. Wasn't it, Anna?'

'I don't know. I was dreaming, I'm afraid.'

'Deuce,' Maurice said.

Bill managed to win that game. His face was shiny and flushed, his close-cropped hair was glued to his forehead and from time to time he had to pull away the shirt that was now sticking to his torso as though it were tailored from plastic.

Maurice, whose service it was, took the lead in the next game. When he stooped to pick up a ball near Anna, she noticed that he had gone white round the mouth and nose; but otherwise he looked as unruffled as when he had first walked out on to the court.

'Out, I think,' Bill said at forty-thirty against him.

'Was it? I couldn't see too well. Deuce then.'

Again, Anna knew that Bill had cheated.

With a skilfully sliced service and then with a lob to the baseline after the briefest of rallies, Maurice won the next two points. Five-four.

It was in that last game that a sudden change came over Maurice. It was as though he were saying to Bill: 'So far I've been toying with you, now this is how one really plays,' and the demonstration filled Anna with a surging conflict of emotions: admiration for the way in which this man, thirty years older than her husband and the survivor of a coronary attack that by all accounts had all but killed him, raced about the court, putting home one shot after another with devastating accuracy; bewilderment as to why he should have kept this mastery in reserve until this moment; and pity for her husband, who was now like a bull, enraged and groggy, at the moment when the toreador is finally positioning him for the kill. Point succeeded point, culminating in a gloriously angled half-volley, which Bill just failed to reach with a choked cry of 'Damn!'

His chest heaving and a hand pushing his hair away from his eyes, Bill ran to the net. 'Terrific,' he said. 'A love game. The fiver's yours.' Years of training in 'sportsmanship' at public school and university made his expressions of pleasure in his opponent's victory sound almost authentic; but Anna knew what must, underneath, be the bitterness of his humiliation.

'That was a good game. But you must forget all about the fiver.'

'Good God, no. If I'd won, I'd certainly not have forgotten about it.'

'We must have a return match some time. When you come over to my place. I'm afraid that in singles a set is about as much as I can manage. I do better at doubles.' He drew a handkerchief, with his monogram on it, out of the shorts and dabbed first at his forehead and then at his cheek. 'Yes, I enjoyed that,' he said. Then, turning to Anna: 'I hope you weren't too bored, young lady?'

'On the contrary. It was tremendously exciting.'

Bill had gone ahead of them, first slashing again at the long grass, and then, when he had entered the garden, hitting his racket hard against one thigh.

'Bill's quite some opponent.'

'Your game's in a totally different class.'

'Oh, I've played for so many years that I've picked up some tricks. That's all.' He held the gate open for her, smiling gently as she went through. 'I'll tell you what's the secret when you reach my age. Throw away the unimportant points, don't worry about them. But when a vital point is at stake, then do everything you can to win it.'

'It's as simple as that?'

'Yes, as simple as that.'

'I don't know what's the matter with my knee. It seems to be stiffening.' The two men had changed and had baths; Maurice was back in his silk shirt and lavender-grey suit, but Bill was wearing slippers and a dressing-gown over vest and pants. Anna had prepared them each a Pimm's. 'I have this cartilage trouble,' he explained. 'They don't seem able to make up their minds as to whether I should have an operation or not. I want to avoid it if possible.'

Anna had noticed – as she was sure that Bill, who lacked self-knowledge, had never noticed – that this cartilage trouble, like his stiff shoulder, always seemed to afflict him after some game that had been not won but lost.

'You're really a tremendous all-round athlete, aren't you?' Maurice said.

Bill shrugged. 'Well, I play a lot of games, if that's what you mean.'

'Didn't you get a blue for rugger?'

'For rugger *and* cricket. And a half-blue for fives. But never, I regret to say, a blue for tennis.'

They chattered on desultorily until Maurice looked at his watch and said that it was time that he was going.

'No, don't bother to come out to the car with me, not with that leg of yours. Please!'

Bill had got to his feet and had made his way, with an exaggerated limp, to the front door. 'I think I'll put an elastic bandage on it. That sometimes helps.'

'I'll walk with you to the car,' Anna said.

Anna and Maurice crossed the lawn in silence. Then, at the gate, Maurice turned to her: 'Well, this has been a most enjoyable visit. Most enjoyable. And the game of tennis was great fun. I only hope Bill's knee will be all right.'

'Oh, yes. It often plays him up. But never for very long.'

'It's marvellous, the way he *hurls* himself into every activity. I envy him that. I wish I had his energy.'

'So do I. Heavens! He's forgotten to pay you the fiver.'

'Oh, that doesn't matter.'

'But of course it does. I'll go and fetch it.'

'You'll do nothing of the kind. Bill can buy me a drink some time instead. You can remind him.' He climbed into the Bentley, started the engine and then lowered the power-operated window between them. 'Thought any more about the Ethiopian jaunt?'

She nodded.

'And what have you decided?'

'Oh, I'm coming, of course.'

She said it as though the decision, reached on an impulse while the glass had whirred slowly down between them, was something that had been established irrevocably from the first moment they had met.

The Collectors

MURIEL BEESTON was one of those people who from time to time engage servants for others but never have occasion to engage them for themselves. Thus it was that she had first come to meet the Rushtons when a dying friend of her dead father, to whom she used to go and read in his huge Edwardian flat behind the Albert Hall, had asked if she could find a couple to look after him.

At the agencies she had been told that the salary offered by this wealthy man was 'wholly unrealistic'. Next, as a result of an advertisement in *The Times* – for which her father's friend forgot ever to pay her – some strange and even frightening people had trooped into the little drawing room of her mews cottage: a loud-voiced man with a soft-voiced wife, both smelling of drink, who suddenly, inexplicably, began to hiss invective at each other; two willowy middle-aged men, who had been in the merchant marine and were now eager to go into domestic service together; an obese hulk, obviously in the early stages of Parkinson's disease, with a worried wife, all jutting bones, who whined on incessantly about the business they had had to sell; a young, well-spoken, well-dressed couple, who had no references and were politely imprecise about providing any. . . .

Muriel had been in despair when the Rushtons had arrived. They were small, rosy and neat, with deferential manners that made them select two upright chairs when Muriel invited them to sit, and vague West Country accents. They took Muriel back to her childhood, when she used to go and stay with one of her grandmothers and just such a couple, though on a heavier, more robust scale, were the butler and cook. The Rushtons had impeccable references, many of them on paper as stiff as board, with the letterheads of great country houses. Their last post had been with a peer, now dead, somewhere in Derbyshire. They did not reveal to Muriel what she only learned later, that the peer had died of alcoholism, his estate mortgaged and his dependants unpaid for several months.

The Rushtons did not seem interested in the size, or lack of size, of the salary offered to them. But in the discreetest and most courteous manner they made it clear that they were interested in learning all they could about their possible employer.

'Could you perhaps tell us, madam, what kind of gentleman this General Mortimer would be?' Rushton ventured, as he turned his grey trilby hat round and round in his small, soft hands.

Muriel told them and what she told them seemed to be satisfactory.

'Of course, we should really prefer to work in a house,' Mrs Rushton said.

'There's less to do in a flat, surely?'

'Yes, that's true, madam, of course. But Mr Rushton and I don't really care for flats.'

'Certainly not modern flats,' Rushton put in.

'This isn't a *modern* flat – well, not what one means by a modern flat. Not at all poky or boxy. There are eight rooms,' she added. 'And the servants' quarters are quite separate.'

'We'd have preferred the country,' Mrs Rushton said. 'But Mr Rushton's sister is ill in hospital in London. We want to be near her.'

'I think I'd better mention – to save misunderstanding – that General Mortimer's flat is terribly overcrowded.'

'Overcrowded, madam?' Rushton raised his silvery eyebrows.

'Not with people, of course. With things.'

'Things, madam?' He now sat forward in the upright chair; the hat all at once ceased to rotate between his hands.

'Antiques. Pictures. Old books, too. General Mortimer has always been a great collector.'

'We have always worked for collectors,' Mrs Rushton said surprisingly. 'We wouldn't wish to work for anyone else.'

The General was delighted. Emaciated, stooped, grey and racked with coughing, he would stagger round the flat, from one dimly-lit, crowded room to another, Muriel in his wake, exclaiming, 'It's a marvel, a bloody marvel! They love these things as though they were their own.' With palsied hands he would unlock one of the display cabinets to show her some piece of silver – 'That hasn't shone like that since my mother died.' Gently he would stroke the surface of a bookcase or table, with a long-drawn sigh – 'They must have spent hours polishing that.' Then he would gyrate slowly with the jerky movements of a mechanical doll, as he exclaimed, 'It's all clean! Spotless! Shining!'

Eventually the General was so ill that he could not get out of bed. But the devotion with which the Rushtons nursed him was surpassed by the devotion with which they continued to burnish all the multitudinous possessions he would now never see. What astonished Muriel was not merely that they loved all these inanimate accretions of a long, selfish life but that they knew so much about them – far more than she.

Eventually the General died; and some of his things then had to be despatched to the museums to which he had bequeathed them, while others had to be despatched to Sotheby's for auction. He had 'remembered' both Muriel and the Rushtons in his will, adequately but not generously; he had never been a generous man.

At his death-bed, and later at the funeral, the Rushtons had looked glum. They said more than once how much they were going to miss the dear old gentleman and she knew it to be true. But their real show of grief had come when the moment had arrived to take away the General's possessions.

At first they had been too busy telling one of the porters to mind this and another to put that in a stronger box, to express or perhaps even to realize the depth of their feelings. But when everything had gone except a set of six Chippendale chairs left to Muriel and a Sheraton chest of drawers left to the General's doctor, Mrs Rushton suddenly collapsed into one of the chairs, threw an arm over the chest of drawers and burst into torrential weeping. 'Oh, oh, oh!' she sobbed. 'It breaks my heart to see the last of all those lovely things! Never to see them again.'

Rushton, though he did not actually sob, seemed equally moved.

'I loved them as though they were my own,' he said more than once to Muriel, recalling the General's words.

Muriel found the Rushtons another post without any difficulty; and when that elderly employer had to sell up his great house and everything in it, they asked her to find them another and then another.

If she enquired if they were happy on the occasions when they visited her, they would never speak directly of the people for whom they worked but only of the objects in their keeping. 'Of course, that china must be worth a fortune,' Mrs Rushton would say. 'A king's ransom. But then she has American money, hasn't she, madam?'

'And yet there's a certain – well – a certain lack of *taste*, I should say,' Rushton would take up.

'Definitely a lack of taste. Not like the General. Every piece of the General's was in perfect taste.'

'There's this Van Dyck now. Now I've seen Van Dycks that were as fine as any Rembrandt. Well, almost as fine. But there are Van Dycks that you can only call' – he coughed discreetly behind a small raised fist – 'vulgar.'

'One shouldn't say it, of course, madam.'

'We'd never say it to anyone but you, madam.'

Eventually Mrs Rushton had the first of her heart attacks; and then a second, which reduced her to almost total invalidism. By that time years of devoted service had brought the couple a modest sum of capital and Rushton decided to retire, in order to look after his wife instead of looking after strangers. They bought themselves a little cottage in Rottingdean, and having visited Muriel once before their move, they then vanished from her life, an annual Christmas card apart, for more than three years.

But now Muriel had read of the calamity in the newspapers,

Mrs Rushton was alone and she was on her way to visit her.

'Mean' was the only adjective that adequately described the row of stunted Victorian cottages, at the end of which was No. 12; Muriel had not expected any cottage quite so mean. Poor things! She parked her little car and then walked stiffly – her arthritis was troubling her – up the little path, framed by over-hanging, unpruned fronds of privet, that led to the front door.

'Yes?' the voice of the young woman was as sharp as her face. She was wearing a padded house-coat and low-heeled slippers, and her hair was in curlers.

'Is Mrs Rushton in?'

'Are you Miss Beeston?'

'Yes. That's right.'

'She said you were coming tomorrow.'

'Oh, there must have been some kind of misunderstanding.'

'I expect she got it wrong. . . . Gran!'

Muriel had never known before that Mrs Rushton had had any children.

A door opened at the end of the narrow, dark corridor and Mrs Rushton appeared. 'Miss Beeston! Is that you, madam? I thought that – '

'You thought wrong, Gran. It was today, not tomorrow.'

'Oh dear! Oh dear, oh dear!'

The old lady's agitation gave Muriel a pang.

'It doesn't matter, Gran.'

'But we've got nothing ready. And my room. Such a mess. Even the bed.'

'Never mind. What does it matter?' Muriel forced a reassuring smile. 'I came to see you. Not your bed or your room.'

It was a tiny room, with a view on to an even tinier yard, across which trailed a diagonal line of washing. Everything in it was gimcrack and dusty and *ugly*, yes, ugly most of all. The bed was a low divan, pulled near to a coal fire that was almost out, and the only armchair was a wicker one with a seat that sagged in a jagged bird's nest of broken cane. The young woman had vanished.

Mrs Rushton dithered, still muttering under her breath, 'Oh

dear! Oh dear, oh dear!' Then she opened the door again: 'Eileen! Make us some tea, there's a good girl.'

'What do you think I'm doing?'

'My son's daughter. He's dead, you know. She and her husband came here to look after me, after Mr Rushton – went away. She's a good girl.'

'Why don't you get back into bed? Wouldn't that be best?'

It took a long time to persuade the old woman; but eventually she scrambled back, drawing the clothes up to her chin with hands that – Muriel suddenly noticed – were grey with grime. No less surprisingly the white hair around the pinched, lined face was wispy and straggly. In their references the Rushtons had always been specially commended for their cleanliness and tidiness.

Muriel perched on the edge of the bed. 'I feel ashamed that I've allowed so much time to pass without coming to see you. How long is it? About three years?'

'About that.' Mrs Rushton talked as though her false teeth no longer fitted her, her tongue repeatedly passing over them and then under them. 'Yes, it must be about that. We last visited you just after my first attack. We'd just left Dorchester. That was a lovely house. Lovely things.'

'When I read about your troubles in the paper, I thought that – well – I thought that perhaps there might be something I could do to help you.'

Again the tongue moved about the ill-fitting teeth, while the grey, arthritic hands still held the bedclothes close up to her chin. 'It was terrible. They shouldn't write all that. Every paper it was.'

'People soon forget.'

'The neighbours don't.'

'It must have been a dreadful experience.'

'He did it for me, you know. It was for me. And then he took all the blame. Well, he knew that I liked to have nice things around me, he knew that I missed the nice things. Of course, he missed them himself. Missed them terribly. And that was how it started. The police said in court that he'd never sold a single thing for gain and that was the truth. Not a single thing. We had them all here. Everything. This house was full of them. An Aladdin's cave, the papers said.'

'But didn't you know that he had – where they had come from? Didn't you wonder?'

The old woman jerked her head sideways, drawing her lips back from her sunken mouth, in a mixture of craftiness and alarm. 'Well, of course, I asked him. I used to say to him, "Where does all this come from, all this stuff?" But he had this story about being in the dealing business. And, well, I believed him. I thought he was in the business. He knew enough about things like that to be a dealer, didn't he?'

'I suppose he did.'

Muriel was sure that the old woman was lying, as she must have lied to the police. She was as knowledgeable as her husband about antiques and could not have failed to know the value of treasure looted from almost every country house of note in the home counties.

'I should have guessed. I should have stopped him. That's what they all tell me. And now I lie here and I think it's all my fault, he did it all for me. To cheer me up, seeing as I was ill and couldn't get up and about.'

'I can't imagine how he managed to go on for so long without anyone catching him.'

'Well, you wouldn't really suspect anyone like Mr Rushton, would you?'

Muriel had to admit that one wouldn't.

'Of course, the security in those stately homes is a real disgrace. The police agreed with us. Why, he'd just walk round with the crowd and pop anything he fancied into a pocket. Just like that. They should do something to tighten things up. It's not fair, madam.'

'I must say it does seem most extraordinary. Didn't he even get something out of the Royal Pavilion?'

'Oh, such a lovely little miniature of the Princess Charlotte! How I loved that miniature! I could have cried to say good-bye to it!'

Mrs Rushton now sat up, propping herself on an elbow. 'Of course, madam, he looked after everything ever so carefully – well, you know how he is. Nothing was damaged. Some of that silver looked better when the police fetched it away than it had looked in years and years. And the furniture!'

'Furniture?' Muriel was astounded.

'There wasn't much of that, of course. But he used to call and say he'd come to fetch this or that piece to be repaired and you'd be surprised how often the butler or the housekeeper or whoever was in charge would let him go ahead. But it was risky. He always had to be sure the family were away.'

'Two years does seem an awfully heavy sentence.'

Mrs Rushton nodded. 'It's not as though they didn't get every single piece back again.'

At that moment the grand-daughter came in with a tray, kicking the door shut behind her so violently that tea splashed out from the chipped spout of the large brown tea-pot. There was a plate of biscuits and a flaccid Swiss roll, untidily cut at one end.

'Thank you, dear.'

'Back in bed, Gran?'

'Miss Beeston persuaded me.'

'Best place for you in this perishing cold.'

Muriel shuddered involuntarily; the fire was now almost out and she wished that there was a bed into which she herself could also climb.

As they sipped the bitter, black tea, the two women began to talk about the General; or, rather, not about the General but about his possessions. Did Muriel remember that Copeland dinner service? The George III cream jug that Queen Mary had wanted? That pretty little Victorian card-table that he could never decide whether to sell or not? The old woman became gradually animated; she sat bolt upright in the bed, her back against the wall; her sallow, sunken cheeks began to glow and the dull eyes took fire. From the General's flat they passed on to the other houses in which the Rushtons had worked: the Elizabethan manor in Warwickshire; the home of a wealthy

Peruvian couple in Chester Row; the Lutyens farmhouse near Birmingham. The time passed quickly.

When Muriel at last said that she must start on the journey back, the old woman insisted on scrambling out of bed. Suddenly she seemed embarrassed.

'Oh, Miss Beeston. There's something. I don't know rightly how to tell you.' She went to the rickety chest of drawers and began to tug at one of the handles. 'Drat this drawer!' Her breath was coming in painful little sobs; Muriel was afraid that she was about to have another heart attack.

'Shall I try it?'

Muriel pulled and at last the drawer yielded. But as it flew open the whole chest rocked from side to side.

'That's how they make furniture nowadays! Just look at it!' Mrs Rushton was venomous in her contempt.

She inserted a hand into the drawer and drew out a little bundle. Muriel watched her, fascinated, as she peeled off first a yellow duster, then a stocking and finally a handkerchief.

Muriel gasped.

The old woman was holding out a Meissen china jug in a hand that trembled slightly, the veins at the wrists purple and cordlike. 'It's yours, madam,' she said in a low voice. 'It must have escaped the notice of the police. We'd forgotten about it.' She turned it round, staring down at it. 'Such a lovely thing.' She drew a deep sigh. 'He shouldn't have taken it, madam. But the temptation was too much for him.'

All at once Muriel realized that Rushton must have stolen the jug on the last visit they had paid her; and that proved finally that, for all her protestations of innocence, Mrs Rushton had been his accomplice.

Again the old woman turned it round in her hand. 'The police missed it. Just fancy that.'

They missed it because you managed to hide it, Muriel thought; but she thought that without any anger or indignation or shock.

'You'd better take it with you, madam.'

'But it's not mine,' Muriel said on a sudden, saving impulse.

'I've never had anything in the least like that. I wish I had.'

'Not yours, madam?'

Muriel shook her head.

The old woman stared down at the piece, her eyes clouding over. She shook her head vigorously two or three times. 'That's odd,' she said. 'Are you sure?'

Muriel gave a laugh. 'Of course I am.'

Again the old woman shook her head; then she echoed Muriel's laughter. 'Well, I don't know where he got it from. But he could always pick up a first-class piece. Couldn't he?'

Slowly and with immense care she began once again to wrap up the jug first in the handkerchief, then in the stocking and finally in the yellow duster.

The Tree

How I loathe the WC. It has its uses, of course; civilization would be unthinkable without it. But it's so unreliable in performing its necessary functions. It's so unaesthetic. And, let's face it, it *stinks*. . . .

An old, famous, rich politician thinks these things as he lies out in the late afternoon, distended from too much food and depleted from too much conversation, after a Sunday luncheon party. They are the kind of thoughts that an English politician only acknowledges to himself when he is still half-asleep and that he will never acknowledge to others. *How I loathe the WC.* How I loathe the working class.

Dry thoughts of a dry old man in a dry season.

He had said good-bye to the last of the guests, a simpering newspaper columnist and his broad, energetic opera-singer wife, crunching with them down the gravel drive and, firm hand shading firm eyes against the glare, watching them as they squeezed themselves into their Mini. Then, not wishing to go back to the disorder of half-filled ashtrays and quarter-filled glasses and coffee-cups (the women, his women, could see to all that), he walked round the Georgian house, past his youngest grandchild's tricycle and his oldest two grandchildren's bicycles, past the garden shed (one of his wretched women had left the door open again), the greenhouse and the outdoor lavatory that no one ever used now that Mrs Parkin no longer came to 'do' for them, and down to the tree. Just as the women were his women, so the tree was his tree. It was a lime and at this time of year it seemed to him always to be enveloped in a cloud of scent. One of his women, his daughter-in-law, had told him only that morning that she could smell nothing at all – 'You're imagining it,' she had said. But how could she expect to smell anything so subtle and exquisite when she was always puffing at those filthy Gauloise cigarettes? The chair was there for him, because another of his women, the Spanish *au pair* girl who would so often sigh inexplicably when the two of them found themselves alone together, had been told to see that it was there on any day of fine weather. Sometimes, although the chair was there, he did not use it, because he was kept at the House, because he was attending some committee meeting or because he was opening a charity bazaar or a hospital or an antiques fair.

He stretched himself out in the chair and looked first around him at the long grass undulating as the warm breeze slid caressingly across it, and then up into the black branches, with the brilliant green leaves crowded about them. He could hear, since despite his age his ears were still preternaturally acute, the bees buzzing in the lime-flowers. He liked that sound and the absence of any other sound of any kind whatever. Though the house was in Canonbury, the road was far away; and the grand-children had mercifully been taken by the Spanish *au pair* to the swimming baths. 'You might be in the depth of the country,' the simpering newspaper columnist had gushed. His own pad (that was the word that he used as he spoke about it) was an eyrie above Shaftesbury Avenue, from which he never ceased to be aware of the unending turmoil of motion and emotion down there far below him. A rubbishy little man, the big man had thought; but the big man had none the less been charming to the little one, with the charm of someone for whom charm is a habit acquired from the best of parents, nannies, schoolmasters.

Lynton loved that tree as much as he loved any of his posses-sions; and when he was disheartened, fearful or depressed, its consolatory power was quite as great as that of his Rembrandt, his string of racehorses or his two pointers. Rembrandt, race-horses, dogs, tree: in his life of fretfully conscientious usefulness it was not often that he could pay attention to any of them. But he was not sure that that tree did not mean more to him than any other of his possessions. Beautiful tree. The breeze made a gentle susurration in the branches as he looked up, up, up, through a pulsating tunnel of green to the eggshell blue of the sky above it. As a child he had played in its shade; as a boy he had read under it, lying out, not in a chair placed there by one of his women, but in the deep grass; as a young man, late one evening, the tree a shuddering mass above him, he had held in his arms the woman whom he had loved but who had failed to become his wife because she was a divorcée at a time when that mattered, because she was so many years older than he and because she was poor and (comparatively speaking, of course) of humble origin. He would like to die under that tree, exhaling his last breath as the tree exhaled its perfume, on some late summer afternoon, at once distended and depleted . . .

It was as he was thinking that, that he heard that horrid common voice.

'Excuse me, your lordship.'

Mrs Parkin, who had lived for so many years in that house, the last of a mean, squat row, and whose husband had helped to tend the garden until a stroke had felled him, had always called Lynton 'your lordship'. But that had been in respect, with none of the irony that this old cow's mooing contrived to insinuate into the phrase.

'Yes, Mrs Sparks.'

She was the other side of the wall, in the narrow alley in which the residents of that row of slum houses dumped their lidless bins, their shopping-bags overflowing with rubbish, their cardboard boxes, broken crates, rusty tins. Sometimes the stench of all that garbage would mingle with the scent of his tree; but miraculously, even on a day as hot as this, it could never completely overpower it. She was on tiptoe, her brown, shiny face peering between the trailing arms of the Albertine rose; and even today, in the middle of August, she was wearing that knitted pixie-bonnet. She was ageless, shapeless, charmless; she was also unappeasable.

'That tree,' she said.

'Yes, Mrs Sparks.'

He could see her fingers, cracked and deformed from years

of peeling potatoes, scrubbing floors and washing up for others, gripping the top of the wall. She's hanging on by her fingernails from the window-ledge of life, he thought; she always has. He liked that image, it amused him.

'Yes, Mrs Sparks?' he prompted again, since she was still peering at him silently, as though she had forgotten what it was that was on her mind. But, in fact, both of them knew, he quite as well as she.

'That tree. All that sticky stuff is coming off it worse than ever. Everything's sticky in my garden. The bushes are coated with it. Like a kind of slime. I daren't put my washing out. I said to Mr Sparks only this morning that that tree has made our yard quite uninhabitable.' The voice whined on, mingling now with that consoling buzz of the bees and that even more consoling scent of the lime-flowers. He had heard it all before, so often. He closed his eyes, his hands joined over his slightly protuberant stomach and his chest rising and falling as he breathed evenly and deeply. He might almost have been asleep.

'Are you listening to me, your lordship?'

He opened his eyes. The green, green leaves flickered above him. He made an effort, and then, with that elaborate courtesy of habit, replied: 'Yes, Mrs Sparks, I am listening. I've been listening to every word. I wish that I could do something to help you. But as I have already told you, that tree has a protection order on it. Even if I did want to lop it, prune it or have it cut down, I couldn't do so. I'm forbidden to do so. If I did so, I'd be liable to a fine.' What he did not explain was that he himself had sought the protection order just as soon as she, that oaf of a husband of hers and those two hulking brutes that were her sons had started their moans. 'I'm extremely sorry but there it is.'

'I don't understand about these protection orders. Who are they protecting?' Her hands moved at the top of the wall almost as though she were preparing to heave herself over.

'They are not protecting any *person*. They are designed to protect trees.'

'It strikes me that it's *we* who need some protection. Against that tree of yours. Mr Sparks was saying only on Sunday last there's nothing will grow in our yard. It stands to reason. No sun can get through.'

He wanted to say, 'The weeds seem to grow well enough.' He wanted to say, 'Mrs Parkin and her husband had no difficulty in creating a charming cottage garden.' (Often his guests, the politicians, journalists, writers, bankers, artists, actors, would peer over the wall and say how pretty it all was. None of them would be caught growing those giant dahlias in their own gardens, of course, but somehow they were just right for nice old Mrs Parkin and her husband, two Cockneys full of sly obsequiousness and quaint homespun wisdom.) He wanted to say, 'Somehow, Mrs Sparks, it seems rather appropriate that that once charming cottage garden should now be all overrun with loosestrife. Loosestrife: that strikes me as an excellent indication of the kind of sloppy, malevolent lives that you and your family lead.' But instead he smiled at her and said, 'I do feel awfully sorry for you. But there it is. If you want to have a word with them down at the Town Hall, do please do so. If you can persuade them to agree that the tree should go, then of course . . .' (Hideous, ignorant woman, determined to amputate the one beautiful thing that redeemed that shocking row of houses.)

'I think that's for you,' she said.

'What's for me? What's for me, Mrs Sparks?'

The hands at the wall now reminded him, in their intrusive greyness and rubberiness, of the tentacles of an octopus in an aquarium. If one took a bill-hook and hacked one of them off, at once seven would sprout in its place.

'To see those Town Hall people. After all, it's your tree.'

Pointless to argue with her. But the habits of charm and courtesy persisted: 'I'd certainly speak to them if I thought that any good would come of it. But I know that it wouldn't.'

The pixie-bonnet bobbed as she tossed her head; there was a rustle from the trailing arms of the Albertine as she nudged a shoulder between them. 'They'd not be likely to send you away with a flea in your ear. They'd do what you told them.'

He laughed. 'I'm afraid, Mrs Sparks, that you're very much exaggerating my importance and influence.'

'You was a Minister, wasn't you?'

He nodded. 'Yes, Mrs Sparks, I was.'

'Well then?'

'There's no "Well then?" about it, I'm afraid. The fact of my having been a Minister doesn't mean that I can set aside a preservation order.'

'So you won't do anything?'

There must be some gypsy blood there, he thought, as he had often thought before when enraged with her. Her skin and that of her two sons, though not of her husband, was almost Indian in its swarthiness. Although she must be, oh, at least sixty, the thick eyebrows that met across her forehead were jet in colour, as was her hair.

'It's not that I won't do anything. I can't do anything.'

The tentacles uncurled from the wall. There was a flash of sun on the bilious green of the pixie-bonnet and then she had retreated, back past the overflowing bins and bags of rubbish and through the gate, fissured and creaking, that led into her yard. The gate slammed. He heard her speaking to one or more of her invisible menfolk, in a voice that was, he was sure, pitched purposely loud so that he should hear her. 'Stupid ole cunt! No change out of *him*! Might have guessed it!'

'Sh!' That must be her husband, a decent enough man when she was not there to goad him on.

He looked up at the tree, still now in the perfectly still air but for those eager bees that drank at its flowers. Beautiful, beautiful tree, so unlike that hideous, hideous woman. He closed his eyes. Sighed. Dozed off. It was as he awoke from that doze, like some diver emerging from the depths of ocean, that he began to think: How I loathe the W C . . .

2

Her face puffy, the wiry hair falling across it, old Mrs Sparks ('Ma Sparks' to Lynton's cool women) emerges from slumber like some deep-sea creature hurled floundering and gasping up into the light of day by a depth-charge. Ooh, oh, oh . . . She clutches at her head, the vee of her nightdress falling away to reveal udder-breasts streaked with purple veins. Mr Sparks ('Steptoe' to Lynton's cool women) sleeps on, humped and gently snoring, beneath a mound of bedclothes, a trail of saliva glistening down his chin as though a snail had crawled there. How can he bear the thick woollen pyjamas and all those army-issue blankets ('fallen off a lorry') at the start of an August scorcher like this? He is always chilled, wearing layer upon layer of vests, pullovers and cardigans even when he is playing bowls with his cronies. This morning, as on every other morning, he does not have to get up. He will kip on until the pubs open.

Ooh, oh, oh . . . Mrs Sparks staggers to her feet and almost falls, inadvertently kicking out as she does so at the chamber-pot, its enamel pitted and scratched from generations of scouring, that stands beside the bed. What looks like a strong solution of iodine splashes the rug. 'Fuck!' She pushes away her hair and waddles to the window, raises a flaccid arm and tugs the curtain aside on its bangle-like brass rings. It is so dark here; but beyond the tree the sun is brilliant. Now she raises the net curtain and peers beneath it. The yard is in shadow except for a dappling, as though a handful of gold coins had been scattered as largesse about it, where the light falls, hot and bright, through the crowding leaves. The breeze gently pulls the loosestrife, leggy and etiolated, now left and now right. There are some tenuous pale pink blooms on the murderously trailing arms of the rambler roses. She fumbles for the rusty catch of the window and then pushes it outwards, letting the freshness invade the frowstiness of this dim, dank lair.

She can now hear voices but, because of that bloody tree, she cannot see the children from whom the voices, as sharp as knives newly honed, are coming. The knives slash at her. Children . . . She frowns, still holding the edge of the curtain up with one hand, and begins to remember. Her dream. She was a child again, barefoot and in a grubby pinafore, and she was stooping among the bluebells, snatching at them with a ravenous greed for their unexpected brilliance. The sun rested like a warm palm on the

back of her neck as it filtered down through trees. The bluebells
are against her chest and in the crook of her arm and on the
ground all around her. 'You silly girl! You shouldn't be picking
those.' She hears the voice and tilts up her head in an effort to
see more than a pair of legs and a walking-stick. Then she gives
a little scream because a dog with a long body and long drooping
ears is sniffing at her. 'She won't hurt you,' says another voice,
this time a man's. It is kinder but it, too, carries with it a certain
disdainful authority. Plus-fours, another walking-stick. 'But do
leave those bluebells alone. If you pick them, they'll only die. If
you leave them, all of us can enjoy them.' The bruised stalks
tumble from her as she clambers to her feet. Her hands are green
and sticky. 'There's a good little girl,' says the woman, who is
dangling the leash of one of the dogs from her firm, competent
hand. 'Isn't anyone with you? You shouldn't be all by yourself
in the woods, should you?' The little girl squints up; she cannot
see the face because the sun is in her eyes now, like a warm palm
pressing on them. 'My bruvver . . .' she says vaguely, gesturing
up the path. The two walkers, with their two dachshunds, pass
on. . . .

A dream or a memory? Or both? She cannot be sure. The
uncertainty of it disquietens her. She never had a brother.

Again she stares out, trying to penetrate that screen of leaves
to see what is going on beyond it. The mystery of it tantalizes
her. There is a glint, which she knows, from what she has seen
in the winter, to be an oval-shaped pond, stocked with goldfish.
There is a blur of grey which must be the flagged path. There is
the red and white of the canvas chair on which the old geezer
lazes away his afternoons when he has nothing else to occupy
him. She wonders what the children are doing to make their
voices so excited and shrill. Once, on a winter's afternoon, she
caught them trying to throw the Siamese cat into the pond. She
was glad when the cat scratched the cheek of the older boy. If
that cat ever finds its way over the wall, as once it did, she knows
what she is going to do to it.

She stares down now into the yard. Well yes, it would be nice
to have something growing there other than that purple weed

thing and those unpruned roses and those giant clumps of rhubarb. Now that spuds are so dear, they could have some of those. Carrots. Broccoli. Or geraniums. Geraniums would cheer things up. But she can understand why Dad and the boys don't want to put in any work on the yard. What would be the point with that bloody great tree sucking up all the goodness out of the ground and shading all the light from the sky? Below her, she can see the two Yamaha motor-bikes, each gleaming and glistening within its caul of plastic. Behind them lies the rusting carcass of a Norton Villiers. Lynton, director of a number of ailing and failing companies, would find a facile symbolism there. But that is beyond literal Mrs Sparks, who sees only two new motor-bikes and an old one.

She drops the net curtain and, leaving her husband to go on snoring under the mound of bedclothes, she makes her way downstairs. She puts on the kettle, having decided that she need not call the boys for another ten minutes (the boys are, in fact, men in their thirties), and then she wanders out in her bare feet into the yard. Her toes are oddly crumpled, the nails brown and horny. Suddenly she feels the tackiness under her soles; and when she pulls at a head of loosestrife, that too is tacky. Disgusting. The tackiness reminds her of something nasty but she prefers not to speculate what it might be.

'Children! Children! Breakfast!' One of the cool women, either the one with the blonde hair to the shoulders or the other with the dark hair piled up on top, is calling through the swelling heat of morning. 'Come along! At once!'

She would like to see which of the two cool women it is. She would like to see the children hurrying up the path from the pond. She would like to see if they are eating their breakfast on the terrace, if the *au pair* is waiting on them and if the old geezer is there too. She would like to see the garden, with its regular patterns of rose-beds and, beyond them, its brilliant herbaceous border. But that fucking tree is always there. As she now confronts it, it is like some high, high wall; or like a net woven of green and dark brown cords. Beyond it is the mystery that it guards; the secret rites that she can never join.

Each day the tree seems to approach nearer and nearer to the house. One day, she knows (though her reason tells her that it is only a silly fancy), it will come so near that it will begin to push against the brickwork, slowly tilting the house backwards until the walls crack, the windows buckle and rain down their glass on to the loosestrife below them, the plaster starts to trickle like sawdust to the ground and, behind their own house, the house of old Mrs Emerson begins also to disintegrate. The tree presses harder. The tree is inexorable. The roof rises, like a hat plucked off by a gale, and then crashes downwards. There are fissures snaking up the walls of Mrs Emerson's kitchen . . .

She shakes herself and smiles. Silly. What an idea! But as she still confronts the tree, she feels once again that it is somehow advancing forward. But this time it is pressing not against the shoddily built little house but against her own fat, unlovely, sixty-six-year-old body in its fluttering baby-doll nighty.

3

Two or three days later, as he lay out under the tree with a book, open but unread, propped on his stomach, Lynton heard from beyond the wall, the alley and the other wall, the sound of steel ringing out on stone and deep men's voices saying things that he was just too far away to catch. Still half-asleep, he thought: What are they doing? Digging a grave? That sound of steel ringing out on stone had reminded him of the burial of his wife in the Dorset churchyard where, for many generations, all his family had been put to dignified rest. He lay back and listened with a strange feeling of trepidation. He had experienced that same trepidation when, many years before, he had felt the first faint judder of an earthquake while holidaying on one of the Ionian islands.

Eventually he got up and, wading through the deep grass, he ascended the slope on which the tree stood. From there, the trunk firm against his back, he could see what he wanted over the wall, across the alley and over the other wall. It was those two sons, who would never even give him a sulky good morning

H.F.—F

unless he forced it from them, and who would never look at him unless he stared at them insistently. He had never discovered what work they did. Sometimes singly and sometimes in pairs they would be absent for several days on end; and then they would again be hanging about their home for periods no less lengthy. When at home, they spent hours on end tinkering with their motor-bicycles. They seemed to have no other interest – though the Spanish *au pair* had once said (giggling, not really minding it at all) that they had been 'cheeky' to her when she had been walking past the house. Now each was stripped to the waist to reveal long, muscular arms, the skin Indian in its darkness, and no less dark chests, broad and with heavily defined pectoral muscles, on which the nipples stood out like pennies and the hair grew thick. Each had a beaked nose, predatory under a low forehead; each full, very red lips. They were digging at the garden, hurling their spades into the earth with a murderous ferocity. It was a long time before they realized that Lynton was watching them and then, without gazing at him, they muttered to each other.

Lynton called at last from the protection of the tree against which he was leaning:

'I see you've made a start on the garden.'

The two men looked up reluctantly, their spades poised. Again one muttered something to the other. Then one of them replied, 'That's right, squire. We thought it was time.'

'What are you going to do?'

'Well, the first thing's to get rid of all this.' An arm, glistening with sweat, indicated a pile of leaves, bruised grass and trailing stalks. 'Then level. Then lay the concrete.'

'You're going to concrete it all?'

'Yep.'

'All of it?'

'That's right, squire. Seemed the best thing.' Neither of the men had ever smiled at him before but now the speaker did, revealing brown, broken teeth behind those full, red lips. 'Nothing'll ever grow here right. Not with that tree of yours. So we decided to make things tidy.'

Suddenly Lynton was aware that Ma Sparks had come out from the kitchen and was standing, legs wide apart and arms on hips, on the top of the steps that led down into the garden. From their two eminences they surveyed each other, as the men resumed their work, with that din of hacking, chipping and scraping. Then she gave a seemingly jolly smile, raised an arm and waved to him. 'Morning, your lordship!'

He had never known her to be so pally to him.

4

All that stifling day, as his voice had echoed around him in a half-empty hall, as he had pretended interest in what he was being told over luncheon at the club by a boring American businessman, as he had shopped for a birthday present for one of his women and had gone round a gallery with another of them, he had thought of the tree. The chair would be out under it and the children would be away, staying with a grandmother. It would be cool and silent there and Concepcion, dear little Concepcion, heaving her inexplicable sighs, would bring him a glass of iced China tea with a slice of lemon in it, just as he liked it. He would read that book of political memoirs; or he would do *The Times* crossword; or, better still, he would do nothing at all.

At first, it was all as he had promised himself. The air was fresh and faintly perfumed under the spreading branches; Concepcion hardly spoke, since she knew that, when he was tired, he preferred to be left in silence; and the Earl Grey tea was deliciously chill and astringent on his tongue. The book and *The Times* lay in the grass beside him; perhaps later he would pick up one or the other but not now, not now.

He lay back, the half-empty glass icy in his grasp, and stared up through that pulsating tunnel of green to the eggshell blue of the sky beyond it. Peace. Perfect peace. But then he saw the brown, like rust graining the sides of that tunnel here and there. Leaves dying or dead. Curled up. Brittle, juiceless, lifeless. Christ! He jumped up from the chair and hurried into the house, still clutching the glass of tea.

5

The man called himself a 'tree-surgeon' and he was recommended by one of Lynton's friends, a professor of forestry. He was not a very impressive man, timid and inarticulate, with small womanish hands and a pear-shaped body; but the professor, whom Lynton trusted, had said that there was no one better.

'Well, there's certainly something wrong.' Which seemed obvious.

'What do you think it is?'

A shake of the head, a blinking of the eyes. The lashes of the eyes were short and thick and sandy. 'We've had a very dry summer. Haven't we?'

'Yes, we have.' Which also seemed obvious.

'I'd recommend soaking of the roots. For several hours each day for a start. And I'll give some nutrient.'

'Nutrient?'

'I've got it with me.'

'But you've no idea otherwise . . .?'

Again the short, thick, sandy eyelashes blinked. 'Limes are usually immune to disease. Not like elms. I can see no indication of any kind of disease. The tree *looks* healthy. Very healthy. Except for that dying-off of branches here and there.' He fell silent. He did not often say so much at one go.

Lynton stared up into the beautiful, ravaged tree, 'You don't think . . .' The tree-surgeon, who was getting something out of his canvas rucksack, looked up in enquiry. 'You don't think that the tree could have been, well, poisoned?' He lowered his voice to ask this question since he had no wish for old Ma Sparks or one of her menfolk to hear him.

'*Poisoned?*'

Lynton put a forefinger to his lips, since the man had said the word quite loud. Then he indicated the house the other side of the alley and, in a whisper, told the story. 'I suspected something when I saw them digging up the garden. After all, that would have made it easy for them to get at the roots. The roots must reach that far, mustn't they? They could have dug during the day and then have put down the poison – weed-killer or whatever it was – during the night. Easy.'

The man was looking oddly at him, almost as though he suspected some paranoiac fantasy. But of course he did not know that evil old woman and her brood. 'Well, it's *possible*,' he agreed at last grudgingly, hitching at the trousers that rested low on his childbearing hips. 'But I shouldn't have thought . . . There's no way of telling.' He stooped now and began to fumble in his canvas rucksack. 'Have you got some steps?'

'Steps?'

'I have to get up high on the trunk. The nutrient.'

'Oh yes. The nutrient.'

Lynton began to call for Concepcion. (That morning the Spanish girl had said that she was sure that Ma Sparks was a witch and that she had put some kind of spell on the tree.)

The tree-surgeon climbed up the ladder and hammered into the trunk a number of small aluminium pipes that each had a plastic phial attached to the end of it. 'If anything will do the job, those will.' The tree no longer looked beautiful, its trunk stuck with those plastic phials and its branches drooping and withering here and there.

As he looked up at it, Lynton experienced exactly the same desolation and despair that had overwhelmed him when his wife had gone into the London Clinic for the first and least cruel of her operations.

6

Mrs Sparks has been standing for a long time at the bedroom window, the net curtain raised in a swollen hand and her body bent low to peer out from under it, so that her back has grown stiff and aches. 'Come away from there!' Mr Sparks has told her from time to time. Once or twice he has joined her for a few seconds of her vigil, sucking ruminatively on his false teeth in a way that always gets on her nerves. But now he has put on his stained and battered trilby hat and tottered off to the pub where shortly, sweaty and grubby, the two tree-fellers will also be

calling in for a jar. Mrs Sparks's 'boys' are away on a job. She
has heard from old Mrs Emerson, who heard from the lady who
does for the big house, that the old geezer is away in America.
He gave orders for the tree to be cut down while he was abroad.

It is thrilling to hear the mechanical saw rip through the
branches and to see them tumbling downwards. At a safe distance, the three children, the two pallid boys and the plump
girl, are standing watching. The Siamese is stalking up and down
before them, her ears cocked and her tail erect, as though
indignant at the destruction of the tree beneath which she has
so often skulked in the long grass in ambush for birds. It is
thrilling to feel the light grow brighter and the air grow warmer
as yet another limb is amputated and falls away. She suggested
to the old geezer that the 'boys' might do the job for him; but
he answered coldly, in his most la-di-da manner, that he thought
that it would be better if he got 'professionals' in. The 'boys'
could have made a good thing out of it, getting paid for the
work and then selling the wood. Mrs Sparks wonders if the old
geezer has ever suspected how the tree died. But she does not
really care. No one can prove anything. After all, people can
spill what they like in their own yards.

That younger of the two men is not bad-looking. Golden
hair on his chest just like Dad's all those years and years ago.
Nice, long golden hair on his head. Nice narrow waist. Briefly
she is lost in an erotic reverie, in which she is somehow the tree
up which the man is shinning, its branches her arms and legs, its
leaves her toes and fingers. Nice.

'Come away from there! Don't stand so close!' It is one of the
cool women, the one with the dark hair piled on top, emerging
from the house, a hand raised to shield her eyes.

'They're all right there, ma'am. Nothing to worry about.'
Mrs Sparks now despises the man over whom she has just been
gloating; she does not like that note of deference in his voice.

Another branch crashes downwards and the youngest of the
children, the little boy, gives a squeal of excitement.

There are two cool women now, walking together down the
path. Mrs Sparks hears, or thinks she hears, one say to the other,

'It's so sad. He loved that tree, so terribly sad'; and the other answers, 'I'm glad he's not here to see it. He must have planned it this way.' Mrs Sparks finds that thrilling, too. It gives her a feeling of power, such as she has never had before in her life. She has not only caused that giant of a tree to be razed to the ground but she has driven a famous lord across the Atlantic.

The tree is now little more than a pole, smooth and straight, with some tufts of leaves sticking out from it here and there to break that smoothness and straightness. The room, usually so chill even on the hottest days, now seems full of scorching air. Her cheeks are burning, as are her bare arms and her forehead. She leans far out, no longer caring if they see her, the ledge of the window pressing into her flabby belly. The men have placed that savage saw of theirs against the trunk. This will be the end.

The teeth gnash deep and deeper, spitting out sawdust in all directions. The three children and the two women watch, bemused into silence. There is sweat gleaming along the spine of the man stooped to the saw beneath her. For a moment she has another erotic reverie of her lips brushing away that sweat. The teeth grind and champ. The grass all about the tree is thick with the yellow sawdust. Her heart is beating uncomfortably fast and she feels a curious pressure in her forehead, just at the point where the jet eyebrows meet each other over the short, blunt nose. There is a strange guttural yell from one of the men, as though he were exploding at a climax of pleasure or agony. There is a crackling, tearing sound and then what is left of the tree veers over, slowly, slowly, slowly, and crashes into the grass.

'That's it,' one of the women says.

'Yes, I'm glad he didn't see it,' says the other.

Bored now, the children are already moving off, followed by the cat.

One of the men says, 'Phew! It's hot!' wiping his forehead on his forearm. The other straightens. 'Let's go round to the pub for a pint.' He turns to the two women: 'We'll be back to clear all this up.' But the two women appear not to hear him. They, too, are now making their way, arms linked, back to the house.

Soon Mrs Sparks is all alone at the window, looking out to the place where the tree once stood. The sun bounces in sharp splinters off the new-laid concrete of the yard. There are two tubs in it now, in addition to the two Japanese motor-bikes and the carcass of the English motor-bike, and one day, when she has time to get round to it, she will put some geraniums or perhaps two hydrangeas in them. Everything seems strangely open and strangely glaring. (A small girl in the bluebell wood lifts up a stone and worms wriggle convulsively away from the light, insects scuttle and scrabble in all directions.) She has a sense of falling, because the tree is no longer there to prop her up. She has a sense of the house itself falling, that green retaining wall suddenly removed from it.

She can see the whole garden now, surveying it from end to end: the symmetrical pattern of the rose-beds; the pond, with the water-lilies floating their fleshy discs upon it; the flagged path; the brilliant herbaceous border; the terrace with its white tables and chairs and its blue-and-white striped awning; even the old house itself. But it now all looks so small; and there is no longer any mystery in it. It might be her own house, her own yard.

She still feels triumphant over what she has achieved; but there is an undertow of disappointment, regret, sadness, fear. Yes, most of all she is afraid.

'Well, that certainly makes a difference,' Mr Sparks grunts, as he breathes the fumes of several pints over her at the window.

'Yes, it makes a difference,' she agrees. But she is still not quite sure what kind of difference it is and whether she really wants it or not.

Brothers

SEATED beside his brother in the tank-like air-conditioned Cadillac, Tim wanted to cry out to him, 'Oh, it's wonderful to be together again!' But it was his brother, Michael, in his rumpled jeans and open-necked khaki shirt, a middle-aged man who still dressed and behaved like a young one, who said it for him.

'Oh, it's wonderful to be together again!'

Tim could not say things like that, any more than he could free himself from the bondage of starched collar, tie and suit in a heat that all but felled one to the pavement as one stepped from the cool cavern of the car out into the glare.

Michael pressed a metal flange set into the door beside him and the window began to glide downwards with a faint sound as of a moth's wings crepitating against a lampshade. Once there would have been no sound at all but the car was an old one. He laughed delightedly; and Tim, who so often scolded his students, 'Oh, don't do that! Please! It's pointless to have air-conditioning in a car if you then open the window', now only gave one of his rare, lop-sided smiles.

'They do you well. Or is it that you do yourself well?'

'Neither. The car was a silly buy. It seemed to be a bargain when I got it off an American officer returning to the States. Less than five hundred. But it guzzles up petrol, there are streets here too narrow to take it, and when anything goes wrong with it – as it often does – no one knows how to put it right and I end up by having to send to the States for spares.'

'Still. I like it. Very posh.' Again the thin, nicotine-stained forefinger pressed the flange, this time not down but up, and the whirring glass slowly interposed itself between his eager face and the faces on the pavement.

'How womanish they all look!'

'Who?'

'The Japanese men.'

Tim did not answer. He was bemused by his sudden happiness, almost dizzy with it, as though the arrival of this brother whom he saw so seldom and loved so much had been like a drink gulped down on an empty stomach. Those three weeks alone in the house that smelled like a cigar-box had been very long.

'And they're ugly, I'd never realized that they were so ugly. You should see the people of Indonesia. Marvellous!' His hand descended on his brother's, caressing it lightly; and strangely Tim felt none of that embarrassment that overwhelmed him even when his wife or one of his children made physical contact with him. Instead of shrinking or shifting uneasily, he accepted this demonstration of affection with a profound gratitude and relief, even joy.

Later, as they held slender, ice-pearled glasses in their hands and looked out into a garden that exhaled a vaporous greenness – the maid, showing them into the sitting room, had slid the door back along its groove with the same near-silence with which the window of the Cadillac had glided up and down – Tim said: 'How long are you staying?'

'How long do you want me to stay?'

'*Forever!*' No, he did not say that, because he could not say it, even though it was the truth. 'For as long as you like!'

'Let's see how I like Japan. I've no fixed programme for my Mr Sponge's Sporting Tour.' Michael lived frankly and blithely on others; and the others rarely resented it, acknowledging that in some intangible way they had also been living on him. He gulped at his gin-and-tonic and gulped and gulped again. Finished. He held out his glass.

'Shall we eat now?' Tim asked. He always had one drink before luncheon and two drinks before dinner; that was the rule.

'Oh, couldn't I have another of these first? Please!'

'I don't see why not.'

Over the tough lamb cutlets and the lacklustre beans, Michael said, 'I suppose you've missed them.'

'Yes. Yes, I have.' Tim might have added: 'But strangely I miss them no longer, not since you arrived.'

'Funny that. I'm so glad to be rid of all that nonsense. Sometimes it seems as if I never had that awful woman – or that awful brat.' Woman and brat were both now living in Canada with the rancher to whom the woman had scuttled from the wreckage of her marriage. 'It's as though for years I had had two lodgers – inconsiderate, always complaining of something or other, never paying their whack. And now I can hardly remember anything about them.' He leant across the table and helped himself to some more of the wine. 'But you like your lot, don't you?'

'Yes. Yes, I do.'

'Strange.'

'I've missed them. There hasn't been a day since they left, hardly an hour, that I haven't missed them.'

'Poor old chap.' Again that hand, its palm cool in that searing heat, slid over Tim's; and again Tim felt none of his usual uneasiness at a physical contact, but only a profound gratitude and relief, even joy.

Tim went to his office that afternoon, leaving his brother asleep in a rickety deck-chair, the once jaunty green-and-red stripes of its canvas now faded and blurred, out in the porch. The hair on Michael's bared chest was fluffy and white and he was wearing a pair of baggy bathing drawers, rucked up tight against his crotch as he stretched his long, bony legs out into the sunlight. When Tim, an airmail copy of *The Times* shading eyes screwed up against the glare, ventured out to say good-bye to him, Michael fumbled with a hand as he said, with no trace of embarrassment: 'Oh Christ! I'm having a coming-out ball.' There was a glass – whisky? brandy? – beside him. He had helped himself.

In his room the rucksack and the small, battered suitcase, its handle secured with string, still remained unpacked. When Tim had peeped in on his way from the lavatory, the sight of them, his brother's only luggage, had vaguely exasperated him, as he was now vaguely exasperated by the view beyond the porch of waist-high weeds ravenously choking the flowers bedded out, only two or three days before her departure, by his wife.

'Would you like something to read?'

'I don't think so.' Unlike his brother, Michael could remain totally unoccupied for hours and hours on end.

'Here's an airmail *Times* from Friday.'

'Oh Christ, *no!*'

Tim returned from his office after seven and still Michael lay stretched out, idle, in the chair, the evening sunlight now glistening on his upturned face. The glass, refilled many times in the intervening hours, rested on his stomach, both hands clasped around it. In contrast to his brother's sunburned one, Tim's face was the colour of tin.

'You look tired.'

'I *am* tired. There's always so much to do. They're like vampires – the most courteous of vampires.' Tim sighed. Then he called to the maid in the recesses of the house: 'Imai-san! Imai-san!'

He told her that he wanted a gin-and-tonic, but when she returned he saw that what she had brought was a dry martini – his usual evening drink. He shouted at her, hating himself even while he did so, and she cringed, as his mongrel bitch, Tricia, cringed when one raised a hand or a newspaper to her. She took the glass from him, the skin over her high cheekbones taut and flushed, and scurried away with it.

Tim leant back against the dusty wall and shut his eyes. 'I shouldn't have shouted at her like that,' he said in contrition.

'You stretch yourself too far. That's always been your trouble. You stretch yourself too far and so inevitably the elastic gets frayed. Try not to do quite so much for quite so many people. Sometimes tiredness makes you do all your good deeds with, well, less than a good grace, and then it would have been better if you hadn't attempted the good deeds at all.'

Tim knew that his brother was right. He sighed. Then he

straightened, the wall leaving a smear of ochre dust on a shoulder of his suit, and said: 'Would you like to come to the vet with me or would you like to go on sitting here?'

'The vet?'

'I've got to pick up Tricia – our mongrel bitch. She's been having an operation.'

'Why not?'

In the tank-like Cadillac, Michael asked: 'What's been the matter with this bitch of yours?'

'Oh, nothing serious. We decided to have her spayed.'

'Oh, no! You couldn't! How *could* you?'

'It's a very simple operation.'

'But it's so cruel. It's so – so unnatural.'

'She's had two litters of puppies. You've no idea of the trouble we have whenever she comes on heat. Every stray in the neighbourhood finds its way into the garden.'

'Oh, but I think that's a terrible thing to do to any animal.'

Tim almost reminded Michael of his refusal to let his wife have more than that single 'brat', but he refrained from doing so. Michael had once owned a Great Dane, now dead, of whom he would often say: 'I prefer dogs to humans and Caesar prefers humans to dogs. So we get on perfectly.'

As the vet, in a white coat, with rusty stains on it, reaching almost to his ankles, wandered off down a long, narrow corridor, it seemed to Tim as if sharp shards of glass were being scraped against each other somewhere deep within his skull. But it was only the dogs squealing and yapping out in an invisible compound.

Tail between her legs and body brushing the floor, the bitch, Tricia, sidled up to her master. Michael put down a narrow hand and she turned to sniff at that, her disproportionately long tail thumping the boards so that the dust eddied upwards in a shaft of sunlight.

In the car Michael took her on his lap and examined the place where her matted coat had been shaved for the injection of the anaesthetic. As his fingers explored, she gave a little squeal that could have been expressive of either pain or pleasure, perhaps even of both. He put his face down to hers and a long rubbery tongue unrolled to sweep across his nose and lips.

'I shouldn't let her do that. Dogs carry all kinds of parasites in Japan.'

'Tim! I do believe you're jealous!'

Tim grunted, but Michael had been right. Tim himself never took the dog on his lap, never allowed it to lick his face or even his hands, upbraided the children if they allowed it to do so. But when Michael permitted all these things he wanted to cry out: 'She belongs to me! Put her down! Don't let her do that to you! She's mine!'

As they drove home through the gathering dusk, Michael peered out through the window, open now though the air that blew through it was still dust-laden and scorching, and again exclaimed in a tone of wonder: 'How womanish they look!' His hands fondled the ears of the bitch, as she sat on his knees, her beady eyes staring, hypnotized, ahead of her. Then he turned to his brother, under the armpits of whose suit the pale grey mohair was darkening with sweat, to say: 'Tell me about Rosie.'

'I suppose she's dying.'

No one had ever said it before, not even the stern-faced American doctor at the Mission hospital who had first diagnosed leukaemia, not even Laura in her moments of most extreme anguish, not even Tim to himself. But of course it was true; and that Michael should have faced and forced that truth somehow made it far more bearable than the talk of that middle-aged missionary sister about this little boy, a patient of hers, who had recovered, yes, totally recovered, from the dreaded illness, or of the doctor himself about all these marvellous cures that were being discovered every day for seemingly incurable maladies.

Again Tim's face was the colour of tin, except for the bruise-like shadows under the eyes, as he said: 'Yes, I suppose she is.'

'Poor Tim. And poor little Rosie.'

As the narrow, nicotine-stained hand went on massaging the bitch's ears and as the dust-laden air seared Tim's averted cheek, he all at once felt a strange, stagnant peace within him, as though previously turbulent waters had suddenly subsided to leave an all-covering, all-choking sludge. He swallowed, the prominent Adam's apple jerking up and down above the collar-stud that pressed into his throat like a spike (Michael had once benignly mocked him, 'You must be one of the few men left in England who still wear detachable collars'), and then blurted out: 'I think that Laura knows. And, even worse, I think that Rosie knows. But we've never spoken of it.'

'Perhaps it would be better if you did.'

'Perhaps.'

'And then perhaps not. There are sometimes things that are too big to talk about. It's like two people trying to hoist a weight too heavy for them. It imposes an unendurable strain on them. It can inflict' – he gave his singularly sweet smile – 'all kinds of ruptures.'

But the weight is not too heavy for the two of us. The words were not spoken but they were there between them, loosening the tight line into which Tim had stretched his mouth in his attempt to suppress the agony behind it.

'When do they return?'

Tim shook his head, again hearing, deep at the centre of his brain, that clash and crunch of jagged shards of glass against each other.

'Not planned?'

'There are tests – all that kind of thing.' He swallowed. 'One can hope for remissions, of course.'

And miraculously, seated beside his brother in the tank-like car as it lumbered down a street so narrow that one expected it at any moment to scrape against the wooden houses on either side of it and snap them to fragments as an elephant snaps the branches in its jungle path, he had himself all at once experienced a remission of that previously unsleeping agony of loneliness, longing and futile despair.

'What are you doing now? You never write. I never know what you're up to.'

The dog slept, occasionally snuffling or grunting, in Michael's lap, its silvery-grey tail, disproportionately long for its dumpy

body, curling over a bare arm. Again there was a drink beside
his chair – tomorrow I'll have to order some more whisky
and gin, Tim had thought, as he had shaken the last drops
from a White Horse bottle full that morning – but he was
wholly sober. A low moon hung over the garden fence; that
greenish vapour that the garden had exhaled during the long,
burning day, had given it an opalescent halo. Gnats, their
stings like tiny burning darts, clouded about them in spite of
the coil, a snake tipped with fire, that released an odour com-
pounded of mould and camphor.

'But I sent you that postcard, such a pretty postcard, from
Bangkok and another, admittedly far less pretty, from Hong
Kong.' But the postcards had said nothing other than that he was
travelling closer and closer.

'I meant, what job are you doing? And are you writing?'

From time to time Michael took a job – schoolmastering,
with the BBC, with UNESCO, with an advertising agency.
He was paid well; he worked brilliantly, which was to be
expected, and conscientiously, which was not. But then a weariness and restlessness would overcome him, as it had overcome
him in his once happy marriage and in so many of his friend-
ships. There would then be no sudden disruption but a slow,
almost imperceptible gliding away. 'Aren't you happy with us?
Do you feel we're not making proper use of you? Do you want
more money?' To each of these questions he would shake his
head, giving that singularly sweet smile of his, so unlike his
brother's bitterly lop-sided one. Oh, no, he would say. I just
feel, well, that I'd like a – a *petit changement de décor*.

'Job?' He drew one ear of the dog through his fingers, taking
pleasure in its silkiness as he once had taken pleasure, no more
and no less, in the silkiness of the hair of that wife whom he
could now hardly be bothered to remember. 'No, I've got no
job at present and none in the offing. I've got a little money
stashed away. You know me. My needs are very simple. Provided
I can eat well and have all the booze I want. . . . Which reminds
me . . .' He stooped down to retrieve the empty glass and then
held it out.

'The Scotch is finished,' Tim said, thinking, Hell, surely he could have bought some duty-free drink on the plane. 'I can give you some gin or brandy.'

'Couldn't that fetching little maid-san of yours pop round the corner to the nearest pub or off-licence or whatever they have in Japan?'

'I'm afraid she's gone home. She doesn't sleep in.'

'Well, then, give me some gin. I never like to change horses in midstream but there it is.'

When Tim returned with the drink, he pursued: 'Your writing. Are you writing?' Suddenly resentful both of this endless drinking at his expense and of his brother's sobriety despite it, he was deliberately asking a question that he hoped would hurt.

'Writing? Oh, no, my dear fellow, I never write now. The infirm glory of the positive hour . . . that's all over.' Suddenly he tweaked savagely at the dog's ear and it gave a little yelp; then he resumed that hypnotizing stroking, stroking, stroking. 'Poetry, like sex, is really only for the young. But –' he sighed and gulped at the glass '–oh, I sometimes scribble this or that. Just to amuse myself.'

'What kinds of things?'

'What I call my commonplace book. And it *is* commonplace – most of it. Trite, boring, insignificant. Like my life these days.'

Out of the whirling vortex that had all at once encompassed him, a fire-tipped needle stabbed at Tim. He clapped a hand to his cheek, then rubbed it with a forefinger. 'Let's go in,' he said. 'I'm being bitten to death.'

Michael stooped for his drink, rose and threw an arm around his brother's shoulder. 'Poor old chap! It's strange how every insect feeds on you and I always remain immune. Your blood must be sweeter than mine, I suppose.'

Hands reached out to him from a palm-fringed shore, quivering through the haze of heat that veiled the straits between. There was coolness there, reconciliation, oblivion. But he could not get across. He waded out into the water, but as it reached his chin, its taste bitter and brackish, the hidden current jerked at him, a tether at a frantic animal . . .

He opened his eyes and stared up at the wooden ceiling, behind which (how the sound always terrified Laura) the rats would often scuffle and patter back and forth. Something was missing; and what was missing was not only Laura's body beside him, the sweat trickling off her sleeping face and glistening along the arm that trailed to the floor, and not only the children, whose empty rooms on either side of him now contained nothing but a smell like that of ash long resting in a burnt-out grate. What was it? What? Then he realized. The bitch Tricia was no longer snoring beneath the bed. That regular sound, which so much exasperated Laura that she would often get out of bed in the middle of the night and drag the cringing beast, her claws scraping the bare boards in her protest at being banished, down into the kitchen, had never troubled him. Indeed, during those long three weeks in the subaqueous dimness of the prison in which his life had been passing it had seemed somehow to palliate, though it could never remove, his loneliness and longing. When he had slept, it was as though it was on that regular sound that he floated out and out to that distant palm-fringed shore; and when he had not been able to sleep, gazing up at the ceiling as he was doing now while the sweat ran off his body, it still supported him so that he did not wholly drown. Sometimes, as the dawn slowly, imperceptibly, began to define the fly-blown mirror of the gimcrack dressing-table, now empty of all Laura's bottles, boxes and tubes, opposite the window, he would stretch an arm down and call softly 'Tricia! Tricia!' and the bitch, roused from her slumber, would slide along the floor, her tail thumping, to wreathe her tacky, rubbery tongue around his fingers. There were occasions when she would even try to climb on to the bed, straining and scrabbling with her short dachshund's legs while her spitz's muzzle would seek for his face. But then he would order her 'Down, Tricia! Down! Bad dog!' and, furtive and ashamed, she would slink away from him back under the bed.

He threw his legs off the bed and called her name softly into the darkness. 'Tricia! Tricia! Where are you?' He might have been calling 'Laura!' There was no answering scamper. He got up and went to the open window, feeling suddenly chilled despite the heat that had previously caused his sweat to saturate the sheet rumpled beneath him. He ventured out on to the shaky balcony, forbidden to the children in case it should collapse beneath their weight. In the moonlight the three huge earthenware pots trailed blackened fronds that looked like the legs of giant spiders. He had forgotten Laura's instructions to water them, just as he had forgotten her instructions to keep the garden free of weeds. Imai-san, to whom the same instructions had been given, had also either forgotten them or deliberately ignored them, as she ignored any duty that she felt to be either beyond her or beneath her. He leant recklessly against the rail, all at once seeing it snap beneath his weight, the rotten wood disintegrating into an acrid dust and then his body plunging downwards on to the terrace below, to lie there spreadeagled. The image brought him a brief, self-indulgent pleasure.

There was a square of lemon-coloured light between the two crowded flower-beds. Either Michael had gone to sleep with his light on or else he was still awake.

Feet bare, Tim pattered back into his room and pulled on his pyjama jacket, thrown over the back of a chair, with jerky, exasperated movements. He went out into the hall and again called softly through the silent house 'Tricia! Tricia!' No response. He looked in the bathroom, where a tap dripped desolately into a bath streaked with an orange stain of the same colour as the nicotine on Michael's fingers, into the empty rooms of the children, into a lavatory that always smelled, as Laura put it, 'of drains', in spite of all her emptying of powders into it and all her squirting of aerosols.

He went down the creaking stairs, pausing from time to time, his hand on the banister.

Michael's voice called from the downstairs bedroom: 'Tim? Is that you?'

'Yes.'

'Aren't you asleep?'

'I was looking for Tricia – for the dog.'

'Oh, she's with me.'

Tim slid back the door; and there was his brother, lying completely naked outside the bedclothes, his knees drawn up with a
notebook laid across them. He made no move to cover himself.
The dog rested under his knees, almost supporting them. Her
little beady eyes slid from brother to brother; she did not wag
her tail.

'Oh, she shouldn't be there, Michael!'

'Does it matter?'

'Laura doesn't like her to get on the beds or the sofas and
chairs. She knows that.' *And you know that too*, he almost added.

'Well, Laura isn't here. So Laura needn't know. Poor little
thing!' He fondled the dog, running a hand along that sharp,
overlong muzzle. 'She's had a bad time – having those ovaries
scraped out of her. She deserves to be spoiled.'

'There's always the likelihood that she has fleas. In this hot
weather it's virtually impossible to keep a dog free of them.
And she always picks them up at the vet's.'

'Well, as I said earlier this evening, insects never show any
interest in me. So I don't mind.'

Tim stared at the long narrow body, with the greyish tufts
of hair on the chest – they looked as if they had been glued
there, haphazard – and the strangely boyish legs. He's older than
I, he thought, five years older, and yet he's aged much better,
that greying of the hair apart; and at that Tim was suddenly conscious of his paunch, across which his pyjama trousers strained
themselves, and of his breasts, like a pubescent girl's.

'Why aren't you asleep? It must be terribly late.'

He looked at his watch; the tone was similar to that which he
used to the children when, in the middle of a dinner party, he
heard them chattering or scurrying about upstairs.

Michael now looked at his own old-fashioned watch, inherited from their father, and worn on a faded nylon strap that
had also once been his. 'Not yet three. That's not late for me. I
only sleep three or four hours each night.'

'I didn't know that you also suffered from insomnia.'

'I don't. Insomnia's when you want to sleep and feel you ought to sleep. But I'm perfectly happy – reading or writing or thinking or just, well, lying and waiting pleasurably for another day.'

Tim approached nearer to the bed; and the bitch, expecting to be punished, pressed her body deeper and deeper into the bedclothes, her little eyes peering up at him fearfully. Suddenly he felt a hatred for her, so craven, so disloyal and so easy for any chance comer to seduce. 'What are you writing?' he asked.

'Oh, just some commonplaces in my commonplace book. Things like how womanish the Japanese men look and how I travelled for the first time today in an air-conditioned Cadillac. I've never been in an air-conditioned car before and I've never been in a Cadillac. So that's something rather important, isn't it?'

Tim did not know whether he were being teased or not.

Michael patted the bed. 'Sit down.'

Tim shook his head. 'No. I'd better try to get to sleep again.' He thought of those hands reaching out from that unattainable palm-fringed shore with a sudden access of longing and despair. 'It was just the dog,' he muttered. 'Just the dog. I was . . . worried.'

'You worry too much, dear Tim. What's the use of worrying? It never was worthwhile.'

'Men used to sing that when they went to their deaths in the trenches.'

'Sit down. *Please!* Let's talk.'

But Tim was backing, a squat and unhappy figure, his plump feet making the boards creak beneath them, towards the door and the dark hall beyond it.

During those first days the lives of the two brothers for the most part twined in a gentle harmony that made it possible for Tim to forget for long periods on end that Laura and the children were far from him; that there was no certainty when they would come back, if indeed they ever did so; that Rosie was doomed; and that Laura probably already knew that, as he did, though they would not admit it to each other. But from time to time, jarring that harmony, he could hear, sometimes near at hand and sometimes almost out of earshot, that sound of jagged shards of glass scraping and screeching against each other.

There was his jealousy over the bitch, which manifested itself in his either dragging her ferociously off the chairs or sofas on to which he knew that Michael must have coaxed her or remonstrating with Michael himself: 'She's been taught *not* to sleep anywhere but on the floor or in her basket. You're spoiling everything that Laura's achieved with her in these last months.' But Michael paid no attention to such protests; even in front of his brother he would say: 'Come on, old girl! Come to your uncle!' and hoist her up on to his lap, where she would stretch out, grunting and sighing pleasurably.

Then there was Michael's endless drinking, for which, a further annoyance, he never paid in either money or hangovers. One night they went on a round of bars and nightclubs and the next morning, his wallet empty, Tim could barely raise his head from his pillow. But Michael gleefully devoured a huge breakfast of fried eggs and bacon and round after round of toast. He never now asked if he could have a drink but would merely either go over to the drinks cabinet and help himself or order Imai-san to fetch him what he wanted. 'This looks rather pale,' he said on one occasion, holding the glass that Tim had handed him up to the light and peering disapprovingly at it as though he were a doctor examining a medical specimen. Tim all but retorted, 'You'd have a better chance of getting a stronger whisky if you occasionally bought a bottle.'

Finally there were the perpetual trivial irritations of clothes scattered about the guest-room; of the bath unscoured; of the plastic raincoat – intermittently the rain poured down those first days – thrown, still dripping, into this or that corner of a room ('What's become of my French letter?' Michael would demand as he searched for it); of newspapers left on the floor and cigarette-ends tossed into the grate or abandoned, exhaling a vile

smoke, on the edge of an ashtray. All these things were negli-
gible, Tim told himself; it was not as though there were no
Imai-san to glide about the house to put everything to rights.
But, fanatically tidy himself, he hated all the mess; and knowing
how much Laura would have hated it, he felt that, in overlooking
it, he was somehow betraying her. On one occasion he had
found Michael giving the dog some milk in the porridge-bowl
with the Womble on it that was Rosie's and that no one else
must ever use. Only then did he show his anger, shouting 'Oh,
for Christ's sake!' as he snatched the bowl off the floor and held
it under the tap, splashing his suit as he did so.

'Why, what's up?'

'That bowl belongs to Rosie.'

But then he thought: What does it matter? She'll probably
never use it again. And his hand stiffened on the bowl as he
stared bleakly down into the miniature whirlpool that the water
was making in the sink.

There was a party for a number of Japanese dignitaries and
their twittering, tittering wives, and to Tim's horror his brother
appeared for it in those same blue jeans in which he had arrived
and in that same khaki open-necked shirt. Surely he could have
changed into a suit, Tim thought angrily, forgetting that neither
that bulging rucksack nor that suitcase that appeared to be made
of some thick and tough kind of cardboard had contained one.
But then, in wonder, he had watched as his brother had gone
from one to another of these guests, none of whom Tim had
ever found in the least bit charming or charmable, and had
suddenly transformed them, so that the puppets he had known
all those years had all at once, by some magic, been changed into
human beings. Blessed are the charmers, for theirs is the kingdom
of heaven.

'You're so much better at this job than I,' he said despond-
ently when the last of the guests, the mayor of the city, his face
scarlet from too many unaccustomed martinis, had staggered
into his chauffeur-driven Mercedes and the two brothers had
then waved a final good-bye to him from the steps.

'I suppose I am. But only for an evening. I couldn't take it for more than an evening. Whereas you have to take it – or something like it – for the rest of your working life.' Michael spoke, as always, with a quiet truthfulness that carried no sting with it. He had summed it all up. But that night, the palm-fringed shore shimmering in the distance, Tim had wondered why he himself, with so much effort, achieved so much less than his brother with none at all.

For the whole of the three and a half years that he had spent in Japan, Tim had been served by the same secretary, Michiko Kuroda. It was only in the past few months that he had come to call her Michiko, after a summer school at which the rest of the English staff, most of them young and unmarried, had at once assumed on arrival that everyone would be on first-name terms. Tim suspected that she did not at all care for the new familiarity; though frequently urged not to do so, she still called him 'Mr Hale', still called Laura 'Mrs Hale' and still always prefaced the children's names with a 'Master' or 'Miss'.

She was usually already seated at her desk when he arrived at the office and she often stayed on there long after he had left it. He would remonstrate with her – this or that job could be left for the next day, there was no urgency whatever – but she would coolly shake her head, her helmet of sleek, black hair swaying as she did so, and would tell him that really, Mr Hale, she had nothing else to do that evening, she hated to leave a job unfinished, he must not worry about her. Laura had made bitter, barbed fun of this devotion, just as she did of the brothers' devotion for each other, telling her husband and even friends of theirs that it was obvious that the poor girl was secretly in love with him. But Tim himself had always doubted that. It would have been flattering, of course, if behind that glacially composed exterior a fever of longing raged: but if Laura were right – and admittedly jealousy always sharpened her sense of smell for such things – then why did Michiko perform all her duties with the efficient distaste of a hospital nurse attending to some particularly unattractive patient and some particularly unattractive malady? She rarely looked directly at him and the nearest

she came to smiling was a curious drawing-up of her upper lip
that gave her face the look of a startled hare.

In the event, he had been proved right and Laura wrong. He
had learned that the Japanese woman was, indeed, devoted to
him; that she admired him and respected him so much that she
thought first of him when desperate for advice and comfort. But
she was not in love with him, for the simple reason that she was
in love with someone else. This someone else was a young
English physicist, working at the university under the legendary
Professor Yukawa and lodging at the house, a labyrinth of
wooden boxes placed at angles to each other to make odd-
shaped courtyards and little gardens, in which the Kuroda
family, father, mother and daughter, lived in the foothills of
the lonely mountain that soared up to dominate the sprawling
and seething city. The old General, Michiko's father, whom
Tim had met only once over an elaborate meal eaten in almost
total silence and served by the two women of the household who
took no part in it, had spent several years in gaol at the end of
the war. The mother suffered from some liver complaint that
had given her face a bronze-like sheen and that had bowed and
emaciated her. Impoverished, they let out the most distant of
the boxes in their domain to foreign students, artists and disciples
of judo, karate or Zen, looking after their meals with the same
coolly efficient distaste with which Michiko looked after Tim's
needs in the office. They served their lodgers only in the sense
in which Tim served the mongrel bitch or Laura served the
peonies and azaleas in the garden.

The young man, who was called Morgan, dressed with an
attempt at formality that gave him an almost laughably old-
fashioned air among the other young lodgers, chiefly American,
from whom he kept aloof. His suits, tightly buttoned even when
the summer was raging at its hottest, were crumpled, baggy at
the knees, stained with oil from his bicycle and with the food
that slipped from inexpertly wielded chopsticks. The first time
that he had visited Tim and Laura, both the Hales had simultaneously found themselves staring at the sole that was flapping
loose from one of his shoes; and he, unfortunately, had seen

them staring and his face, already red and puffy from his bicycle ride up to their house from the university, had grown even redder and even puffier.

He was, in fact, as Laura often declared, a nice enough boy; and as a physicist he was said to be outstanding. But even if Tim had not known from Michiko's *curriculum vitae* that Morgan was thriteen years younger than her – perhaps Morgan himself did not know this, since like so many Japanese middle-aged women Michiko had remained physically little marked by the passage of the years and all the tribulations of her family – the relationship seemed an improbable one. To the Kuroda parents it seemed not merely improbable but monstrous. Two other daughters were married, their single beloved son had been killed on Iwo-jima; they had expected this daughter, now in her forty-third year, to look after them and after the houseful of lodgers, as they grew increasingly infirm. If she must now conceive the mad idea of marrying, then they were well able to select for her some well-born, well-to-do widower from the small circle in which they moved. This young man, they could see for themselves, was certainly neither well-born nor well-to-do; and, worst of all, he was not Japanese.

Michiko, who had never before told Tim anything about her private life – of the General's years in gaol he had learned from a gossipy liberal professor – had poured all this out to him, not once but many times. In consequence he had come to dread her entrances into his office, followed by the desperately composed plea: 'May I disturb you for a moment, Mr Hale?' Even more he had come to dread her calls at the house, sometimes with Morgan, who would falter behind her on the doorstep and would then sit almost wholly silent, wringing his large, sweaty hands, as softly, insistently, implacably she talked, talked, talked. She did not wish Laura to be there; any advice that Laura might proffer to her she obviously regarded as worthless. Laura soon realized this and, seeing Michiko, would flounce out of the room, saying that she must attend to the children or the supper or the garden. 'Do we *have* to let her in whenever she chooses to call?' Laura demanded more than once; and Tim had then patiently explained how sorry he felt for her; how according to the Japanese code, an employer was held to be responsible for the personal happiness of an employee; how she had no one else to whom to turn. He had too strong a sense of duty, Laura retaliated; and of course she was right. Most of the good actions that he performed were performed out of that unsleeping, nagging sense of duty, a kind of perpetual psychic toothache, and not out of kindness or love or gratitude. He wished that it were otherwise.

After dinner on the fifth night of Michael's stay – Tim was just reluctantly pouring out a glass of brandy for his brother – Imai-san glided in to announce: 'Lady is at door.' There was only one lady who, now that Laura was away, would call unannounced at such an hour.

Before dinner the two brothers had had the quiet tussle that now preceded each of their meals together.

'Let's go in to eat,' Tim had said, draining the second of his martinis, and 'Already?' Michael had replied. 'Oh, do let's have just one more drink. What's the hurry?'

Tim had then explained that Imai-san would be eager to get home; it was not really fair on her to keep her waiting any longer; she would miss her last bus and then he would have to offer to drive her.

'I can't think why you don't have a living-in servant,' Michael had retorted. 'It's not as though she's all that good, is it?'

Rising to his feet and carefully placing his empty glass on the tray, Tim had replied in a voice of weary patience: 'Actually, she's very good by Japanese standards. And servants are becoming almost as difficult to find and almost as expensive here as back at home.'

Over the meal, Michael's hand had gone out repeatedly to the bottle of wine. Tim, who alone usually drank only a single glass and resented that between them they now finished off a bottle at every meal, had decided that, next day, he would offer his brother the choice between sake or beer.

Michael had chewed laboriously on a piece of steak: 'She's overcooked this steak. I've noticed she tends to overcook things.'

Tim had resisted the urge to retort: 'If the food seems to you so unsatisfactory, why don't you take me out to a restaurant one evening?'

Michiko, for all her apparent submissiveness and shyness, was ruthlessly egotistical in achieving any aim important to her. Over small things – the care of the lodgers or the care of Tim – she would sacrifice herself without stint or qualm; but over anything of moment, it was others who must be sacrificed. Tim and Laura had learned this previously unsuspected truth just as soon as the Japanese girl had decided to make her English employer her counsellor.

When she now slid into the sitting room, her head lowered and turned slightly sideways, she had all the appearance of someone overcome by humility and shyness; but Tim knew that the presence of a stranger would in no way deflect her from her course.

'Ah, Michiko!' he exclaimed in a tone devoid of any pleasure. He might have been saying 'Ah, some more letters!' when she brought in the second post to him in the office. 'I don't think you've met my brother yet. My brother, Michael.'

She put her hands on her knees and gave a little bow, the bell of sleek black hair swinging forward to conceal all but the tip of her nose and her forehead. 'I am afraid that I am disturbing you at this hour?'

'No, no. Not at all. Sit down!' It was not Tim but Michael who said this.

Michiko glanced sideways at Tim, her head still lowered, and then carefully seated herself on the edge of the sofa, her knees and ankles both close together and her hands resting, one on top of the other, nervelessly, in her lap. She did not speak.

'A drink?' Tim suggested, not because he felt well disposed to her, intruding at such an hour, but because that perpetually nagging sense of duty told him to do so.

She shook her head. 'I do not wish to be a trouble. No, thank you.'

If she did not wish to be a trouble, why had she come in the first place?

'I can get you some coca-cola.'

'No, thank you. Really, Mr Hale. It is too much trouble.'

Suddenly Michael flopped down on the sofa, not at the other end but close beside her, his knees wide apart in the threadbare, faded blue jeans that Imai-san had washed out for him with obvious distaste that morning, and the brandy balloon fondled in both hands between them. He looked at the Japanese woman, appraisingly but kindly; and when she at last turned her head sideways to return his gaze, he gave that extraordinarily sweet smile of his, the chilly pale blue eyes deepening in colour and acquiring a sudden warmth. Slowly, Michiko smiled back, the upper lip tremulously retracted to give to her face that look of a startled hare.

'Something's on your mind, my dear?'

'Please?'

'There's something worrying you.' He leant towards her, all sympathy and solicitude.

'Mr Hale has told you about me?'

'Nothing. Nothing at all. But I can see. You're not happy. What is it?'

She turned completely to him now, swivelling round, so that Tim could see only her narrow back and sloping shoulders. Then, in a patteringly rapid, soft voice, she began to tell him everything. Michael, apparently absorbed, listened to her without a word.

'. . . . Mr Hale – your brother – tells me that it is better to forget about this friend. He thinks that for a little time I shall be happy and then after that I shall be unhappy. He says that it will be difficult for me at first but that after a while I shall be thankful that I did not leave my family and leave Japan. That is what he says. But I' – one of the small, still hands suddenly gave a little jump like a fish in its final death-throe – 'I think that maybe he is wrong.'

'Of course he is!'

Tim was first astounded and then furious.

'And of course he'd give you advice of that kind,' Michael went on. 'That's how he's always lived his admittedly admirable life – very cautiously, very prudently. But if you do what he says, you're certainly not going to be thankful in the years ahead – far from it. No. You're going to say to yourself: "Christ, what a fool I was! I had my chance, I had my one big chance in life, and what did I do with it? I messed it all up." That's what you're going to say to yourself as you get older and older and your parents get frailer and frailer and you have more and more to do as you look after them and that house of yours.'

Tim stepped close to them, his hand trembling as it held his balloon of brandy right against his chest. 'You don't know the General and his wife, Michael. You don't know this boy – Morgan. You don't really know Miss Kuroda. Do you?'

'And I don't have to know them. Well, for God's sake, Tim, what are the things we all regret in our lives? Not the things we did but the things we failed to do – the things we passed up because we just hadn't got the courage to grab at them.'

Michiko seemed not to have heard Tim. She did not look at him; and when she next spoke, it was as though he had never intervened. Yet, on every occasion in the past, she had hung on his every word, however ill-considered or trite.

'I think you are right.' She looked closely at Michael, her long-lashed black eyes meeting his blue ones unflinchingly, in a way that she never looked at Tim. 'I must have courage. I must not let them frighten me. This is modern Japan, this is not feudal Japan. I have a right to marry the man I wish.'

'That's the spirit! . . . Now let me get you a drink.'

'No, no. I do not drink! Never! Never! Mr Hale knows that. I have never drunk in my life.'

'Well, it's time you started. Just a drop. The weakest of gin' – Michael got up and began to pour out the gin – 'with lots and lots of ice and lots and lots of tonic. Just what you need in weather like this.'

Michiko began to giggle, shaking her head from side to side, the hair swinging with it, in a way that Tim found repellent. He had never seen her giggle like that before. 'No, no!' But she took the glass when it was extended to her and put it to her lips. The upper lip retracted. 'Hm. Nice.'

'Now let's drink to your new resolution.' Michael raised his glass. 'To love. And, after love, to marriage.'

Again she giggled, putting down the glass and covering her mouth with one of those nerveless hands. Then she picked up the glass again: 'To love. To marriage,' she said.

When she had gone, her face flushed from the unaccustomed drink and her gait slightly wavering, Tim confronted his brother: 'That was bloody silly advice, I must say!'

'Not at all. You're so conventional and so cautious, that's your trouble.'

'It won't work. It can't work.'

'Why the hell shouldn't it work? She seems a sensible enough sort of girl. She'll adapt to life in England. Or perhaps he can get a job over here.'

'Her parents will disown her.'

'Nonsense! They'll *say* that they'll disown her. But when it comes to it, when the chips are down – you'll see.'

'You know so little about Japan and the Japanese.'

'I have my instincts. And intuitions. And you know they're usually better than yours.'

Tim went to the window. 'You're so irresponsible,' he muttered, looking out into the parched moonlit garden, which he had once again forgotten to tell the driver to water or to water himself. That dryness out there of drooping peonies and yellowing grass and a pond, now empty, at the base of which a few dead lily-fronds spread their friable orange discs, seemed to have become a part of a choking dryness within his own self.

Later, in his bedroom, once again looking out into the silvery wilderness, he found himself banging with a fist on the wooden shutter beside him. Michiko and her problem had been things of which he had often longed to be rid – 'Oh, how she *bores* me!' he had more than once cried out in anguish to Laura. 'That ghastly self-preoccupation!' But now that, effortlessly and painlessly, Michael had taken both Michiko and her problem from him, he could feel only this arid, suffocating rage and resentment. Still banging with that fist on the wall – the whole wooden house reverberated with it and no doubt downstairs, naked on his bed with the dog beside him, Michael heard the reverberations – he suddenly remembered the chess set, the chess set that a bachelor uncle, ignorant and a little timorous of the ways of children, had given him on his seventh birthday. His father had tried to teach him to play and dutifully he had done the best he could. But his lack of both interest and aptitude were so apparent that soon his father desisted and the chess set was pushed away into the back of a cupboard containing playthings and pastimes more exciting.

There, eventually, the elder brother had found it, had taken it out and had begun to teach himself from a book.

At that, the younger boy's interest had at once been re-kindled. 'That's not your set, that's mine!' he had shrilled on discovering what had happened. 'Uncle Roger gave it to me, not you!'

'Well, let's have a game together,' came the equable answer.

'No! No, I don't want to play with you. Hand it over!'

'You never use it now.'

'Hand it over!'

They first bickered, then came to blows – with Michael, of course, the victor.

By taking for himself the things that his brother did not want, Michael invariably made him want them.

Sunday came and the brothers went for a long walk along the foothills of the mountain. Tim wore a suit and tie and carried a guide-book in case they visited any of the temples that had a way of suddenly revealing themselves at the far end of a pulsating tunnel of greenery. Michael had on the faded and rumpled jeans, a cheap short-sleeved check shirt that he had bought off a stall in the market and a pair of gym-shoes.

There had been an argument as to whether they should take the dog or not – Tim had said that she always vanished into the undergrowth and one spent most of one's time whistling and shouting for her; and then there had been another argument when Tim had put her on the lead.

'She doesn't need that thing,' Michael had said. 'I took her for a walk right through the town yesterday and she was no trouble at all.'

'All dogs have to be on leads in Japan. It's a law.'

'A bloody silly one.'

'Well, there it is. Whether you like it or not. As soon as we get away from people, then of course I'll let her off.'

After they had walked for a few minutes, leaving the main road for a path, Michael took off his shirt and draped it over an arm. 'Let her free now.'

'There are still houses here.'

Without arguing any further, Michael stooped and released the dog. Tim said nothing, mastering his sense of outrage.

'Poor little beast!' Michael halted and watched as the bitch scampered from side to side of the path. Then, all at once, she ran up the moss-grown steps that led to a shack-like cottage and having squatted, proceeded to deposit a large, greenish-yellow turd almost on the doorstep.

'Oh Christ! Come here! Come here, Tricia!'

Tim raised the lead over the cringing back of the bitch, who had sidled up to him at this call, her long tail sweeping the path. But his brother caught his hand before he could strike her.

'It's not her fault. She can't differentiate.'

'Of course she can! She's been taught to differentiate.'

'Poor little brute! She must have been longing to have that shit. I can sympathize.'

'You sympathize too much.'

'Think of all the mess that humans leave around them. Like that.' He pointed to a beer can rusting in the undergrowth. 'Tricia's shit will vanish into the earth and enrich it. But paper and tin cans and plastic won't.'

'Think of the people who find that mess on their doorstep.'

'Serve them right!'

'For what?'

'For being revolting humans instead of attractive animals like Tricia.'

Suddenly and simultaneously the absurdity of the argument struck them and they both began to laugh.

Later, on a narrow ledge of rock, Michael tore off the blue jeans, removed the gym-shoes and stretched himself out in the sun. Tim stared down at the long, narrow body; Michael blinked back at him.

'What are you doing?' Tim asked, as he had already asked once, receiving no reply, when Michael had begun to unzip his fly.

'Having a little rest. Roasting my carcass. Sit down. Come on!' He patted the rock beside him; ants scampered in all directions.

'But why? You're not tired, are you?'

Tricia had already lain down beside Michael, her tongue trailing from her mouth and her sides heaving from her incessant racing up and down the mountainside.

'No. But Tricia might be. And it's so beautiful here.'

'We'll be late for dinner.'

'Does that matter?'

'Imai-san said she'd come in specially to get it for us. She doesn't usually come in on a Sunday. She's doing it for you. We can't keep her waiting.'

'It's not so late, is it?'

'Nearly five. If we want to go round by that temple . . .'

'Oh, let her wait! Come on.'

Tim stared again at the long, narrow body, the sweat glistening on it as though it had been smeared with oil. The fingers of a hand went to the top button of his shirt; then he thought better of it. Uncomfortably he perched himself on a rock; he might have been a nervous teetotaller taking a stool at a bar. He peered around him.

'You look terribly uncomfortable there. And terribly hot. Why don't you take off your shirt?'

Tim shook his head and looked away.

'You can't enjoy yourself, Tim. It's so sad. Like so many people, you've lost the knack. You can't enjoy this view' – he pointed down the hillside to the city shimmering in a haze of heat – 'and you can't enjoy this marvellous sun or the smell of pine-needles or those birds calling to each other. All you can do is to think about the time and that we must be home by seven if we're not to keep Imai-san waiting. What does it *matter*?'

'It matters to her.'

'You're an admirable person, Tim. But, oh, I find it all so sad.'

Michael closed his eyes and appeared to fall asleep. Tim watched him, bitterly conscious of the truth of what he had said and yet no less bitterly conscious of the passing of time and of his horror at its passing. He was a creature of time as Michael had never been. He was always peeping at his watch, always considering if there was enough of it to get this or that job done, always wondering if it were early or late and if he were early or late.

At last Michael woke, opening his eyes on the sunlight that, filtering now through the trees, from low in the west, dappled his bare legs with sunlight, giving them a faun-like aspect.

'Oh, wonderful! Wonderful!' he exclaimed, stretching bony arms high above his head and then, as he sat up, out towards the glorious view. The bitch raised her head at the sound of his cry and her tail thumped the ground. 'And what have you been doing? Haven't you moved from there all this time?'

Tim shook his head. 'I was thinking,' he said. But what he had really done was to sink lower and lower into a bog of self-dislike and self-contempt.

Imai-san did not seem to mind their lateness, as she would have minded if it had been Tim and Laura and not Tim and Michael who had been late. At first hostile to the visitor, she now herself would ask him each day if he had anything that he wished her to wash for him and, careless about dusting out the master-bedroom in the absence of Laura, was scrupulous in her daily attention to the guest-room.

In between courses, Michael lit a cigarette.

'Don't you want to eat anything else?'

'Of course I do. After a walk like that, I'm feeling bloody hungry. But can't I smoke a fag first?'

'Imai-san . . .'

'Don't worry, my dear. *Don't worry!* She's perfectly happy.' And what galled Tim even more than the cigarette was the obvious truth of that assertion. He could hear the maid singing to herself in the kitchen, something he had never known her do before, her voice not unattractive as it lingered over the pentatonic melody of a folksong that he bafflingly remembered from somewhere or other, he did not know where.

Michael eventually threw his half-smoked cigarette into the grate. 'You mustn't always be in a hurry,' he said in a gentle, affectionate voice, as though advising a child.

'I have so much to do.'

'Yes, I know. You must try to take on less.'

'How can I?'

'Divest yourself.'

'That's easier said than done. One can't divest oneself of duties and obligations with the ease with which you divest yourself of your clothes.'

Without thinking, Tim then rose from his chair, crossed over to the fireplace and recovered the smouldering butt. He went to the window and flung it out into the night in an arc of showering sparks.

'Silly of me,' Michael said; but the tone implied that it was really silly of his brother to bother about something so trivial. 'I forgot that you don't like me to throw cigarettes into the grate.'

'I don't like you to throw them *lighted* into the grate. They smell so unpleasant.'

'Oh, yes, of course.'

After dinner, Michael went over to the drinks cupboard and stooped for the bottle of brandy. 'A snifter for you?' Now in a reversal of roles it was usually he who offered drinks to his host.

Tim shook his head. He did not think that he had betrayed his annoyance but Michael turned to ask, with raised eyebrows: 'You don't mind if I have one, do you?'

'No, of course not. Go ahead.'

'Poor little Tricia. All that chasing after those monkeys chattering way, way above her head, has completely worn her out. Come here, sweetie.' He sank on to the sofa, put down his drink and patted a knee; and at once the dog roused herself and, with vainly scrabbling paws, struggled to hoist herself up. Laughing, Michael lifted her; and again she gave that squeal –

Tim had never heard it before his brother's arrival – that might be expressive of either pain or pleasure, perhaps even of both.

Tim picked up a book, turning away from the unwelcome sight of the dog in the crook of his brother's arm, her tail trailing over the Japanese damask cover that he and Laura had spent so much time in choosing and so much money in buying. Rarely now did he ever read for pleasure. Next week he would have to give a lecture to the Japanese Association of Teachers of English and they had asked him to make Mark Rutherford his subject – a writer whom he had never read and of whose existence he had hardly been aware until then.

Michael sighed contentedly and no less contentedly the bitch grunted as he stretched his legs out yet further in front of him and pressed his head yet further back into the cushions. The two noises, of brother and bitch, produced that old, familiar sensation of jagged pieces of glass scraping against each other somewhere deep within his skull. But why should they upset him? Everyone always marvelled at his powers of concentration – writing reports to the London office against a background of the children milling and screaming round him and Laura listening to music.

The door glided back; and there was Imai-san, her ageless face drooping on its overlong neck. She looked across to Michael, not to her master, as she said: 'Lady is here.' It was strange that they had not heard the bell. Perhaps, since the door was always left unlocked except at night, Michiko had merely walked in; or perhaps she had met the maid as she was leaving.

'Lady? What lady?' Michael asked.

'It can only be Michiko,' Tim replied.

Imai-san inclined her head. 'Kuroda-san.'

Like the servant, Michiko addressed herself first to Michael when she entered the room. He might have been the host. 'I am sorry to trouble you,' she said in that tone of false humility that Tim had come to know so well.

'Not at all,' Michael replied, at once assuming the avuncular role, formerly Tim's, for which she had now cast him in her personal drama. 'Where would you like to sit?'

As always she took a straight-backed chair; and as always she sat in it with feet and knees together and nerveless hands resting, one on top of each other, in her lap.

Tim stared at her until she had to acknowledge his presence. In the past it had been Laura's presence that she had always put off acknowledging for a similar, insulting long interval. 'Good evening, Mr Hale.'

'Good evening, Michiko.'

She sensed a disapproval. 'I hope you do not mind my coming to see you on a Sunday evening.'

'You're always welcome.' He answered as one of her fellow-countrymen would have answered her in similar circumstances. The wintry politeness of the tone implied the exact reverse of the actual words. But she was not for long put off.

She swivelled herself round, presenting her back to Tim as on the previous occasion – the bony shoulder-blades stuck up through the flimsy blouse, he could have counted each of the vertebrae of her spine – and then began to Michael: 'Mr Hale, last night an idea came to me. Maybe you will think this a crazy idea. But I believe that possibly it is not. I want you to help me. Maybe I am crazy and maybe this idea is crazy but, as you say in England, nothing venture, nothing gain.'

'What is this idea?' Michael asked gently, his fingers tugging at one ear of the sleeping bitch.

She told him: not him and his brother but him alone – and once again, Tim might never have been there. If Michael would speak to her father, just speak to him, just explain what he thought about the match, she was sure that he could win him over. Her father was a hard man and an obstinate man but she felt convinced that Mr Hale – an outsider, who had nothing to gain if his advice were taken, a man so, so intelligent and so, so charming (she blushed faintly at this point) – could change his mind for him. Was it too much to ask? Could he possibly . . . ?

'Well, I don't mind having a try,' Michael conceded. 'As you say – or as *we* say – nothing venture, nothing gain. I don't know how the old boy will react to a total outsider interfering in family matters. But if you think it might do some good . . .'

'I am sure that *you* can do some good. I am sure of it. Do not ask me why but I have this feeling.' As she spoke that *'you'* the fishlike hands once again gave their death-throe twitch.

She went on to say that her father was away in Tokyo until the Tuesday. He was at 'a reunion' – the word conjuring up for Tim a picture of other elderly, upright, arrogant men like the General reminiscing about the war and plotting for a future in which all this American democratic claptrap would be buried and forgotten. Perhaps on Wednesday Michael could call at the house with her? Any time that suited him would suit her. Nothing was said about what would suit Tim or the office.

Michael made an appointment for that hour, between his brother's return home and dinner, when he made his deepest inroads into the drinks cupboard.

After she had gone, her upper lip retracting as she said good-bye to Michael and then trembling a little as she said good-bye to Tim – perhaps she had suddenly realized that she had forfeited his protection and wondered if she might not need it at some future time – Michael turned to his brother with a smile: 'Do you really think I can achieve anything?'

'Do you really think that you can achieve anything?'

Michael shrugged. 'Perhaps. Yes. Why not? I'm quite good at winning people round.'

'Very good, I should say.'

'Oh, Tim!' Michael threw an arm round his brother's shoulder and hugged him to him, as his clear, delighted laugh rang out through the open windows and out into the garden.

The next morning it began to rain after days of drought. The huge yellow discs now floated on top of the pond instead of disintegrating at the bottom of it. Tricia had to be dragged out, her claws rasping on the wooden boards, in order to relieve herself in a single panic-stricken gush. Thunder kept booming out, as though a temple gong were being struck somewhere just overhead. Looking out of his office window, Tim saw the lightning racing like a flame across a jagged escarpment of the mountain.

When he came home, Michael was not there. Imai-san said 'Gone out,' when he asked her, but more than that she did not know. She was ironing the blue jeans and the khaki shirt. That morning she had lent Michael one of his brother's handkerchiefs without asking permission and Tim had only just restrained himself from remonstrating with her. When Michael was there, stretched out on the sofa, often with a glass in his hand and with the bitch asleep beside him, Tim found himself wishing that his brother were somewhere else: in the garden or in his room or even (though he seldom acknowledged this to himself) in another city or another country. But now, as he settled down by the streaming window, with his copy of *The Revolution in Tanner's Lane* (how could the growing pains of the Dissenters be of any interest to the Japanese, since they were of absolutely no interest to himself?), he suddenly experienced a sense of loss, almost panic, that his brother was not there. He put down the book on his knee; he stared out of the window. A brilliantly coloured paper umbrella, a giant peony, jogged above the fence. But it was not Michael.

Tim got up and went along the narrow passage to the guest-room, half-persuaded that Michael might be in there, absorbed in writing or even asleep. But the room was empty; and empty of that now disconcertingly restless and now totally relaxed presence, it seemed even more forlorn than Rosie's empty room above it. Tim stood in the centre, his hands clasped before him, and gave a little shudder, despite the clinging, cloying heat of the thunderstorm. Then he saw the open exercise book on the rumpled bedspread. Michael had lain there and written down his commonplaces.

Tim slowly approached the bed, his hands still clasped before him; then he wrenched the hands apart and stretched one out with thumping heart. He began to read:

. . . *This absurd and pathetic attempt to achieve order when all natural life is so disorderly. Shit on a doorstep, cigarette in a grate, newspaper on a floor: these for him are like the nails driven into the feet and palms of Christ.*

(Suddenly Tim could feel nails driven into his own feet and palms.)

Oh, I love him and I think that he loves me. But I don't think I can stay here any longer — not a day, hardly an hour. I have a bath and I hear him calling out to Imai-san to come and clean it. (On Sunday I heard the poor devil cleaning it himself.) I smoke a cigarette and at once he empties the ash-tray. I drop The Times *to the floor and at once he picks it up. I lie on this bed and at once he straightens the counterpane.*

(Involuntarily one of Tim's hands began to twitch the cover: the other held the book, the fingers trembling.)

He doesn't really care about food, except as a way of keeping body and soul together. He scoffs it down in twenty minutes flat and is impatient when I can't — or won't — keep pace with him. Eating at that speed, it's amazing he doesn't vomit.

(Tim felt his gorge rise; only an effort of the will suppressed it.)

He has no use for drink, except as a pick-me-up after a wearisome day at the office. And so we have this nightly battle of wills. I want to have my three or four gins at leisure before we eat — what's the hurry? But he wants to gulp down one — or two at the most — and then start on the business of stoking up.

(Tim was mastered by a sudden craving for a drink of extreme cold and extreme potency. He could almost feel the icy rim of the glass against his trembling lower lip.)

He has buttoned and tied himself into all these multifarious duties and responsibilities just as he buttons himself tightly into those suits far too small for him and all but strangles himself in those ghastly ties.

(His tie had become a noose round his neck; the suit and the shirt beneath it and the underclothes beneath that had become the successive layers of a bandage covering a suppurating wound.)

He does so much that, in effect, he does nothing. He gives so much of his time and his money and himself that, in effect, he gives nothing

*at all. I want to laugh at him and I want to weep for him. I never
know which to do.*

(Tim sank on the bed. Something was welling up out of the
sludge within him, just as the water had welled up out of the
once arid throat of the pond, bringing life to those friable orange
discs and setting them afloat; but whether it was laughter or
tears he did not know.)

'Oh, gosh! Yes, I know, I know, I know. I'm late and Imai-san
wants to catch that last bus and the steak will be even more
overcooked than usual . . . But I must have a drink and change
out of these shoes and socks.' Michael stooped to the drinks
cupboard; Tim had heard his shoes squelch as he had hurried
across the room and now there were muddy footprints on the
carpet, cleaned shortly before the departure of Laura and the
children. 'An umbrella and raincoat don't protect one's feet or
even one's legs in downpour like this.' He poured out the gin
until the tumbler was almost full and the bottle almost empty;
then he gulped it neat, gulped and gulped again. His eyes began
to water.

'That's better,' he said. 'That's more like it. Much more like
it.' He was about to raise his glass to his lips; then stared at his
brother. 'What's the matter?'

'Nothing. Why?'

'You look so – so *odd*.'

'Do I?' Tim put a hand over his eyes as though in an attempt
to shield himself from this scrutiny.

'As though you'd had bad news. Or were not feeling well.'

'I've had no news, good or bad. And I'm feeling as well as I
ever do. Perhaps it's just that I'm hungry.'

'Poor Tim. You want to stoke up. I'll only keep you a moment.'

Stoke up – that was one of the jagged, rasping, fragments of
glass from the diary. Tim went to the window and looked out at
the pond. The rain drops beat down on the water-lily discs, no
longer orange now but a greenish-yellow, the colour of bile,
with a force so vehement that it seemed as if they would pierce

them like buck-shot. 'Where have you been?' he asked eventually, still not looking round.

'To the Japan Air Lines office.'

The water, black and metallic under the livid sky, was now thrusting out of the pond in ever-widening circles.

'The Air Lines office?'

'Now that the weather has broken like this, I think the time has come to strike camp again. I've been extravagant – I felt I could afford to be after all these days when you've not allowed me to spend a single penny. I've bought myself an air-ticket to Manila. I know this man there – well, I hardly know him. But he's an American professor of sociology or something like that and he told me that if I ever came his way, I must be sure to look him up. No doubt he'll be surprised that I've taken him at his word. But he seemed a nice enough chap – a bit of a bore but nice enough. I expect I can be his unpaying guest for a week or two.'

Still Tim did not look round. 'When are you going?' His voice sounded attenuated against the swish of the rain across the window.

Michael's hand, very firm and yet very gentle, almost caressing, closed on his shoulder. 'I thought tomorrow, old chap.'

'Tomorrow!' Tim swung round.

'Does that seem terribly abrupt? But you know me. I like to do things on impulses. It's not that I haven't loved every minute of my stay. And I'll miss not having made that trip to Nara that we promised ourselves. But you'll be able to get on with all your duties – and all your obligations – much better without me to add to them. Won't you?'

Tim looked back into the garden; and then he saw that what he had imagined as happening and had then told himself could not possibly happen, had in fact done so. The disc of one of the water-lilies, split in half by the battering of the rain, had opened what looked like the fleshy mouth of a wound, pink at its centre and greenish yellow, as though putrescent, at its lips.

He turned, incoherent in his fury. 'That girl . . . The girl . . . What about . . . ? Your promise . . . you promised . . .'

Amazed and bewildered, his brother stared at him. 'What girl?'

'Michiko. Michiko Kuroda. You told her. You promised her. Her father. She's relying on you.'

Michael laughed, totally unconcerned, and raised his glass. 'Oh, you can speak to the father for me. You know him, after all. And you have the full, formidable authority of the British Council to back you up. Whereas I – I'm just a nobody.'

'You know I . . . And she doesn't want . . . It's you . . . . You . . .'

Again Michael gave that clear, ringing laugh of his.

'Nonsense, old fellow! You have far too little confidence in yourself. You can deal with the matter far better than I.' His hand reasserted its grip on his brother's shoulder; he began to propel him towards the dining-room door. 'You're not upset at my going so abruptly, are you? Are you? But you know me. I'm rather like a bird. I peck around in one garden for a while and then, though there are still lots of juicy worms in it, I fly off and peck around in another garden. That's *me*. You know that, Tim.'

Although, by the next morning, the rain had ceased to fall, the atmosphere was still haunted by its lingering presence. One could smell it; one could all but feel it on one's skin, soft and moist; one could all but hear it, in the sound of water racing down the mountain or thrusting against the banks of the river and the network of canals. Everywhere moss seemed to have been splashed like an emerald dye: at the base of trees, up the steps of temples, on garden walls and fences. Of course it had always been there, waiting for the rain to illuminate it as objects in a darkened room suddenly leap into life at the touch of a switch, but Tim gazed at it in amazement.

Michael was happy in the trundling air-conditioned car, the dog in his lap. He stared out at the passers-by, a perpetual smile on his over-thin, over-long mouth, and then he stared down at the dog, drawing her silken ears through his fingers. He rarely looked at Tim and then only for a moment at a time. They hardly spoke to each other.

'I hope you'll have some good news of Rosie.'

'Thank you. But somehow I doubt . . . it seems pretty certain . . .' Tim found that, since reading the commonplace book, he could talk to his brother only in these disjointed phrases. He might have been their father after the first of his strokes.

Michael hummed to himself (Tim recognized the melancholy falling-away of the folksong that Imai-san had sung to herself in the kitchen and again he sought in vain for a recollection of the occasion when first he had heard it) and then he put a hand over Tim's in that old gesture of affection and protection, though now the touch had become meaningless and somehow chill and chilling even in that temperature. 'Cheer up.'

'Oh, I'm quite cheerful.'

'Are you?' Again he hummed. Then: 'Poor Tim. Don't drive yourself so hard. That terrible puritanical sense of duty!'

'One is what one is.'

'Oh, dear, yes!'

They came to the station, where Michael was to catch the express to Tokyo. He searched through his pockets and then took out his wallet and peered into it. He laughed, gaily and good-naturedly. 'Be a dear, as you always are, and lend me two or three thousand. I don't want to cash another traveller's cheque and I *would* like to have a bite on the train and a taxi to the air-port.'

'You'd better have ten thousand.'

'Oh, but that's far too much!'

'Japan is a very expensive country.'

Michael seemed not to have got the implication of that remark; and, strangely, it pleased Tim more that way than if he had done so.

'Oh, you are kind.'

The two men and the bitch walked down the crowded platform in total silence.

'At least you won't have to wait,' Tim said at last. 'The trains are always on time, you know.'

'So I'd heard. What's important is that *you* don't have to wait.

I know how much you have to do. And you always hate waiting Waiting never bothers me.'

The train came in exactly when due.

'How narrow it looks!'

'Yes, the gauge is narrower here than in Europe. There's a funny story about how that came about but if I start to tell it to you, you'll only miss the train. Quick!'

'Dear Tim! A thousand thanks!'

Then suddenly and amazingly, Michael did something he had never done before, not even when the two of them were children. He put his face close to his brother's and, throwing both arms around him, kissed him full on the lips. After that he gave a short, breathless laugh, looked closely into Tim's eyes for a moment, and bounded into the carriage. Tim stood frozen.

A whistle blew, its sound falling away strangely like the end of Imai-san's folksong. The train began to glide forward, while Michael stood at the window and waved, waved, waved. Everywhere people were waving: an elderly woman, the sleeve of her iron-grey kimono falling away to reveal an emaciated arm; a group of schoolchildren, many of them with banners; two young girls, giggling and swaying. But Tim did not wave.

Suddenly there was a jerk at the lead that he was holding; and then Tricia was off down the platform, racing through the crowds at an incredible speed. But she could not keep up with the accelerating train. Faster and faster she drove herself; then all at once, near where the platform ended, she came to a bewildered halt. She stared into the distance; pattered a few feet back the way she had come and pattered once more to where the platform ended; then she raised her head and let out a single, long howl.

Tim had heard nothing like it from her before; he was never to hear anything like it from her again. It was a human wail, expressing an unbearable intensity of loss, longing and regret; and it seemed to him to come, not from the bitch, but spurting from somewhere deep, deep within the dust-choked cistern of himself.